Between the Moon and the Tide

Haven Island Series Book One

Erin Cantrell

Erin C. Grandorff

This is a work of fiction. Names, characters, places, events, and incidents are products of the author's imagination or are used fictitiously. Any resemblance to actual persons, living or dead, or actual events is purely coincidental.

Publisher: Erin Cantrell Grandorff

Developmental Editor: Julie Mianecki

Ebook Cover Artist: Issa Muhammad

Paperback Cover: Erin Grandorff

ISBN (eBook): 979-8-9941875-1-7

ISBN (print): 979-8-9941875-2-4

For information contact: ecantrell17@gmail.com

Printed in the United States of America

First Edition: 2026 Unabridged

Contents

Dedication

This book is dedicated to the summers that changed us, the way the moon shifts the tide—slowly, silently, and forever.

Early 2000's Playlist

RUN DON'T WALK TO DOWNLOAD THESE FROM LIMEWIRE (IYKYK)

1. Vindicated by Dashboard Confessional
2. Swing Swing by All American Rejects
3. Sugar, We're Goin Down by Fall Out Boy
4. Dammit by Blink-182
5. In Too Deep by Sum-41
6. The Middle by Jimmy Eat World
7. Mr Brightside by The Killers
8. We Belong Together by Mariah Carey
9. Don't Cha by the Pussycat Dolls ft. Busta Rhymes
10. Cool by Gwen Stefani
11. Caught Up by Usher
12. Breakaway by Kelly Clarkson

13. Shake it Off by Mariah Carey
14. That's What I Love About Sunday by Craig Morgan
15. Anything But Mine by Kenny Chesney
16. Some Beach by Blake Shelton
17. Nothing on But the Radio by Gary Allan
18. The Woman with You by Kenny Chesney
19. Must Be Doin' Somethin' Right by Billy Currington
20. She Let Herself Go by George Straight

Part One

Chapter one

The drive from Clemson to Haven Island, South Carolina, was dragging on—four hours of sun glare, asphalt, and overthinking.

Emily Kennedy was restless from more than just the caffeine in her iced latte. She was done with college, done with Ryan, and not at all ready to fit into her mom's new life. It felt like being stuck between point A and point B with no map, no plan, just her own second-guessing for company.

She fumbled with the dial, coaxing cold air from her finicky AC, and tried not to think about what waited on the other end. Something buzzed beneath her skin, an uneasy, expectant feeling. She didn't know it yet, but this summer would reroute everything—her plans, her heart, and the person she thought she was.

Along the winding two-lane highway, hand-painted signs offered boiled peanuts and fresh peaches, while sun-faded billboards advertised beach rentals. Closer to the coast, traffic thickened to stop-and-go misery. A long line of minivans strapped with cargo carriers and SUVs towing jet skis or golf carts on trailers stretched out ahead of her. Families were headed for vacation while she was headed for… what? Purgatory? Or straight-up hell, as hot as it was.

Emily glanced at her reflection in the rearview. Her dark hair was swept into a haphazard bun, slightly sun-lightened at the ends. No mascara, no foundation, not even lip gloss. Pretty? Maybe. But she wasn't trying too hard to be.

She cranked the volume on her freshly burned CD, letting Blink-182 and Jimmy Eat World drown out the maddening crawl of traffic. Her fingers drummed on the steering wheel as she half-sang along.

Law school in the fall. Fresh start. But first, I've got to survive this summer.

She shifted in her seat and turned the music up.

Home wasn't supposed to mean the coast. Home used to be a suburb outside Charlotte. She could picture the familiar bungalow with its creaky porch swing—the place where her bookshelf overflowed with stories she could disappear into for months, where her mom hummed off-key in the kitchen over something questionable simmering in the crockpot. After her dad died, it had become their two-woman world, cozy and perfectly imperfect.

She'd give anything to be headed north on I-85, back to that life. Instead, she was driving south—toward the one her mother had built without her.

Emily had visited Haven Island once or twice before, tagging along when her mom, Marinda, drove down for an annual charity golf tournament. The island had always seemed quiet, almost tediously so. The kind of place that made Emily itch for some excitement after a day or two. Her mother loved it, though. Maybe that was why she kept coming back.

It was on one of those outings that Marinda had met Greg. Polite conversation over cocktails turned into dinners, long weekends, and eventually, a proposal. Within a year, they'd slipped away to Charleston and eloped. No fuss, just the courthouse followed by champagne at a rooftop bar.

Emily hadn't been surprised. Her mom had said, after losing her first husband so young, she never wanted another big production. She'd just wanted someone steady, a companion to laugh with—Greg fit the description.

Thinking about Greg made Emily roll her eyes, almost instinctively, before she immediately felt guilty about it.

Greg was a nice man.

That's it! He's too nice. He's just so... derivative.

"Someday I'll learn not to be such a cynical, snarky bitch," she muttered to herself. "Mom is happy, I should just let her be happy."

The mixtape's track rolled to Sum 41's "In Too Deep" as the green highway sign for Haven Island crept into view.

Once she made the turn, a suspension bridge, rising at least 200 feet over Haven Inlet, loomed steep and intimidating.

Please make it over this bridge, baby.

Emily sent up a prayer to the General Motors gods and kept her eyes on the lane lines.

From the bridge's highest point, she risked a peek over the side. The sunlight flashed off the channel below; above, the blue sky was fading into brilliant shades of red and orange.

The minute her tires reached flat ground, she let out a long exhale.

The streets on the island were packed with summer tourist traffic—cars idling and golf carts darting between them. Emily laughed out loud as a police officer on a bicycle came flying up and pulled one of the golf carts over.

When she finally rolled up to the gated golf community called Haven Lakes, an elderly guard checked her license, printed a pass, and waved her through.

The Spanish revival beach house looked nothing like home and felt even less like it. White stucco was adorned with terracotta trim. Arched windows poured golden sunlight across pale hardwood floors. A wrought-iron balcony curling off the second story gave it the look of a Mediterranean postcard.

Emily's school photos lined the stairwell—awkward bangs, bad dye jobs—curated like artifacts. The rest could've been staged: linen slipcovers, seashell art, and not a magazine out of place.

It was her mother's dream house.

I'm only here for three months. Maybe it will be nice to try something new.

It wasn't what Emily was used to, but she could admit she was impressed.

Marinda—slender as ever, a stack of mail in one hand and a margarita in the other—swept into the foyer and wrapped Emily in a warm hug. She had always been beautiful in that refined, effortless way: medium-length ash-blond hair framing well-defined cheekbones, still stunning even if age had dulled the girlish shine of her youth. In her all-white tennis dress, with a cardigan draped around her neck, Marinda looked like she belonged in this house, this neighborhood, this life.

Emily suddenly felt self-conscious in her frayed jean shorts, tiger paw t-shirt, and worn Chuck Taylors. She liked to throw on clothes and go, not overthink a wardrobe. She didn't quite fit in at Clemson with the sorority girls, and now she was worried she didn't fit in at home either.

She had Marinda's bone structure—the same small features, the soft mouth with full lips—but her coloring was all from the Kennedy side. Dark hair, eyes a deep emerald shade framed by dark lashes and brows, and pale skin that rarely kept a tan. Her heritage gave her a look that was feminine and yet… wild.

"You have his wit, Em," Marinda had said once, regarding Emily's father. "Owen was always a fan of sarcasm and dry humor."

The unfamiliarity of this place magnified the loss Emily always felt, but usually kept carefully contained. Today, she let herself miss her father more than she had in a long time.

Chapter two

Emily's new stepfather appeared beside her mother and offered to escort her upstairs.

Greg was the picture of easy confidence, sporting a permanent golf tan, careful Botox, and teeth a shade too white. At the beach, polos and khakis replaced his suits. He wasn't unattractive. Just… country-club perfect. Always smiling, always agreeable, always cordial. A well-mannered Southern gentleman.

"You'll like it here," Greg said, after he set her bag down. "Small town, friendly people. Lots of tourists, but we'll be rid of them by September."

"Her room" looked suspiciously like a guest space in a vacation rental.

"I'm not sure about that bridge. I may have to stay on this island forever," Emily said half-jokingly.

"They built it after a storm took out the old swing bridge in the '80s," Greg said. "Takes some getting used to."

There was a pause before Greg continued.

"Do you have any plans this summer, Emily? A lot of places are looking for seasonal workers. I know the clubhouse could use some servers, and your mother mentioned you have experience."

I'm not a golf club girl! He really doesn't get me.

Greg must have seen the look on her face.

"If not," he said smoothly, "there's a summer place called High Tide down by the marina. Mostly a beach bar, but they serve some tasty pub grub. I know the owner, Jeanne, and she's been looking for reliable help."

"I'm not sure, I hadn't really thought much about it," Emily answered truthfully.

"Summer gig," Greg said with a shrug. "Jeanne says the place is slammed June through August. Should be an easy way to make a little money before law school!"

Greg was himself a lawyer, mostly retired now, but he still owned his firm and occasionally stepped in on tough cases. As a high-profile defense attorney, he had made a fortune.

While he launched into a story about his law days back at LSU, Emily's mind wandered.

I don't want to be that type of lawyer. I want to help people who can't help themselves, not keep rich assholes out of jail.

Still, she couldn't help but like Greg. He was growing on her with every interaction. His slow, soft drawl was nearly impossible to be mad at. She could see the charm and the appeal. He was a safe bet, exactly what her mom deserved after fourteen long years of being alone.

"Thanks for the suggestion about the bar, Greg," Emily said when he finished, and she meant it. He was trying to be helpful, and that was something.

"Go ahead and unpack, get settled in," Greg said as he headed out of the room. "Dinner will be ready in a little while. I have to go man the grill, and your mother is making margaritas!"

Emily smiled politely while internally her brain fired the comeback: *Fantastic. Make mine big enough to drown in.*

After Greg's footsteps had faded, she looked around again. At the neat bedspread, the little vase of fake flowers on the dresser, and the neutral walls. It was a room that could belong to anyone. The only personal touch was an oil portrait her mother had insisted on—Emily posed in Chanel tweed and her mother's pearls.

The painting didn't show the resentment in her eyes. The whole thing made her look like someone's grandmother on her way to tea with the Queen.

They should hang a little placard beneath it: Our daughter, future Supreme Court Justice. That might impress someone.

She exhaled loudly as she flopped onto the bed.

Maybe I do need a job or... something.

She rolled onto her side, propping herself up on one elbow.

Something that belongs to me, not mom or Greg. Something that feels... normal.

Dinner was the kind of meal that reminded Emily why Greg had been such an easy addition to her mother's life—he was a fantastic cook. While Marinda could barely make a casserole without burning down the house, Greg ensured the ribeyes were seared but pink in the middle, the rosemary potatoes crisp at the edges, and the asparagus still bright and glossy with olive oil.

Marinda had contributed to the meal by mixing margaritas—strong and tart—with salted rims that left Emily licking her lips between bites.

Her mother was flushed from the tequila and sunshine, laughing more freely than Emily had seen in years.

They really do seem so happy together.

A pang of something she couldn't quite name pressed behind Emily's ribs.

The house itself came alive in a homey way at twilight: gas lanterns glowing softly on the patio, crickets chirping, the faint gurgle of the pool filter. Somewhere, yacht rock hummed low—Christopher Cross crooning about sailing while Greg topped off their drinks.

Weekend plans were already on the docket: Sunday mass at St. Catherine's followed by a brunch Greg and Marinda were hosting for a few couples from the neighborhood. Emily promised she'd tag along, though it felt more like an obligation than something she was looking forward to.

After the peach cobbler Greg served for dessert was gone, Emily leaned back in her chair, quietly considering her own plans for the summer.

"Tomorrow, I think I'll go down to the bar you told me about, Greg," she said, twirling her straw.

"Which bar is this?" Marinda asked curiously.

"High Tide," Greg replied. "I told Emily that Jeanne needs all the help she can get this season. The island gets more and more popular every year. With all the new condominiums, it's as busy as I've ever seen it!"

"Yes, the crowds and the traffic are terrible in the summer," Marinda agreed with vexation in her voice.

She turned toward Emily.

"Do you think you would like that, Em? Working in a beach bar?"

"I've waited tables before, Mom," Emily said, trying not to sound defensive. "I'm sure it's not more than I can handle."

"Good deal," Greg said. "I'll shoot Jeanne a message to let her know you'll be stopping by."

As Greg and Marinda drifted toward the sunroom for a nightcap, exhaustion settled into Emily's muscles, and her eyelids suddenly felt heavy. She hugged her mom, let Greg pat her shoulder, and headed upstairs.

Maybe I will like it here. The least I can do is give it a chance.

Tomorrow, she'd see what this beach bar was all about.

Chapter three

The next morning, Emily drove the narrow island road that led to the marina. Boats rocked in narrow slips, tall masts and rusted outriggers leaning into the sky like crooked spears. Seagulls wheeled above the docks, their cries cutting through the heavy air. Salt, diesel, and dead fish scents tangled in the heat. It was late May on the Carolina coast, and summer was already pressing in.

High Tide sat at the edge of the channel where the inlet met the Atlantic Ocean. Weather-worn and perched on stilts, it looked like it had been clinging there longer than the tide itself.

The back side faced the marina and the parking lot, but the front had a water view. That detail, Emily surmised, must be the draw. That and the fact that there weren't many other places to go on the island. Not to her knowledge, anyway.

A neon sign, once in red but now faded white, announced **HIGH TIDE** in a block font.

"It looks like it might drift out to sea at the next high tide," Emily mumbled under her breath.

A wraparound deck hugged the building, crowded with mismatched picnic tables, high-top barrels, and brightly colored umbrellas that had seen better days. String lights hung overhead, unlit in the daylight but promising to come alive after sunset.

The screen door at the entrance banged open and shut every few minutes as sunburned tourists wandered in, flip-flops slapping against the boards. The muffled sound of music, laughter, clinking glasses, and someone yelling, "Order up!" rolled through the air.

Emily killed the engine and slid her sunglasses up on her head, staring up at the place for a moment. It wasn't neat and orderly like Greg's gated neighborhood. It was rough around the edges, loud, and lived in. High Tide looked like everything a beach bar ought to be. She decided she liked it.

For the first time since she'd crossed that terrifying bridge, Emily felt a spark of possibility.

Inside, the air smelled of fried shrimp and old beer spills. Strings of Christmas bulbs were tacked along the beams, accenting the bar's dim lighting. Wood-paneled walls were cluttered with hand-painted signs—*No Shoes, No Shirt, No Problem* in peeling teal, *Beer: Cheaper Than Therapy* hung crookedly. The Jolly Roger presided over the bar like a pirate's den.

Overhead, the ceiling fans turned lazy circles, doing little to stir the heavy air, while the radio blared just loud enough to drown out the clatter of plates and the shouts from the kitchen.

Jeanne spotted Emily right away as she hovered near the hostess stand, letting her eyes adjust to the dimness.

The bar owner was short and compact, with a wiry energy that seemed to buzz under her leathery skin. A cigarette stayed tucked permanently behind her ear, and her gray hair was pulled back, but frizz escaped in every direction, wild as sea spray.

“Greg’s stepdaughter, right? Emily?” Jeanne’s voice was raspy, with a Northern accent. Sharp but not mean—just to the point. The kind of tone that cut through the noise of the dining room, whether you liked it or not.

Emily nodded, nerves pricking her stomach.

“Good. It’s Saturday—we’re drowning. Grab an apron.” Jeanne shoved one into her hands. “You know how to carry a tray?”

“Um… yeah, I do,” she stammered.

Jeanne gave her a wry grin. “Let’s see if you can keep up, sink or swim style. Lunch rush is already picking up!”

The place blurred after that. Orders came flying at Emily, and menus were stacked in her hands. She almost dropped a tray after catching her foot on a loose floorboard, but was able to save it.

A slim server dressed as if he’d walked out of a fashion magazine waltzed through the dining room like it was his personal runway. Dark-skinned and sharp-featured, his hair cropped close, Joel stood out, strikingly posh against the bar's shabby backdrop.

He whisked by Emily with a wink and a voice like silk. “Don’t drop the oysters, honey. They’ll never forgive you.”

Emily blinked, halfway between intimidated and charmed.

A young waitress breezed past behind him, balancing a tray of beers with one hand. Her long skirt swished around her ankles, and layered bracelets clinked at her wrist. Where Joel radiated glamorous and sophisticated, Kenzie had an earthy, artsy calm about her.

She caught Emily's eye and mouthed, *good luck*, flashing a grin that was both sympathetic and mischievous.

That's when Emily noticed *him*.

Behind the bar stood a tall guy in a faded Gamecocks T-shirt, the cotton pulled tight across his shoulders. Her gaze lingered—broad chest, sun-warmed skin, tattooed sleeves crawling down his arms like stories he didn't need words to tell.

He moved with the quiet confidence of someone accustomed to being watched. When he reached for a bottle, his shirt sleeve slipped just enough to reveal a scar, thick and jagged, slicing through the ink before disappearing under the fabric. Not an accident. It looked surgical, and a little like heartbreak stitched shut.

When his gaze met hers, Emily's pulse stuttered. His dark eyes—hazel, maybe—lingered on her face intentionally, and he smirked—a slow, knowing curve of his mouth that said he noticed everything. It unsettled her just enough to make her curious.

By the time Emily untied her apron hours later, sweat was running down her back. She was tired, but somehow alive in a way she hadn't been in months. The lunch crowd had moved out, but it wasn't quite time for the dinner rush yet.

She sank into a seat at the bar and poured herself a glass from the pitcher of ice water.

That kicked my ass.

She let out a groan while vainly trying to stifle it.

It had been a while since she'd worked this hard. Still, there was something nice about it. Something almost freeing.

"Hey, baby girl! This silverware won't roll itself." Joel's voice snapped her back to reality.

"Do y'all normally work doubles around here?" Emily asked, doing her best to keep the exhaustion out of her voice.

"Honey, I am a full-time diva," Joel replied sassily. "But I work doubles all summer. I have to pay for SCAD. Unless I can find a sugar daddy."

"SCAD?" Emily asked cluelessly.

"Savannah College of Art and Design," Kenzie chimed in matter-of-factly. "We're both students there. Joel's fashion. I'm cinema."

"Wow, that's so interesting," Emily said with genuine enthusiasm, leaning against the bar top. "I just graduated from Clemson with an English degree. Heading to law school in Charleston this fall."

"Yes girl, get that money!" Joel said, snapping his fingers. "Remember us when you're rich."

The dark-haired bartender hadn't said anything as he cleaned, but as he moved closer to their end of the bar, Emily could tell he was picking up on the conversation.

"Clemson Tiger, huh?" he asked after a minute.

"Yep," she replied. "And judging by that shirt, you must be a Gamecock?"

He pulled up his shirt sleeve to show more of his tattoos. Among the labyrinth of ink, Emily could make out the words "Forever to Thee" winding down his bicep.

She rolled her eyes. “How original.” Her voice came out sounding sassier than she meant to be. She extended her hand, “I’m Emily.”

“I’m Asher,” he said, taking her hand in his. “But everyone calls me Ash.”

His grip was firm; his palm was warm and calloused.

Who is this guy?

A strange electricity flickered through Emily, like she was touching a live wire. Ash had that quiet, unreadable aura. The kind that made her want to know what he wasn’t saying.

“Well, y’all,” he said to Emily, Joel, and Kenzie. “I’m gonna head out for a bit. I’ll be back before dinner service. Jeanne can handle the bar for now.”

Emily watched him go, trying to stop herself from stealing a glance at his ass in those jeans, but it was useless.

Joel caught her gaze lingering and interrupted her thoughts. “Forget about it girl, he’s taken."

“Taken?” Emily asked, only half understanding.

“Mm-hmm. Blond beauty queen, all Lilly Pulitzer and daddy’s money.” He twirled a spoon in the air like punctuation.

Kenzie rolled her eyes. “Mandy Green. They’ve been together since high school—quarterback and cheerleader cliché. He went to South Carolina on a full ride, got hurt, then transferred back here to Coastal State after his dad died.”

“That’s... a lot,” Emily murmured.

“Oh, it gets better,” Joel added in a stage whisper. “Rumor says she cheated. Everyone knows—except him.”

“But you didn’t hear that from us,” Kenzie added, smirking as she slipped out back for a smoke.

Emily didn't have much time to ponder this new information. The silverware was barely rolled, and the condiments hastily re-stocked before they had to throw themselves into dinner service.

The hostess called out that night and Emily stepped in, seating tables and running drinks so the more experienced servers could keep everything afloat.

In all honesty, she was grateful for the break. Her shoulder already throbbed from hauling heavy trays, and her arms were still adjusting to the rhythm of balancing dishes and dodging other servers as they rushed by. Running water pitchers, mixed drinks, and sodas felt like a mercy.

Unfortunately for her nerves, it also meant constant trips back and forth to the bar. The same bar Ash was stationed behind again.

He moved with an ease that made it all look simple—pouring, shaking, sliding drinks down the polished wood counter. He was relaxed but commanding. Unbothered even as ticket after ticket printed and the orders stacked high. She could easily picture him on a football field, calmly reading the defense and making the play.

He'd changed and showered. The worn T-shirt was gone, replaced with a button-down rolled at the sleeves. The fabric was stretched across his shoulders in a way that made it impossible not to notice how solid he was.

Of course, he cleaned up nice, and of course, she'd noticed. He wasn't the type Emily normally went for. Her preferences usually leaned more toward guys in Vans and band tees, not men who wore cowboy boots and tight jeans. But damn, there was just something about him.

I wonder what he looks like without a shirt on?

Heat pricked her face, and she spun on her heel before he caught her staring.

"You good?" Kenzie asked, appearing at her side, eyes narrowed. "You look a little red. Like… startled red."

"I'm good," Emily lied quickly, tugging at her apron strings. "It's just hot in here."

"God, I know it. They need to keep that damn patio door shut!"

Kenzie snatched her tray of drinks and weaved back into the crowd.

The dinner rush rolled on like an avalanche. Jeanne's bark cut through the music. Chairs scraped. Glasses clinked. The printer never stopped spitting tickets. Emily barely had time to think, just move. Breathe. React.

In the blur, she caught sight of Joel weaving between tables with effortless charm. He bent down to talk eye-level with kids, and their parents relaxed around him, grateful for the distraction. She had to admit—he was great at this.

She took note of the rest of the crew. Most of the servers were local women in tank tops and jean shorts, hair yanked back with pens stabbed into ponytails, skin browned by the relentless island sun. They moved with a confident rhythm Emily hadn't learned yet.

By the time her shift ended and the last table was wiped down, Emily's feet ached, her shirt clung to her skin, and she smelled like fryer oil. She collapsed into her car, windows rolled down because her AC seemed to be on the fritz again.

Her body throbbed with exhaustion, but beneath it, something stronger pulsed—anticipation, maybe, or a warning. Somewhere between the lunch rush and a handshake across the bar, her summer had stopped following the plan she'd made for it.

As she drove away, the cool night air brushed softly over her skin, and she tried—and failed—not to picture Ash. The smile. His eyes. The way he'd looked at her like he knew something she didn't.

She shook her head to clear it, but it was useless. He was at the top of her thoughts, and she had a feeling he wasn't going anywhere.

Chapter four

For Ash, the ocean was the one place he could still relax. Early mornings before the bar opened, before Mandy's constant texts, before the weight of everything, this was his reset. The slow pull of the tide and the patience of waiting for a tug on the line grounded him.

He glanced toward shore and caught sight of a lone jogger. The stride, the swing of her ponytail—just for a second, he swore it looked like Emily.

His breath hitched, brisk and unexpected.

No. Couldn't be. I'm losing it.

She'd been in his head since yesterday—that spark, and the sass that came out of nowhere.

Emily was beautiful in a way that didn't need to announce itself. The kind that showed up in jean shorts, a white T-shirt, and sneakers.

An outfit that would be simple on anyone else. But on her? Impossible to ignore. And her lips—God, those lips. Smart-ass sharp, but they looked kissably soft.

Work just got a lot more interesting.

A sly smile tugged at the corner of his mouth.

Clemson Tiger. Trouble written all over her.

Then he dragged a hand over his face, as if to wipe the thought of Emily away.

Mandy was the safe choice. The obvious choice. She'd always been perfect. Old-money perfect. The kind that didn't need to flash it but wore it in every detail: tailored clothes, easy politeness, and the quiet confidence of someone who never had to worry about rent or repairs.

Her family's neighborhood looked like a magazine spread—rows of immaculate homes wrapped by perfectly manicured lawns and driveways free of oil stains and stray toys.

Ash's world was the opposite.

Home was a sun-faded double-wide off a rural back road, the air conditioner rattling, and the porch sagging just a little at the edge. His mama still worked the diner's morning shift and came home smelling like bacon grease and coffee. When his daddy was alive, he'd hauled freight across the country—on the road more often than not, but he made sure his family never went without. It wasn't fancy, but it was honest.

On Mandy's first visit, she had smiled politely, but he'd caught the uncertainty in her eyes. He'd seen the hesitation before she'd sat on the old plaid couch, the way she'd pinched her nose when his daddy lit a cigarette, and the careful way she'd examined the mismatched glass of sweet tea his mama offered. She'd never said she was better than them; the space between their worlds did the talking.

Still, Mandy had always been there. Every football game, every homecoming dance, prom pictures, and then their slow drift into adulthood. Spending summers at her daddy's lake house and sneaking down to the dock after dark. The first time, which had been clumsy, but unforgettable.

Truth was, Mandy was the only woman he'd ever been with. She'd taken care of him after his shoulder surgeries, helped him bathe and dress when he was numb on painkillers and weak as water.

She was predictable in a way that used to feel like comfort. He'd always known exactly what to expect—her schedule, her moods, her outfits, hell, even her periods. Floral prints and pastels lined her closet like candy. Dinner dates were always at the "right" restaurants. Conversations stayed safely on the surface.

Mandy liked order, and for a long time, he loved that steadiness; it was exactly what he thought he wanted. Somewhere along the way, comfort had blurred into boredom. Predictability had started to feel like suffocation. Dinner with her parents became tense, every word heavy under the weight of expectation.

Mandy worried his old truck might embarrass her at the valet. She insisted on driving them everywhere now, in her shiny new Lexus, never letting him touch the keys. It was humiliating, but not as bad as sitting through her father's hints that a bachelor's from Coastal State wasn't good enough for a man planning to marry his daughter.

Lately, Mandy had taken up the same refrain: online MBA programs, fast-track promotions, and a corner office in her daddy's company.

"I'll even do most of the work for you, Ash," she'd said once, casual as a weather report. "Just apply. We can get the degree on paper, and then my father will hire you."

Mandy was smart. Driven. She probably could earn an MBA in her sleep. She handled public relations and marketing for her father's company, effortlessly shaping narratives for a living. She was used to getting what she wanted, and what she wanted right now was a cleaned-up version of Ash. A man in a collared shirt and cufflinks. The kind who wore a watch that cost more than his mama's trailer and drove something German.

Does she really love me, or just the man she thinks she can turn me into?

The thought hit like a gut punch because he didn't know anymore.

Did Mandy even know him now? Had she ever? Or had she only loved the version of him that lived in yearbooks and newspaper clippings—the hometown star, the golden boy who looked good on her arm.

Maybe she hadn't loved *him* so much as she'd loved his potential. The scholarship. The scouts. The easy smile, the clean-cut image. That was the Ash who belonged in her world, but that boy was gone. His shoulder had taken the game, and life had stripped away the shine.

It was obvious by now he wasn't destined for the pros or magazine covers. He was here, behind the bar at High Tide, a twenty-six-year-old bartender. Working hard, paying bills, still a little unsure of what came next. He suspected Mandy didn't want this version of him—*the real one.* She only wanted the dream.

Emily, though… she'd looked right at him and hadn't flinched. That girl was wildfire—messy hair, rolled eyes, and unfiltered honesty. She didn't try to impress anyone, and somehow that was what impressed him most. Just thinking about her made something in him snap back to life.

Ash tightened his grip on the fishing rod.

Don't be stupid. You don't blow up years of history for a girl you just met.

Mandy wasn't a bad person. She didn't deserve to get hurt. She'd been his whole world for so long that he didn't know where she ended and he began. Leaving that behind would feel like cutting off a limb.

Yet meeting Emily had undone him in ways he hadn't been prepared for. It wasn't just an attraction. It was the terrifying sense that she could be someone he might spend a lifetime wanting.

Mandy was everything he'd ever known. Emily was everything he didn't know how to stop wanting. And he wasn't sure which would cost him more—holding on or letting go.

A gull screamed overhead, snapping him back.

Ash reeled in his line, the clicking like a clock winding down.

The sun was glaring over the ocean now, the tide pulling hard against the pilings. He packed up his gear, but the current in his chest wouldn't quiet.

Chapter five

Emily woke earlier than she wanted; the room was still dim, with only a faint pink glow peeking through the curtains. Her body felt wired, restless, the way it got when she hadn't burned off enough energy.

Rolling over, she glanced at her phone through gritty eyes. The sun came up early on the coast. Too early to get ready for church, but she was too awake to sleep in.

Fine. Run first. Then play the dutiful daughter.

She laced up her old ASICS, pulled her hair into a high ponytail, and slipped out the door with the soggy island air clinging instantly to her skin.

She was glad she had opted only for a sports bra and shorts. The sun wasn't completely up yet, but the humidity made it feel like she was running in a sauna. The roads were quiet, only the occasional golf cart humming past.

Emily fell into an easy pace, breath steady, her legs grateful for movement. She'd been in ROTC at Clemson, and though she'd never pursued the military, the training had carved a tempo into her muscles that hadn't left.

Running was as much for her mind as it was for her body. Once in a yoga session, the teacher had called it the "monkey mind". The restless chatter in your head that leaps from thought to thought with no rhyme or reason, like a monkey swinging from branch to branch.

Emily knew that feeling too well. Her monkey mind was loud, constantly replaying arguments, regrets, snarky comments she wished she hadn't said, or worse—things she wished she had said but didn't.

Out here, with her shoes pounding against the pavement and her lungs working hard to time her breathing, the chatter dulled. Each step pounded a rhythm, and for a while, the thoughts inside her head were drowned out by the cadence of her stride. It wasn't oblivion exactly, but it was the closest she got to it.

Her legs carried her to the pier, where the air smelled salty with a hint of wet sand and sea creatures. She slowed when she spotted a lone, beat-up Chevy Silverado in the lot, its black paint faded to a dull, rusty gray. She noticed right away the University of South Carolina sticker on the back window.

Curious, she followed the boardwalk down to the pier.

There he was—*Ash.*

Baseball cap tugged low, rod balanced in hand, his shoulders relaxed in the early morning light. The waves rhythmically lapped against the pylons, and the line disappeared into the glinting tide.

Emily froze, her heart thumping harder than her pace should've made it. For one crazy second, it felt like she'd known he would be here and some part of her had been running toward him without even realizing it.

That's insane. It's just a coincidence. It's a small island. He's just a guy fishing off the pier.

Still, something about watching him this way felt strangely intimate, as if this was a version of him not many people got to see.

He hadn't noticed her, and she didn't call out. She lingered for just a minute before turning away, slow and deliberate.

Emily crept off like a cartoon villain in a Scooby-Doo episode, silently praying no one saw her because she could *feel* how ridiculous she must look.

Once she reached the pavement, she took off again, her stride tightly controlled and turnover quicker—as though she could outrun the unfamiliar electricity buzzing under her skin.

Back at the house in Haven Lakes, Emily showered quickly, dressed in a simple sundress, and sat through church without complaint.

The sanctuary was bright and airy, sunlight streaming through the windows. Her mom beamed beside Greg in the pew, and he shook hands with half the congregation like he was running for office.

To Emily's surprise, she liked the priest. He was younger than most she'd known, easygoing in the way he spoke, peppering his homily with dad jokes that made everyone laugh out loud. But beneath the humor, his message was solid—kindness, forgiveness, not judging people for their flaws.

Emily caught herself thinking, *if only I could live up to that, if only we could all live up to that.*

When they returned home, Marinda hovered by her bedroom door, perfectly put together in a crisp print dress.

She pressed a little too hard, voice sugar-sweet but firm. "Em, maybe something a little more elegant for brunch? That dress is fine for church, but these are Greg's colleagues and some of our neighbors. A linen shift, maybe? I bought you some nicer things. They're hanging in the closet."

Emily bit back a sigh.

Linen shift.

The two most dreaded words in her mother's wardrobe vocabulary. She could practically feel the scratch of the fabric as it choked the life out of her.

Before she could argue, her phone buzzed in her hand.

Jeanne's raspy voice barked through the line the moment she picked up."Emily, thank God. Sunday brunch crowd's eating us alive, and the hostess called out again. Can you get down here now?"

Emily glanced at her mom.

Marinda's smile faltered, disappointment cutting across her face like a hairline crack in porcelain.

Emily was already peeling out of the sundress and tugging on jean shorts and a soft, fitted T-shirt with the logo of High Tide on the back—the one Jeanne had given her at the end of her first shift. No one at High Tide seemed strict about uniformity, but she was the new girl and didn't want to test it.

By the time she slid her feet into a well-worn pair of checkerboard Vans, she was already feeling more like herself.

"Sorry, Mom. Work really needs me. It's crazy around here in the summer!"

It was her best attempt at an apology.

Marinda's lips pressed into a thin line, but she didn't argue.

Emily slung her canvas bag over her shoulder and headed for the door. The relief that washed through her felt almost guilty.

Almost.

Brunch with Greg's friends meant uncomfortable clothes, polite laughter, and pretending to be engaged in conversations that bored her. High Tide meant sweat, noise, and chaos. With Ash there, it felt like the "so wrong in the right kind of way" flavor of chaos she was already anxious for more of.

Chapter six

By the end of Emily's first week, High Tide already felt like a different kind of home—one that smelled like beer and fryer grease, not clean linens and floor polish.

Kenzie and Joel had taken her under their wings, teaching her how to survive the rushes with a deliberate mix of sarcasm, charm, and caffeine.

"Rule number one," Kenzie said, balancing a tray of crab legs like it weighed nothing, "never run unless something's actually on fire. It just causes panic."

"Rule number two," Joel called from behind the bar, "smile like you mean it, even if you want to throat-punch someone."

Emily laughed, shaking her head as she filled water glasses. "You two should write a book."

“We would,” Joel said, “but the brunch crowd leaves us no time for creative pursuits.”

Even Jeanne had softened a little, only grumbling half as much when orders backed up.

“You’ve got grit, kid,” she’d muttered one afternoon. “Most girls cry by now.”

It was the kind of praise that meant more than Emily wanted to admit.

Then, of course, there was Ash. He wasn’t always there, but when he was, she noticed everything about him. The slow, deep drawl of his voice. The way he moved behind the bar. He didn’t flirt openly, but she could feel him watching her sometimes—a flash of eye contact, a half-smile when she cracked a joke.

Once, when she leaned over the ice bin, she felt the weight of his gaze trail down her body, and a shiver ran straight through her.

“You’re getting faster with those drink tickets,” he said one night, voice low enough that she had to lean in.

“Guess I’m a quick learner,” she said, fighting the smile tugging at her mouth.

“Guess so.”

And that was it. Just that. But it hung there like static in the air.

Emily tried not to think about the way his forearms flexed when he poured a draft or the sound of his laugh when Joel teased him about being “the finest straight man in the building.” But her brain didn’t cooperate.

While wiping down the last table one night, she caught herself watching him again. The line of his shoulders under that button-down was distracting—broad, tapered, the fabric pulling just enough to hint at the muscle beneath.

He moved with an easy swagger. Even the simple act of tossing a bar rag over his shoulder somehow looked effortlessly confident. When he bent to grab a crate of empty glasses, his shirt lifted just slightly, enough to flash a strip of tan skin at his waist.

Emily's breath caught, and for one dizzy second, her imagination ran wild.

Stop it. He has a girlfriend.

But logic didn't stop the heat that pooled low in her body, or the way her pulse kicked whenever his voice carried across the bar. It wasn't just a crush—it was something she felt all over.

"Earth to Emily," Kenzie whispered, breaking her trance.

Emily blinked. "What?"

Kenzie smirked. "Girl, I've seen that look before. Just... tread lightly, okay?"

"What? I'm not—"

"Sure, sure," Kenzie said, already turning away. "Whatever helps you sleep."

Kenzie's words stayed with her long after work ended because Emily knew she wasn't imagining it anymore. Something was happening between her and Ash—quiet and unspoken, but undeniable.

One night in June, the sun dipped low, throwing streaks of light across the bar top and turning the whole island honey gold. The air held that sticky summer weight, not unbearable yet, just enough to make everything feel slower.

It was a weeknight, so nobody expected much of a rush. Regulars drifted in—dockhands, sunburned tourists, and couples nursing beers before heading home. The steady murmur of conversation mingled with the clatter of dishes and the faint twang of the radio.

Emily wiped down tables while Kenzie perched on a barstool, methodically refilling condiment bottles. Joel hummed along to an old Jimmy Buffett tune behind the bar.

"You're not doing bad, newbie," Kenzie said with a grin. "You've survived us so far."

"Barely," Emily said, untying her apron strings and stretching her sore shoulder.

Joel playfully tossed her a lemon wedge. "Don't worry, Jeanne only tries to scare the new hires for the first month or so."

"I think she likes me," Emily said.

"Oh, honey," Joel replied, perfectly deadpan. "If she didn't, you'd *know*."

They all laughed.

Even Ash cracked a grin where he stood rinsing pint glasses. He looked relaxed tonight, moving with the same quiet confidence that always messed with Emily's head. Every so often, his eyes would lock on hers. Not for long—just a second here or there—but long enough to feel like a secret passed between them.

Tonight, he looked a little more put-together than usual. Still in his black button-down, but it looked crisp and intentional, like he'd actually ironed it. His dark hair, usually tousled from the humidity, was neat at the edges, still damp from a recent shower. He smelled faintly of something spiced and clean, just enough to catch when he walked past.

Through the window, Emily saw a white luxury SUV pull up outside—quiet, sleek, expensive. The kind of car that cost more than her first year of law school.

She noticed the change before she understood it—Ash's expression tightened as his phone buzzed and his easy smile slipped.

He set the glass down, wiped his hands on a towel, and turned toward the door.

"Excuse me?"

Jeanne's voice cracked through the air like a whip.

"Going somewhere, Ash? It's only six-thirty, and you haven't stocked a damn thing."

He turned, sheepish but grinning. "God, Jeanne, I thought I told you. I've got dinner with Mandy and her parents at The Palm tonight."

"Write it on the calendar next time!" she snapped. "You're lucky it's slow. I won't be busting my ass behind this bar for you like last time!"

"You'll be fine, Jeanne." He flashed a disarming grin and jogged for the door before she could answer.

Through the window, Emily caught the scene unfold—the SUV, the blonde waiting behind the wheel.

Even from here, Mandy looked flawless. Not intimidating, exactly, just too perfect to seem real. She wore her hair in soft, definitely-not-natural waves, and her skin shone with that sun-kissed glow money seemed to buy. Her dress was a shade of pink that probably had a French name, and even the way she sat seemed posed.

Mandy didn't look like she belonged here. Not at a place like High Tide. Not with someone like Ash.

When Ash opened the passenger door and climbed in, Mandy's radiant smile lit up to meet him, and Emily felt something heavy sink low in her chest.

They look good together. Painfully good. Like Barbie and her tatted cowboy Ken.

She looked away.

But good and right aren't always the same thing, are they?

Kenzie noticed first—the way Emily's smile didn't quite reach her eyes after the SUV pulled away. She didn't say anything, just nudged Joel with her elbow.

Joel looked up from rolling silverware, clocked Emily's face, and groaned.

"Oh no. Nope. We are *not* doing that face."

"What face?" Emily asked, forcing casual as she wiped an already clean counter.

"The face that says, 'She's gorgeous and I'm not,'" Joel said, wagging a finger. "Miss Mandy might look perfect from here, but trust me—half of that glow is just money, honey."

Kenzie laughed. "Stop, you're making her blush."

"Good," Joel said. "She's prettier when she's not frowning like she lost her puppy."

Emily rolled her eyes, but a smile crept through. "I'm fine, really."

"Mmhmm." Joel squinted. "You know what? I'm coming over one night. We can do a full glow-up. Hair, makeup, the works. We'll drink wine and play dress-up until you see what I see."

Emily laughed. "You're ridiculous."

"I'm *fabulous*," Joel said, hand to chest. "So are you, baby. You just don't know it yet."

Kenzie leaned on the counter. "You should let him. He did my hair for a festival last year. People wouldn't stop talking about it."

She flipped open her notebook to a photo. Her golden hair—usually loose and a little wild—had been twisted into an undone braid crown, wisps escaping perfectly, on purpose. The bronzy makeup, the soft shimmer. It was effortlessly cool and very *her*.

"See?" she said. "Joel's a magician."

Emily grinned, shaking her head. "All right, maybe. But only if there's wine."

"Oh, there will be wine," Joel said with a wink. "And contour palettes. We're gonna make that boy regret ever dating Little Miss Pastels."

Kenzie choked on her laughter; Emily joined right after. And just like that, the longing in her chest eased, and the night softened around her. For the first time that summer, she didn't feel like an outsider.

Chapter seven

Mandy always drove like she was trying to outrun something. In every other part of her life, she was composed, deliberate, every outfit and gesture curated with care. But behind the wheel? She was a menace in lipstick.

Ash never got used to it. Every sharp turn taken with her high heel pressed to the accelerator made his pulse spike, while Mandy didn't so much as flinch. Her posture stayed perfect, hands steady, eyes forward as the speedometer crept higher, as if nothing in the world could touch her.

It struck him sometimes how someone so tightly controlled could crave speed like that. Maybe it was the one place she let herself loosen her grip on perfection.

Mandy was beautiful, no denying it—blond hair, blue eyes, a symmetrical face that could've sold perfume or beachfront property. Tall for a woman, about five-eight, she was all long lines and ballerina posture. From a distance, she looked effortlessly flawless, but Ash knew better. None of it was effortless. It was hours at the gym, a diet of almond milk, protein powder, and salads without dressing. She treated her body like a project—something to maintain, not inhabit.

Her figure drew attention everywhere they went. Ash had lost count of how many men's eyes went straight to her chest, but Mandy never noticed, or pretended not to.

The white Lexus purred through the night, headlights slicing across the asphalt. Her gold bracelets clinked lightly against the steering wheel, her perfume—something floral and expensive—mingled with the scent of new leather.

Mandy took a corner a little too hard, and Ash grabbed for the oh-shit handle. Without looking away from the road, she tossed something into his lap.

"Put that on," she said, flashing him a quick smile. "You can't wear that shirt to dinner with my parents. It's too… casual."

Ash glanced down at the folded polo in his lap. Crisp, pressed, perfectly sized. To complete the look, a navy sport coat hung in the back seat.

She'd clearly planned this.

No tattoos around the fancy dinner crowd. Wouldn't want too many pearls clutched.

All he said was, "Mandy, we're just going to dinner."

"Yes," she said, with that pointed brightness she used when she was trying to soften a command, "dinner at *The Palm.*" She emphasized the name as if it should mean something to him. "You never know who you'll run into there, or what might turn into a networking opportunity."

He nodded and turned to the window as the town slid past in a blur.

Networking opportunity.

The polite version of *don't show up looking too working-class.*

She'd never say it outright, but the message was threaded through everything from the shirts she bought him to the subtle corrections when he mispronounced words like *filet mignon.*

Ash didn't pretend to be something he wasn't. He didn't wear designer anything, didn't discuss property portfolios, and didn't belong to boutique gyms with eucalyptus towels. He was getting tired of feeling like she was always shining him up for display, sanding down every rough edge that didn't fit her imagined future.

He exhaled slowly, unbuttoning his shirt. It felt surreal sitting in Mandy's luxury car, peeling off the shirt he'd worn behind the bar. The same bar where he'd spent the last few days stealing glances at another woman.

He tugged the polo over his head. The fabric was stiff, synthetic. It didn't feel like him at all.

"Perfect," Mandy said, still focused on the road. "Now you look like yourself again."

Ash almost laughed.

Yourself.

The car surged forward as Mandy accelerated past a golf cart. She was talking—something about the wine cellar her father was building, a new boat they were buying—but her words blurred into background noise.

All Ash could see was Emily. Her hair slipping loose. Her laugh rising over the music. The little crease between her brows when she concentrated on an order. The heat of the bar clinging to her skin. Her soft, feminine scent that would somehow follow him home.

He knew he shouldn't be thinking about her. Not now. Not ever. But she'd cut through him anyway—vivid, impossible to shake, like a song stuck on repeat.

When she leaned over to scoop that ice, so help me, I wanted to—

"Are you even listening?" Mandy's voice snapped him back.

"Yeah," he said automatically, eyes fixed on the highway.

She sighed, flipping down the visor to check her lipstick. "You've been distracted all week. Everything okay?"

"Yeah, babe. Just tired."

"Well, try to perk up," she said gently, though urgency threaded cleanly through it. "Daddy's been dying to ask you about that coaching position."

Ash nodded, but his thoughts were already sliding away again. He pictured Emily, standing across the bar. The smile that reached her eyes. And those eyes—deep, startling green. He didn't know anyone who had eyes like that. Didn't know anyone who could look at him and make everything tilt off-axis.

I want to hold her chin, tilt her face up, and look in those eyes for a minute before...

He didn't finish the thought.

They were already pulling up to the valet, the restaurant lights glowing gold against the water. Every line of the building felt pristine, every detail gleaming as if it were ready for an inspection.

Mandy reached over, straightening his collar and brushing invisible lint from his shoulder.

"There," she said, smiling like she'd repaired something.

Ash stepped out of the SUV behind her, and all he could think about was how much he missed High Tide—the rough edges, the noise, and the girl with the sharp wit whose presence felt like oxygen. He longed for that kind of freedom. He was getting tired of the performance.

Inside, The Palm shimmered with soft light from glass chandeliers. The air carried the layered scent of truffle oil, fresh flowers, and chilled white wine. Round tables held linen napkins folded like origami, polished silver, and centerpieces arranged with architectural precision—everything whispering money and expectation.

Mandy's parents were already seated, smiling in that staged, magazine-perfect way.

Her mother, Elizabeth, looked like an older, lacquered version of Mandy—same blond hair, same blue eyes—but with the faint, telltale tightness of someone fighting a full-time war against aging. Her skin was too smooth for fifty, her lips just a touch too full. Beautiful, yes, but stretched to the point of artificiality.

Her father, Andrew, was coastal old money personified—tan and silver-haired, dressed in a pale linen suit. His Rolex caught the light with every slight movement, the diamonds twinkling like they were in on a joke Ash wasn't.

Together, they looked like a glossy advertisement for "successful living."

Ash straightened instinctively as they waved him over. He hadn't even reached the table and already felt out of place. Still, he played his part—handshakes, polite laughter, easy conversation. He'd had years of practice at making himself palatable.

The conversation sparkled lightly across the table, flowing like champagne instead of whiskey. Bright, light, and bubbly. No burn. Nothing substantial.

"So, Asher," Andrew said, unfolding his napkin, "Mandy tells us you've been offered something with the college?"

Ash nodded. "Yes, sir. An assistant coaching position at South Carolina."

Andrew's eyes lit with legitimate interest. "That's quite an opportunity. SEC football is a big stage. I'm sure with time you could work your way up there."

"Big hours too," Mandy added quickly, her smile tight. "We'll hardly see each other if he takes it."

Ash forced a slight grin. "That's kind of how coaching works, babe. At least during the season. But we haven't ever let distance keep us apart, right?"

Mandy smiled at that, pleased with the reassurance.

Her father chuckled. "Well, that's what ambition looks like. Working hard, putting in the time, and then after you pay your dues, you can write your own ticket."

Ash gave a short nod, but his stomach twisted.

Ambition.

Another word that used to fire him up, but now it just made him feel… tired.

"I was thinking about a trip in the spring," Mandy said lightly, turning her wine glass between perfectly manicured fingers. "Paris, maybe. It's gorgeous that time of year. What do you think, Ash?"

He managed a smile, but he knew exactly what she meant. Paris wasn't a vacation. Paris was a set-up—the kind of city where people knelt under twinkling lights, posed for photos, and made announcements. After almost ten years together, wasn't it time?

The thought made his stomach pitch so hard he nearly winced.

Mandy watched him expectantly; her parents were watching *her* watching *him*, all of them waiting for the correct answer. Waiting for him to hit his mark in the script she'd already written.

He lifted his glass, taking a slow sip to buy himself a breath.

"Paris sounds nice," he said quietly.

In his chest, everything was cinched tight. He could feel the walls closing in—city lights, a ring, a future he wasn't sure he could live inside.

A life with Mandy.

A life of disappointing Mandy.

The guilt hit instantly, knifelike and unforgiving.

He tried to steer his mind somewhere else. Of course, it went back to High Tide. The buzz of the crowd. Jeanne's gravelly smoker's laugh over the blender. Joel cracking jokes while he sauntered by. Emily leaning against the counter, head tipped back, laughing at something silly and small.

Her laugh wasn't polite. It was loud, messy, and unrestrained. Her voice always came out a little too intense, like she didn't know how to hold anything back. Reckless, real, and oh so sexy.

"Isn't that right, Asher?" Elizabeth's soft voice cut into his thoughts.

He blinked. "I'm sorry?"

Her laugh was light and tinkling. "I said, you'll love the lobster here. They fly it in daily from Maine."

He smiled politely. "Right. Can't beat seafood from Maine."

Like we don't have a whole ocean full of fish right outside?

He'd learned rich people always needed things that came from a specific place. Lobster from Maine, Champagne from France, caviar from Russia, leather from Italy, and port from the Douro Valley. But none of that made much sense in his opinion.

Mandy gave his thigh a slight warning squeeze under the table—*be present.*

He lifted his wine glass and took another long drink.

You weren't supposed to chug wine. He was refined enough to know that at least.

But hell, tonight I just might.

Conversation drifted on—stocks, real estate, the next charity fundraiser. Words that used to spark something in him now felt distant, like he was listening from behind glass.

Ash checked his phone under the table and saw no new messages. He scrolled through his contacts until he reached her name—*Emily Kennedy.*

Jeanne had sent an email last week with everyone's numbers for shift changes. He'd added Emily's immediately. Told himself it was practical. He liked the way her name looked on the screen. The sound of it, *Emily Kennedy*, was almost lyrical.

They'd never texted—not once—but still he found himself checking, thumb hovering over the name like maybe if he stared long enough, she'd text first. Ask a question about the schedule. Make a sarcastic comment about the bar. Anything. There was nothing. Still, every time his phone buzzed, some small, stupid part of him hoped.

"Something you want to share?" Mandy asked, her eyes lifting from the menu.

He snapped the phone closed and set it down on the tablecloth.

"Just work."

Her lips pressed into that practiced, polite line—*don't be rude.*

His mind was already gone again.

Emily was probably working right now, twisting a piece of hair around her finger, the humid air clinging to the skin along her neck. The same skin he wanted to run his mouth over while grabbing her waist and pulling her close.

Damn it. Stop.

He forced himself to tune back in.

By dessert, he'd checked every polite box, answered every question, nodded in the right places, and smiled on cue. But when Andrew insisted on paying the check, Ash felt guilty—like he'd been somewhere else all night, and in a way, he had.

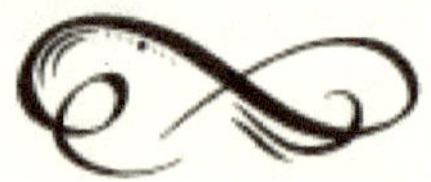

Outside The Palm, Mandy slipped her arm through Ash's as they stepped out together into the sticky, coastal night air.

"See? That wasn't so bad," she said brightly. "You were charming, as always."

He gave her a faint smile. "I've had practice."

She handed the ticket over to the valet and tossed her clutch into the back seat.

The second she slid behind the wheel, her voice dropped, cool and deliberate. "Let's stay together tonight. I've got that whiskey you like. We could get in the hot tub. You look like you need to relax."

Her lips curved into a slow, provocative smile. As she put the car in drive, she tugged her skirt up and guided his hand between her legs. A soft moan slipped from her lips as his fingers pushed her panties aside and pressed into the warm, inviting heat of her body.

Ash sucked in a breath. A jolt hit him, quick and unmistakable. His body craved hers, and he could tell she definitely wanted him.

The air thickened with her perfume, sticky and sweet, wrapping around him in the tight cabin of the Lexus. He felt her hand drifting to his thigh, tracing the hard outline beneath his pants, and sending need rushing through him, low and immediate.

"Mandy, pull over," he said suddenly, voice low but serious. "You shouldn't be driving at night while we're doing this."

She shot him a look. "Oh, so it's fine for me to give you road head on the way to Daytona Beach, but you can't touch me?"

"We were idiot kids," he said softly. "Thank God we didn't kill someone. You need to be more careful. I worry about you."

Mandy's whole body stiffened immediately. She slid her hand back onto the wheel first and then tugged the hem of her skirt down.

Ash withdrew his fingers, painfully aware that it was his fault the moment had collapsed between them.

Damn it. I didn't mean to kill the mood. She was trying to be spontaneous. Why did I have to sound like such a controlling asshole?

Silence filled the car, broken only by soft music on the radio.

After a beat, Ash cleared his throat. "Hey… can you drop me at the marina?"

"What? Why? I'm going to the house."

The house.

She meant her parents' mansion in Haven Lakes. Mandy lived rent-free there and funneled every spare dollar into clothes, shoes, handbags, Botox, facials, massages, manicures, waxes… the endless rotation of upkeep she treated like bare necessities.

"I left my truck there," he said. "I need to grab it. I'm gonna get up early to go fishing."

She shot him a skeptical glare. "How early? You can get it in the morning. You really want me to drive all the way down there?"

"Yeah," he said quietly, eyes ahead. "I really do."

For a moment, he expected her to argue, to press, then to steer him back toward her plan for the night. But she didn't. She let out a jagged exhale, slammed the brakes, jerked the wheel, and laid down rubber like she drove for NASCAR.

The silence for the remaining drive was thick, uncomfortable, and somehow far worse than if she'd screamed at him.

When Mandy finally pulled up beside his old Chevy, the only sound was the hum of the engine and faint country music drifting from the speakers.

"Thanks for inviting me to dinner," he said quietly.

She hesitated, the disappointment plain in her face. "You're sure you don't want to come over?"

"Not tonight."

"Well, you owe me an orgasm then. Maybe multiple."

Ash couldn't tell if she meant it as a joke or a jab.

"Put it on my tab," he murmured, leaning over to kiss her cheek.

He stepped out, closing the door with a muted thud.

The Lexus idled a few minutes, then pulled away, taillights streaking red before disappearing into the dark.

High Tide still glowed faintly in neon across the lot, though most of the crowd had drained out; just a handful of locals lingered over beers on the patio. Jeanne was there, stacking chairs, just like she had every night for twenty years.

Ash's gaze drifted to the parking lot almost without thinking. He scanned the rows of cars, half-hoping to see the rusty red Oldsmobile with a dented bumper and a peeling Clemson parking sticker in the back window.

It was gone.

He exhaled through his nose, the sound swallowed by the crash of waves against the breakers.

When he finally climbed into the cab of his truck, he let his head fall back, his eyes squeezed shut. For a split second, he imagined the passenger door swinging open and Emily sliding in beside him, scooting across the worn bench seat until her shoulder brushed his. It felt so real. He turned to look, but when he opened his eyes, it was just him. Just the dark. Just reality swallowing his fantasy whole.

Ash started the engine. Headlights flared across the lot. He told himself to go home. And he did. Empty, silent, and on autopilot the whole way.

Chapter eight

June slid by almost without notice, the days melting together under the smothering coastal heat. Haven County had a way of getting into a person—salt in your hair and sand ground into every pair of shoes.

At High Tide, summer had settled into its predictable pattern. Rushes and lulls, laughter and humidity, the beer taps hissing like punctuation marks in the noisy run-on sentence of each night.

Emily wasn't drowning the way she had at first, but she still felt like she was chasing something just out of reach. Some nights she walked out with her feet aching and her confidence shaken, convinced she'd never move as effortlessly as Kenzie or Joel.

Kenzie always seemed to notice when she struggled.

"Girl, you're doing better than half the people we hire in the summer," she told Emily one night while rolling silverware, tone matter-of-fact, not pitying. "You just think you're behind because you're a perfectionist. You care too much."

Joel slid her a Sun Drop from the bar fridge after a brutal rush and bumped her shoulder with his.

"You're golden, babe," he said. "Better than golden. You belong here."

She didn't fully believe them—not yet—but their words steadied something in her. She still second-guessed herself, still mixed up table numbers sometimes, still felt a tightness in her chest when the line of customers stacked too deep. But she was learning. She was getting faster. And even if she wasn't fully *there* yet, even if she still felt like she was trying to keep up, she believed she eventually could.

She noticed that Ash was around… just not as much. After the night he cut out early for dinner with Mandy, he'd gone quiet. Still friendly, but distant in a way that made her wonder if she'd done something wrong.

Jeanne had muttered that he'd been staying at Mandy's place exclusively now, at least according to his mama. Emily told herself it shouldn't bother her—it did anyway.

She tried not to listen when people gossiped, but she couldn't help it. Every whispered fragment about Ash clung to her like static.

One slow afternoon, after the lunch rush cleared out, the back of the bar had gone still. Emily restocked the cooler; the only sounds were the hum of the fridge and the clink of glass on metal.

Jeanne's voice suddenly drifted from the office—cutting, familiar, and impossible to tune out when she got going on the phone. "Yeah, I talked to Cindy Bell this morning. Said Ash has been making himself scarce lately. Always has an excuse not to stop by the diner. That boy needs to quit hiding out and go see his mama. You know how she gets."

A throaty smoker's laugh followed, fading into a cough.

"He's got a good heart, though. Too good, if you ask me."

Kenzie filled in a few more details, piece by piece. Ash had an older brother, Arch, a sheriff's deputy, who had a wife, Jessica, and a little boy, Ryker. Ash took the kid fishing sometimes. Sunrise mornings on the pier before work, teaching him to tie knots and cast lines.

His mom, Cindy, worked mornings at the diner by the marina, the place where fishermen and the island's working class showed up for coffee long before daylight. Everyone seemed to know her, love her, or owe her a favor.

A few days later, on her morning run, Emily slowed as she passed the diner. Through the wide front windows, she saw a woman behind the counter—short, soft, blond hair streaked with silver and pulled into a loose ponytail. Her hands moved fast: refilling coffee, sliding plates down the counter with practiced ease.

Even from outside, Emily could see the exhaustion in her eyes—the kind that comes from decades of taking care of everyone except yourself. Still, there was warmth in her face, a gentle familiarity. She didn't need anyone to tell her. She knew that was Ash's mother, Cindy Bell.

Other stories filtered through the grapevine—the kind that made the island feel intimate and interconnected. Jeanne had an ex-husband no one missed. Mean and unpredictable, he hadn't been seen in years, but she kept a .357 Magnum in the safe "just in case."

Joel had his own quiet storm. His boyfriend in Savannah had ended things suddenly, citing "long-distance isn't for me." Joel pretended not to care, but Emily saw the way his smile faltered when the bar slowed.

Kenzie, meanwhile, was living her best, no-strings life. "Labels ruin everything," she'd said once, flipping a braid over her shoulder like a punctuation mark.

Emily was still trying to find her own kind of balance. Life with her mom and Greg wasn't bad—just new and unfamiliar. Greg's polite predictability sometimes grated on her, and her mother was absorbed in the golf-club circuit of luncheons, raffles, and charity committees. Emily tried to show interest, but her head was always half at the bar or half on a run, chasing the burn in her legs and that first lungful of morning air.

Running had become a ritual again. Every sunrise, she hit the pavement, letting her thoughts evaporate. It was easier than thinking about Ash. Easier than naming the way she reacted to his smile, his voice, and the shift in the room when he walked in.

She told herself it was just curiosity. But every time someone said his name, she listened. And every time the door opened at High Tide, she looked up, hoping—without meaning to—that it might be him.

Ash woke up the morning after dinner at The Palm feeling like hell. Not hungover—worse. Heavy, sour guilt that settles in and refuses to budge.

Here he was, fantasizing about another woman while Mandy was trying her best to love him in the only way she knew how. She wanted him to look the part of a serious adult. Wanted him to move forward rather than drift. She wasn't trying to hurt him. She was trying to *help*. And he'd sat there across from her, half-listening, half-wishing he was somewhere else—with someone else.

He rubbed his hands over his face, disgust knotting in his chest.

You're a piece of shit, Bell. A dirty, cheating piece of shit. The kind of guy your dad would've hated you for becoming.

But he wasn't a quitter. Had never been the kind to walk away just because something got hard. He'd played through injuries until his arm nearly snapped. If Mandy was trying, then damn it, he would too. He'd make it right. He'd be better.

Lately, he'd been staying at Mandy's house—her parents' house—most nights. He paid her back for the missed orgasm, and then he gave her several more. Nights blurred into her legs over his shoulders, his mouth between her thighs while she muffled moans with a pillow so her parents wouldn't hear. His tongue knew the exact spot to make her shudder, and she knew how to arch for him at the right moment.

He was getting used to waking up to the smell of Mandy's freshly washed hair on his pillow, and the soft curve of her body pressing into him when she felt like it, or pulling away when she didn't.

Some mornings she'd wiggle back against him, subtle and unmistakable. He'd slide his hands over her breasts, then down between her thighs, finding her ready. They had always moved well together—in bed at least.

"God, Ash," she breathed one morning afterward, still panting against his shoulder. "You're spoiling me. We haven't done it this much since college."

She slipped out from under him and grabbed her phone.

"Shit. It's going to be busy today. I have a ton of PR stuff to catch up on. I need to get moving if I'm going to hit the gym before work."

"We can do that again," he said, grinning. "It's basically a workout if you get on top."

She laughed—freely, unexpectedly. And for a moment, Ash glimpsed the girl he'd fallen in love with years ago.

Then Mandy was back to business.

"Can you not come inside me?" she called over her shoulder, heading naked toward the bathroom. "I know I've said it before, but I'm paranoid."

"Baby, you take birth control," he said. "Isn't that the point?"

"Ash, just please."

He sighed. "Yeah, babe. I'll pull out."

She wasn't wrong. He should be more careful. It wasn't that he didn't want kids—just not now. Not when his own life felt half-built.

He thought about Arch and Jess, exhausted and swapping shifts, surviving on coffee and grit. They loved Ryker fiercely, but the toll was written across every sleepless line of their faces.

What kind of stability could he offer a child? A dad who worked nights, slept half the day, lived off takeout, and hung out with his buddies who coached football at the high school?

If he and Mandy ever had a baby, her parents would swoop in—design the nursery, hire the nanny, oversee every detail. But where would he fit in that picture?

He ran a hand through his hair and exhaled hard.

The bathroom door opened, and Mandy emerged in sleek black leggings and a cropped tank, her blond hair pulled into a glossy ponytail. Even dressed for the gym, she looked done-up, like she'd just walked out of a fitness ad.

"I've got a session with my trainer, then work, and then lunch with Mama," she said, tightening her ponytail. "Will you try to be home for dinner? We can talk about the Paris trip."

He nodded.

Mandy didn't seem to notice his silence. She'd stopped noticing a long time ago. The door clicked shut behind her, and the house fell still.

Most days now, Ash only went to his mama's place long enough to shower and change before heading to the bar. Sometimes he showered at the high school instead, after lifting with his buddies in the weight room. He still made time to work out, but the fishing rods in the back of his truck hadn't moved in over a week.

Two nights ago, he'd even filled out applications for online MBA programs. Thinking maybe—*maybe*—if he could talk about market analysis with Mandy's father, they'd stop seeing him as the washed-up ex-quarterback who mixed cocktails for tourists.

USC had offered him that assistant job weeks ago. He still hadn't answered. Told Mandy he was "thinking on it." But deep down, he didn't understand why he couldn't just say yes. This was his dream; it had always been his dream.

He exhaled slowly and collapsed back onto Mandy's fluffy white pillows—realizing with a sudden, sinking weight that the more he tried to move forward, the further back he felt himself sliding. The less time he spent at High Tide, the more he felt himself losing his grip—like the version of him that laughed easily, lived easily, *felt like himself*—was slipping further and further away.

Chapter nine

By late June, the rhythm of High Tide had finally settled into Emily's bones. She could feel it in the way her hands moved—reaching for glasses, flipping tickets across the bar, and weaving through the crowd without overthinking every step. She still had moments where she hesitated, but they didn't derail her anymore. She was starting to trust in her abilities.

Ash moved around her—close enough to brush past, close enough for their arms to graze, close enough that every shared glance tightened something low in her stomach. But never close enough to break whatever invisible line held them apart.

Until one Thursday.

The lunch crowd had thinned when Walt lumbered in—a regular with gray hair tufting from beneath a faded cap, and a voice gravelly as a bag of marbles.

"Sweetheart," he rasped at Emily, "you must be new. Don't mess up my whiskey sour. Been drinking it the same way for twenty years."

She smiled politely and made it exactly the way the battered recipe notebook behind the bar spelled it out.

Walt took one sip and scowled like she'd handed him poison.

"This ain't right," he barked. "Too damn sweet. They teachin' y'all how to make shitty drinks on that damned internet now?"

Emily froze, cheeks flaming, as Jeanne snapped her head around from the kitchen window. But before she could intervene, Ash appeared—calm, steady, a towel slung predictably over his shoulder.

"Hey, Walt. My fault, man. Should've warned her you like 'em extra sour."

He grabbed a shaker and remade the drink without missing a beat.

"Here you go."

Walt grumbled into a reluctant grin.

"See? I'm still the only one in this place who knows how to do it right." Ash said, flashing a smile.

Emily let out a breath she hadn't realized she'd been holding.

Ash leaned close, his voice low enough only she could hear. "You good?"

"Yeah," she replied quickly. "I didn't need saving."

"Didn't say you did." His mouth tilted—half grin, half trouble. "But Walt's an acquired taste."

Later that evening, the dinner rush hit like a tidal wave. Beer kegs were running low, Jeanne was yelling for more glasses, and Kenzie was swearing she was going to dissolve into a puddle of sweat.

Emily ducked into the stockroom for napkins just as Ash pushed in from the opposite side to grab a liquor box. The space was narrow—barely wide enough for one person, let alone two. She turned to move aside at the exact moment he did, and they collided.

Her fingertips pressed against his chest to steady herself, and his right hand instinctively found her waist. Time slowed. His breath brushed her temple. Her palm flattened against his shirt, and she felt heat radiating through the cotton.

Emily looked up—that was a mistake.

Ash's voice dropped low. "Your eyes… I've never seen that shade of green."

Emily's thoughts exploded inside her head.

He didn't move. Neither did she. Something hovered between them—precarious, dizzying, inevitable.

Then the door swung open.

Jeanne stood in the doorway, eyes widening for a single, blistering second before she snapped back into motion.

"Restock the bar, Ash. Anything else you need to do is on your own time." She barked over her shoulder as she spun away.

Emily jerked back so fast she nearly tripped over the box at her feet, mumbling a sound that barely resembled a sentence. Ash bit the inside of his cheek, trying—and failing—not to smile.

The moment had cracked apart, but the tension didn't fade. By the weekend, it still clung to everything. Emily avoided meeting Ash's eyes, but every time she heard him laugh from across the bar, her stomach flipped like it was doing a complete 360-degree loop.

When Emily came home from work Saturday night, her mother was curled on the couch, a soft throw draped over her lap. The house was quiet, and a half-empty bottle of white wine sat sweating on the coffee table.

Emily kicked off her shoes and melted into the couch as Marinda filled her glass, the chilled stem cool against her palm.

"Em! Perfect timing," Marinda chirped. "We've been invited to a dinner party tomorrow night at Andrew and Elizabeth Green's. You'll come, won't you?"

"Who?" Emily asked.

"They live in the neighborhood," Greg said, strolling in from the den. "Lovely couple. Andrew's a Clemson alum. He knows some people at Charleston College of Law. Might be a great chance for you to make connections."

Marinda nodded eagerly. "Their daughter, Amanda, just took over marketing at Andrew's company. Lovely girl. You two could become friends."

Emily froze with her wine glass halfway to her lips.

"Wait… *Amanda Green*?"

"Yes, that's right!" Marinda said brightly. "I'm sure you've heard of her. She's dating that young man you work with at the bar. What's his name, Greg?"

"Asher Bell," Greg answered. "Good kid. Hell of a quarterback for South Carolina before the injuries. His family's been around these parts forever. One of the Bells founded Bellefontaine, in fact."

Emily didn't have the bandwidth to marvel at Greg's inner Wikipedia; her brain was busy imploding.

Amanda is Mandy.

Mandy-with-the-Lexus.

Mandy-who-looks-like-a-coastal-Miss America.

"Oh," she managed. "I've heard of her."

She drank down the rest of her wine like a shot of tequila and sprinted upstairs. The second her bedroom door clicked shut, she called Joel.

He answered on the second ring, voice predictably dramatic: "Please tell me this is gossip and not a work crisis."

"It's a five-alarm fire," Emily groaned.

He gave her exactly one second of silence.

"You didn't kill someone, did you? I'm not a snitch, but I also just got a manicure. I'm not digging any graves."

"It's worse!" She paced back and forth. "My mom and Greg invited me to dinner tomorrow at their neighbor's house—Andrew and Elizabeth Green."

Joel inhaled sharply. "Mandy's parents?"

"Yes!"

"Oh, bitch, that's a setup!"

"Right?! How can I sit across from her? Miss Perfect? Ash will probably be there too. I cannot handle being compared side-by-side with Mandy."

“Emily, deep breaths,” Joel ordered. “You are not walking into the Greens' palace in a ponytail and a thrifted sundress.”

“I’m not exactly rolling in options over here!”

“Then thank God you called the fairy godmother of damage control. I’ll be over tomorrow before the party. Hair, makeup, outfit triage, emotional CPR. Whatever it takes.”

“You’re a lifesaver.”

“No, darling. I’m your emergency glam squad. And if Ash is there, we’re giving him something he can’t ignore.”

Emily laughed, tension finally loosening just slightly in her chest.

“Four o’clock tomorrow,” Joel said. “Have wine ready. And maybe a prayer, because if Jeanne has to run Sunday dinner service without both of us—plus she’s down one tall, handsome bartender—she may be the one digging some graves.”

Chapter ten

The next morning, Emily was dead asleep when her phone started ringing obnoxiously. She groaned, pawed for it on the nightstand, and squinted at the screen.

"Did you even sleep?" she croaked.

"Darling, beauty never rests," Joel replied, voice fully caffeinated, and entirely too awake for a Sunday morning. "Now listen. Before I come over later, I need you to do something crucial."

Emily rubbed her eyes. "Please tell me this doesn't involve glitter."

"Worse. Open your closet, take a picture, and email it to me immediately."

"What? Why?"

"I need to know what I'm working with. I cannot perform miracles blind."

She sighed, dragged herself out of bed, rummaged around for her digital camera, and snapped a blurry picture of her closet. Basic jeans, tees, a couple of sundresses, and then… buried behind them like forgotten treasure, a rack of pristine designer clothes with the tags still on.

Uploading the images took entirely too long.

Five minutes later, her phone buzzed again.

"EXCUSE ME!" Joel screeched so loudly she had to pull the phone away. "Why are you walking around like a thrift-store delinquent when you have a wardrobe worth more than my life?"

Emily laughed. "It's not *my* wardrobe. My mom bought all that. She was on her 'new husband, new look' kick."

A scandalized gasp. "I will see you after brunch, you beautiful disgrace."

By the time Emily clocked in, the Sunday crowd had already spilled onto the patio. Mimosas clinked, buckets of beer dripped condensation on the tables, and the whole place smelled like bacon, biscuits, and sun-warmed wood.

Ash was behind the bar, shadows cutting across his face. His hair was tousled, and his shirt unbuttoned just enough to make Emily feel slightly off balance. He glanced at her once—just once—and the familiar shock hit her. A mix of panic and pull that left her unsure whether to run or keep pretending to ignore it.

When the brunch rush finally slowed, Joel sauntered up behind Emily, one hand on his hip, already in makeover mode.

"Okay, miss ma'am," he announced as they clocked out, "it's time for your transformation. I can't wait to see this mansion of yours."

Joel stepped one foot inside the foyer of Emily's parents' house and immediately released a scream that could shatter glass. He spun in a slow circle, taking in the arched doorways, the hand-painted tiles, and the wrought-iron light fixtures that threw soft, romantic shadows across the walls.

The entryway flowed into the living room, which opened toward the pool deck and the rolling golf course beyond. Everything was airy and bright, furnished in linen and soft neutral shades that whispered—*don't touch anything.*

"Oh, honey," Joel breathed. "This place is *chic.* Like *Architectural Digest* had a passionate affair with *Southern Living.* Is your mother accepting applications for new gay sons?"

Emily rolled her eyes. "She'd probably love that."

"Tell her she has taste," he declared. "I can work with this energy." He clapped once, eyes sparking. "Now, fashion triage. Show me the infamous closet."

When Emily opened the doors, Joel went reverently silent. Then he stepped inside like he'd entered a temple, hands grazing fabric with awe.

"Why did you not tell me you had an entire Barneys New York annex hiding in here?" He flipped through hangers, muttering. "Tory Burch, Veronica Beard, Alice + Olivia, DVF. Girl, is that a Lafayette 148 blazer?"

Emily flushed. "My mom bought all of it. I've, um… never tried any of it on."

Joel clutched his chest like he'd been shot.

"Never tried it—? THE TAGS ARE STILL ON. Emily Kennedy, this is criminal negligence. I should call the authorities."

He suddenly crouched, spotting the neat stack of shoeboxes. One by one, he cracked them open—Manolo, Jimmy Choo, Valentino, Ferragamo.

He shrieked. "You have a Ferragamo graveyard in here, and you've been walking around in Converse?!"

Emily grinned. "Comfort over couture."

"Not tonight," Joel declared, wagging a finger at her like he was invoking a spell. "Tonight, we honor the gods of fashion."

He began draping fabrics around her shoulders, narrowing his eyes critically.

"Okay," he said finally. "You're a cool winter. Jewel tones. True black and crisp white. Silver jewelry only. Sapphire, emerald, amethyst. None of that pastel Pepto-Bismol nonsense."

He plucked a deep navy silk dress from the rack, held it to her body, and smiled like he'd found the Holy Grail.

"This," he whispered, "and those Jimmy Choos… this is how you walk into the Greens' dinner party and remind Asher Bell exactly what temptation looks like."

Emily swallowed, fingers brushing the fabric. "Joel… I don't know if I'm doing the right thing."

He paused, dress still in hand. "What do you mean, sweetie?"

She sank onto the edge of the bed, voice low. "This feels wrong. Like I'm trying to steal someone's boyfriend. Mandy hasn't done anything to me. I don't want to be that girl."

Joel sat beside her, bumping her shoulder gently.

"Okay, first of all, you're not stealing anything. People aren't stolen. They move toward who they want."

He lifted her chin gently.

"And don't you dare act like you're imagining this."

"I might be," she whispered. "I keep second-guessing and thinking I'm reading into everything."

Joel snorted. "Girl, please. I've known Ash for years. That man never notices women from the bar. They could be naked and on fire, and he'd hand them a fire extinguisher, then go back to pouring drinks."

Emily laughed weakly.

"But with you?" Joel continued, eyes gleaming. "He looks at you like he's trying not to. Like it physically hurts him not to." He pointed a finger for emphasis. "That is not in your head."

Her throat tightened. "Still… he has a girlfriend."

"And that," Joel said, gentler now, "is his business to figure out. Not yours." He squeezed her knee. "You're not chasing him. You're not doing anything shady. You're getting dressed for a dinner party. If Ash has feelings he doesn't want examined, that's on him, not you."

Emily breathed out slowly.

Joel grinned. "Besides… something is going on there. And I am absolutely here for it!"

By late afternoon, Emily's bedroom looked like backstage at a runway show. Joel had taken over completely—clothes spilled across the bed in colorful swatches, makeup brushes lined up in military formation, and a curling iron warming on the vanity like a weapon ready for battle.

"Okay, doll face," he said, giving her hair a firm but affectionate tug. "We're starting with soft waves. Effortless but intentional. The kind of hair that says, 'I woke up like this,' even though it took forty-five minutes and a minor burn."

Emily laughed, lifting the glass of rosé he'd poured her. "You sound like a reality TV stylist."

"Thank you," he said proudly. "Someday you'll see me on Queer Eye."

Joel worked with laser focus—light foundation, a whisper of blush, eyeliner streaked sharp and precise. By the time he finished, her cheekbones looked sculpted, and her green eyes practically glowed. He spun her chair toward the mirror with theatrical flair.

"Behold: the version of you who does not tolerate bad lighting, half-hearted effort, or mediocre men."

Emily blinked. She wanted to joke, but her breath snagged instead. The woman staring back didn't look artificial; she just looked… sure of herself. Different. Unhidden. Aligned. Still, doubt managed to creep in.

Joel clapped once, switching back into glam commander mode. "Wardrobe!"

He shuffled the dresses laid out across the bed before triumphantly holding up the navy silk Alice + Olivia dress.

"Definitely this one," he said decisively. "It hugs, it drapes, it whispers 'expensive' but in a mysterious, I-might-not-even-text-you-back way."

He paired it with strappy, silver high heels and the delicate Tiffany earrings her mother had gifted her at graduation.

"Cool winter palette," Joel declared, stepping back to assess. "Frostbite chic. You're welcome."

When Emily stepped out of the bedroom, Marinda's breath hitched.

"Oh, Emily," she murmured, eyes shining. "Honey, you look absolutely stunning."

Even Greg glanced up from his magazine with genuine surprise. "Wow. You clean up nice, kiddo."

Joel smirked behind her, arms folded. "We don't do mediocre around here."

They walked toward the front door together. Emily hugged Joel tightly before he left.

"You text me *all* the updates," he whispered.

She laughed, then hesitated when she caught a glimpse of herself in the full-length hall mirror.

For a fleeting moment, Emily didn't recognize the woman looking back. Beneath the makeup, a quiet confidence shone. Despite the elegance, something restless lingered in her eyes—a glimmer that suggested she wasn't nearly as easy to figure out as this look implied.

Down at the marina, the late-afternoon lull finally settled over High Tide. The brunch crowd had filtered out, leaving behind only the low hum of half-heard conversations and the clink of glassware being reset for the evening shift.

Ash leaned against the back counter, finishing the last of his sweet tea. When he finally checked his phone, the screen lit up with missed calls and texts—seven calls, four messages.

All from Mandy.

"Shit," he muttered.

He stepped out onto the back deck, away from the clatter inside. The breeze off the water was thick with humidity, but at least it was quiet.

He hit call.

Mandy answered before the first ring finished.

"Where are you?" she demanded, her tone high and tight.

"At the bar," he said, running a hand over his face. "We had a Sunday rush. What's up?"

"What's up?" she echoed, incredulous. "Asher—the dinner party. My parents' dinner party. You were supposed to be here an hour ago! People are already arriving for the cocktail hour, and everyone keeps asking where you are."

He exhaled, long and exhausted.

"Mandy, I told you Jeanne needed me to stay through the afternoon. I'll be there. I just need to shower and change."

Her sigh crackled through the line.

"You knew about this all week. I bought you that new outfit—the linen shirt, the blazer, the tie—and you can't even bother to be on time?"

"I said I'll be there," he answered quietly, forcing calm into every syllable.

“You always say that, and then you’re always late,” she shot back. “Do you have any idea what it’s like to sit here while my mother asks where my boyfriend is in that tone? Like you’re some charity case?”

That one hit him square in the chest.

“Mandy, I’ll be there,” he said again, firmer this time.

Silence stretched for a moment—just her breath on the line, quick and irritated.

“Fine." She said, eventually. "Come straight here. You don’t have time to go all the way back to Bellefontaine. Use the front or side stairs; everything’s already set up on the back lawn. And Ash… please. Try to look like you want to be here tonight.”

He swallowed. “Yeah. I’ll be there soon.”

When the call ended, Ash stayed where he was, staring at his faint reflection in the dark glass of the door.

The linen shirt Mandy had bought was still folded in his truck, untouched. He didn’t set out to screw things up tonight. He never did, but the harder he tried to fit into Mandy’s world, the more he felt like he didn’t belong there.

Still, he grabbed his keys, clocked out, and headed for the parking lot, thinking to himself: *This is what grown men do. They show up, even when every part of them wants to be somewhere else.*

Chapter eleven

By the time Emily and her parents arrived, the sun had dipped low, and the Greens' backyard looked like something Martha Stewart would have envied. The sprawling lawn rolled down toward a small pond where string lights hung from cypress trees. Bright reflections wavered across the still water, doubling the magic.

Long tables that were dressed in pale linen dotted the grass, each arranged with matching place settings and centerpieces of white hydrangeas. Uniformed bartenders glided through the gathering, balancing trays of sparkling rosé and mint juleps with practiced grace. A jazz trio played from the tented patio—upright bass, keyboard, and a smoky-voiced singer in a sequin dress—soft enough to blend with the murmur of polite laughter and the clink of champagne flutes.

A soft breeze drifted past, lifting the sheer white drapery framing the lawn. It was beautiful. Everything here had been designed and planned, right down to the pressed napkins and the floral dresses the women wore—each a soft color but with little variety in style. Even the men's laughter sounded rehearsed.

Greg was already in deep conversation with Andrew Green, shaking hands and grinning like they'd been fraternity brothers in another life. Marinda drifted toward Elizabeth, both of them smiling in that careful, honeyed way Southern women perfected from birth—warm, gracious, and always a little guarded.

Emily followed a few steps behind, moving gingerly in the stilettos. These were the highest heels she'd worn to date, and every step felt like a negotiation with gravity. She half-expected to trip, roll down the manicured lawn, and swan-dive straight into the pond.

Her heart thudded; she knew Mandy was somewhere in this sea of linen, pearls, and polite laughter. If her luck held, Ash was too. Thinking about him made her stomach tighten in a way she couldn't pretend was nerves alone. She eventually spotted Mandy, and recognition hit before anyone had to say a word of introduction.

Amanda Green glowed in the late-golden light like the lawn itself had been built as her personal stage. She stood near the bar, a vision in soft coral silk, her long blond extensions cascading in photo-ready waves. A *Return to Tiffany* heart-tag necklace gleamed at her throat, the silver chain catching every shred of dying sunlight as if it demanded to be admired. Her skin was sun-kissed perfection, and her smile was warm, wide, and practiced. Everything about her radiated ease. Summer in human form—bright, buoyant, born to shine.

Emily could practically hear Joel in her head: *You're a cool winter, baby. You don't compete, you contrast.*

Among the corals, soft cyans, and lilacs of summer, contrast she did. Her navy silk dress caught the last beams of the sun like liquid midnight. The silver earrings glowed against her fair skin. The soft waves Joel had coaxed from her hair framed her face with quiet elegance. She didn't feel like she was playing dress-up. She felt *composed.*

When Mandy's gaze locked on Emily, her mouth curled into a smile that was polite, but careful, a little too precise. "Oh! You must be Emily," she said, gliding closer, her tone sweet-tea smooth. "Your step-father was just telling me you're heading to law school soon."

Emily matched her smile with equal gentility. "That's right."

"How impressive," Mandy replied, her pale blue eyes hovering briefly over Emily's dress before drifting back up. "Law school sounds so… serious. I don't think I could handle all that boring reading." She laughed lightly, as if it were a charming confession.

Emily's own laugh was cooler. "It's not for everyone."

For a moment, they stood there—two women cut from entirely different seasons. One all sunlight and warmth. The other cool shimmer and shadow. Both polite, poised, and suddenly aware of the invisible line drawn between them.

Greg called Emily's name from across the lawn, waving her over to meet someone. As she excused herself, a flash of movement on the other side of the hedgerow caught her eye—a figure was jogging up the side lawn. Tall. Broad-shouldered. Dark hair tousled like he'd run a hand through it a dozen times. Obviously late as hell.

He's here.

A few minutes later, Emily stood near the edge of the patio, balancing a flute of champagne as Greg proudly introduced her to a small circle of men in linen jackets and pastel ties.

"These are some of Andrew's friends from the neighborhood," Greg said warmly. "All Charleston College of Law alumni. Thought you might enjoy picking their brains before the fall semester."

The lawyers smiled politely and asked her about her interests, what kind of law she hoped to practice, and whether she might want to go into politics someday.

As she spoke, Emily reflected on what had guided her career choice. She'd loved earning her English degree, but teaching had never appealed to her. Law school had emerged as a viable option. It hadn't initially been her dream, but it was a place where her comprehension and language skills made sense.

She responded to the questions with practiced grace, striking the right balance of charm and humility—years of being her mother's daughter had taught her how to perform in these kinds of circles. But beneath the calm exterior, anxiety bubbled like a fountain. Every laugh, every clink of glass, every flicker of movement pulled her attention back toward the house.

Finally, as if her patience had been rewarded, a familiar outline caught her eye at the edge of the crowd. Ash stepped out through the French doors, fresh from a rushed shower, hair damp, the faint trace of his cologne drifting ahead of him. His shirt, crisp and white, was neatly buttoned, sleeves cuffed at the wrists. No tattoos visible. The absence of them felt wrong to Emily, like he'd been edited to fit someone else's version.

His khaki blazer hung open. Around his neck was a perfectly knotted pink bowtie, the exact shade of Mandy's dress. Emily's lips twitched before she could stop them. The bowtie. The pressed shirt. The clean shave. It was so… not him. And judging by the stiff set of his shoulders, he felt it too.

Ash's gaze found hers, and for one suspended moment, the rest of the world dropped away as he crossed the lawn slowly, hands tucked in his pockets.

"Hey," he said, voice low, almost cautious.

"Hey, yourself." She managed a small smile. "You look nice."

He let out a half-laugh, tugging lightly at the bowtie. "Well, this wasn't exactly my call."

"I figured," she murmured.

Their eyes held, speaking volumes wordlessly.

"Asher!" Mandy's bright voice cut through the space between them.

She swept in, looping her arm through his with perfect ease. Her silk dress and Tiffany necklace shimmered beside his suit and bowtie. Together, they looked stunning and perfectly coordinated.

Emily saw past the facts and down to the truth—the stiff line of Ash's jaw, the smile that didn't quite reach his eyes. He looked like a man acting out a role he hadn't auditioned for. And for reasons she refused to admit, it stirred something painful in her chest.

Ash felt Mandy leading him away, but he couldn't focus on what she was saying. His mind was still wandering back, like always, to Emily. He hadn't recognized her at first. For a minute, his brain refused to make the connection between the girl in cutoffs traying drinks across the bar and the woman standing beneath the Greens' string lights in navy silk.

God, that dress.

His eyes traced the curve of her collarbone and down the neckline of her dress, which dipped low enough to make his lungs forget their job. Her hair hung loose around her shoulders, brushed and curled into the exact shape he kept imagining while he lay awake in the dark. He'd seen her flushed from the kitchen heat, hair tied up, mouth quick and snappy with a comeback. But this version of her… He didn't have a name for it.

He told himself not to stare, but it didn't work. His pulse kicked hard as his gaze swept lower over her body, taking in the quiet sway of silk at her hips and the way she moved like she had no idea what she was doing to him. She didn't belong in this world of polished silver and perfect manners. She was too real. Too passionate. Too alive.

He admitted to himself right then that he wanted her. Wanted to grab her hand, run straight to his truck, peel out of the neighborhood, and drive until the island disappeared behind them. He would take her somewhere quiet. Somewhere that dress could slide onto the floor, and he could finally—

He dragged in a breath and forced his eyes away.

He had Mandy. He had a plan. He had a whole life mapped out. But standing there, with a bowtie choking him half to death and a plastic smile clamped on his face, Ash realized—fully, painfully—he didn't want any of it.

I want her. To hell with everything else.

As dusk deepened, soft lantern light spilled across the tables, catching on wine glasses and diamond studs. The band shifted into an easy tune, and conversations mellowed into a warm hum.

Emily sat between Greg and a Charleston attorney who wouldn't stop bragging about how he "golfed in the seventies," which she quickly learned referred to his score, not the decade.

Mandy laughed brightly from across the table, her laughter calculated to be just loud enough for everyone to hear. Emily told herself she didn't care, but her stomach twisted anyway.

Ash barely spoke during dinner, offering polite replies, smiling when expected. His sleeves were still buttoned. His bowtie perfectly straight. Now and then, when he thought no one was watching, his focus drifted back to Emily. She tried hard not to notice, but her skin prickled under his attention. The neckline of her dress felt suddenly too low.

Emily forced a smile through the polite dinner conversations, nodding in all the right places. She took in the stiff line of Ash's shoulders and the quiet discomfort in his eyes. Whatever he was holding back edged its way into the silence between them. There was no pretending she didn't feel it too.

He sat close enough to remind her he was there without offering any relief from it. The distance between them became its own kind of cruelty. She wondered if he knew what it was doing to her.

After dinner, her parents decided to stay for another round of drinks, but Emily excused herself, insisting she would walk home. It wasn't far, just a few quiet neighborhood blocks. In heels, however, the distance seemed to stretch and stretch. The night was warm, the air thick and heavy, clinging to her hair and making it fall limp around her shoulders.

By the time she reached the house, the world felt muffled. The soft lamp by the entryway glowed like a beacon. She slipped off her heels immediately, her feet aching as they hit the cool hardwood.

Upstairs, in the bathroom mirror, she saw what Ash had seen all night, and for a moment, she didn't recognize herself. The smoky eyeliner had smudged faintly at the corners. Her lipstick was faded to a soft stain. Her curls had wilted from the humidity. She still looked beautiful but slightly undone.

One by one, she stripped away the evening's armor—earrings first, then the dress, which slipped to the tile in a whisper. Standing there wearing only lace panties, she wiped away the last of the makeup, letting her bare face emerge unmasked.

She pressed both palms to the cool sink, breathing through a mess of champagne and emotions. She named them all—anger, desire, shame, want. She wasn't supposed to want him. But she did. She wanted him with a fierceness that scared her—wanted his body pressed close to hers, his mouth on her throat, his hands everywhere. Wanted him like she'd never wanted anything. It wasn't a crush. It wasn't curiosity. It was *hunger*. A need she felt powerless to satisfy or control.

Emily turned off the bathroom light and crawled into bed, the sheets cool against her bare skin. Sleep refused to come. She could still feel the ghost of Ash's gaze—hot, searching, devastating—sweeping over her before meeting her eyes like he could see straight into her soul. She wanted him to look again.

Chapter twelve

Emily woke with a start, her heart thudding in panic. The sunlight was already streaming through her blinds, far too bright for early morning. She grabbed her phone off the nightstand and shot upright.

11:47 a.m.

"Shit, I'm late—"

Then she remembered it was Monday—her guaranteed day off. She groaned, flopping back into the pillows, one arm thrown dramatically over her eyes. The anxiety fizzled into a half-laugh, half-sigh.

Her phone buzzed, and this time she noticed the notifications: six missed calls and about a dozen texts—every single one from Joel.

Her eyes skimmed the texts:

JOEL: *Are you asleep right now or what bitch??? Pick up!?!?!?!*

JOEL: *Kenzie and I stayed up til 3 reading tabloids and we need DETAILS.*

JOEL: *Was it scandalous? Did anyone get slapped?*

JOEL: *Forbidden romance update STAT! We are perishing!*

Emily couldn't help but laugh.

She texted back: *Calm down. No scandal. No drama. No romance.*

Her phone immediately lit up again with a text.

JOEL: *Get on Skype! We need to see you!*

Emily sighed. The technology was new and a little clunky, but it was the best way to see someone's face from a distance. She threw on a robe, dragged her laptop out of her bag, and logged in.

Joel accepted the video call instantly. His face filled the screen, head wrapped in a silk bonnet. Kenzie peeked over his shoulder with a bowl of Fruit Loops.

"GIRL!" Joel pointed straight into the camera. "You're telling me you walked into that posh-ass dinner looking like Anne Hathaway cosplaying Carrie Bradshaw and *nothing—absolutely nothing—* happened?"

"Nothing happened," Emily said, her voice raspy with sleep. "It was just… tense. Like a staring contest from hell."

Kenzie burst into a laugh. "He just stared at you all night? What is THAT?"

Emily hesitated, chewing at her lip. "Basically. He said 'hey.' And then it was just—build-up. All night. And then nothing."

Joel slapped a hand over his chest. "Oh, it's always the build-up. But for real… are we SURE he's straight? Asking for a friend."

"Joel!" Emily shoved her face into her pillow to muffle her laugh. "Y'all are too much!"

“You love us,” Kenzie said with a smug mouthful of cereal.

Joel waggled his eyebrows. “So. What’s the plan today? You’re off, right? I vote self-care. Brunch, mani-pedi, then a little retail therapy.”

Emily rolled onto her back, staring at the blur of her ceiling fan.

“Tempting…”

She sat up, sweeping her hair into a messy bun.

“But I think I need quiet more than anything. I’m gonna take the ferry over to Amber Isle. Hit the natural history museum, maybe the aquarium. Just wander, and breathe.”

“Solo adventure?” Kenzie asked.

“Yeah,” Emily said with a slight shrug. “I need a break from… everything. Including my own overthinking.”

Joel clucked his tongue but nodded. “Fine, but if Ash figures his life out and comes chasing after you, I expect IMMEDIATE updates.”

“Not likely,” Emily laughed. “Y'all have fun at work tonight without me.”

She blew a kiss and disconnected the call.

Emily padded to the kitchen, made quick scrambled eggs and toast, and inhaled them between sips of too-hot coffee. The caffeine cut through her fog, jolting her awake. By the time she pulled on jean shorts, sneakers, and a flowy tank, she felt lighter—more like herself.

She tossed a paperback, sunglasses, and a notebook into her tote, slung it over her shoulder, and stepped out into the blazing midday sun. She had a whole day to disappear. A whole day to stop thinking about him, or try to, anyway.

When Emily reached the ferry landing, the sun was baking the asphalt and setting the water aglow. A long line of cars snaked down the dock, inching toward the loading ramp. She pulled up behind a white pick-up and let the warm sea air wash through the open windows—salt, diesel, sunscreen, all mixing into that familiar coastal smell.

When the attendant waved her forward, she eased her car into one of the narrow steel lanes. The space seemed to shrink around her. The ceiling dipped low overhead, the air thick and unmoving, and the rumble of the boat's engines vibrated through the floorboards.

It was so tight she could barely crack her door without hitting the car beside her. Her chest tightened. She hated small spaces. Hated the feeling of being pinned in with no easy escape. Forty minutes like this felt impossible.

The horn blared, deep and echoing, and as soon as the ramp clanked shut behind them, she unbuckled and bolted—slipping out through the narrow gap and up the metal stairs until sunlight hit her face.

On the upper deck, she drifted to the railing, letting the wind cool her skin. The ferry cut a clean path through the gray-green water, the sun's reflection scattering like diamonds across the waves. Behind her, Haven Island grew smaller—a watercolor blur of docks, rooftops, and sparse pine trees.

Emily breathed in deep, feeling her shoulders fully loosen for the first time since the night before. Here, with the engine vibrating beneath her and the gulls crying overhead, she didn't feel like a woman caught in the middle of something she didn't understand.

She watched as a man held a torn piece of bread high above his head. Within seconds, a fat gull swooped down and snatched it from his fingers, sending a ripple of delighted screams through the kids gathered nearby.

Emily laughed; the sound carried off by the wind. Amber Isle ahead. Haven Island fading behind. A quiet afternoon that belonged only to her was waiting.

Ash sat at the kitchen island, half-awake, stirring creamer into his coffee like the repetition might jolt him into feeling something. His body was present, but his mind was still back on that lawn, wrapped up in navy silk and green eyes.

Across from him, Mandy perched on a barstool in a matching pastel-pink workout set. She was scrolling through her iPod playlist with one hand, the faint click-click of the wheel under her thumb filling the kitchen. A perfect ponytail hung down to her waist, and a green smoothie was sweating on the marble countertop next to her, untouched.

"Last night was nice," she said, her tone breezy, eyes glued to the screen. "Mama and Daddy thought it went really well."

"Yeah," he said, voice flat.

He took another sip of coffee, hoping she wouldn't notice that the omelet she'd plated so carefully for him was only half-eaten.

Mandy finally glanced up, resting her chin delicately against her palm.

"I saw you talking to that girl," she said. "The one from the bar. Her name is Emily, right?"

Ash's spoon paused mid-stir; he brought the mug to his lips to buy a second.

“She's cute,” Mandy continued, casual tone laced with more than mere curiosity. “That dress, those earrings—she looked like some old Hollywood starlet. Like Natalie Wood, but edgier.”

She took a sip of her smoothie.

“She also looked like she was one step away from breaking both ankles in those Jimmy Choos. Poor thing probably hasn’t worn heels a day in her life.”

Her smile was light, but not warm—this was Mandy probing.

Ash set his mug down slowly.

“She’s one of the servers,” he said evenly. “Just here for the summer.”

“I know,” Mandy replied, the words soft as a dagger. “You spend a lot of time at that bar. Around her.”

There it was—jealousy, sugar-coated and slipped in sideways. She wasn’t asking for reassurance; she was testing him and seeing if he flinched.

He had. He felt it—tight in his chest, sharp in his gut.

Mandy wasn’t wrong. He *was* around Emily a lot. And he thought about her even more. More than was loyal. More than was smart. More than was safe. But he couldn’t bring himself to say any of that.

Ash leaned back and flashed the best smile he could manage. “You don’t have to worry about her, Mandy.”

He told the truth, and the truth was uglier than a lie. Mandy didn’t have to worry about *Emily*. Emily wasn’t the problem. Emily wasn’t scheming or flirting or trying to wedge herself between them. Emily was just… Emily.

Ash was the one who nearly lost control every time she walked past him. He was the one who’d almost kissed her in the stockroom. He was the one who couldn't get her out of his head—not that he even bothered to try.

Mandy returned his smile, but her pale eyes remained cold.

"Oh, I'm not worried," she said lightly. "I just notice things."

Then she stood, smoothed her ponytail, and kissed his temple. To Ash, it felt like a test, like she was patting a dog she trusted not to bite.

"I'll see you tonight, babe."

The front door clicked shut, and silence filled the kitchen in her wake.

Ash set his mug down and exhaled, long and slow. He didn't know what the hell was wrong with him. Actually, no—he knew exactly.

Chapter thirteen

Amber Isle was less than an hour ferry ride from Haven Island, but to Emily it felt like another world—bigger, louder, unapologetically alive. The streets buzzed with tourists and beach bikes, pastel storefronts lined the sidewalks, and window boxes overflowed with hibiscus and bougainvillea.

First, she lost herself in the natural history museum. Kids zigzagged between glass cases filled with conch shells, fossilized shark teeth, and dioramas. Their squeals bounced around the cavernous atrium, but the noise didn't bother her. It settled her. Reminded her that the world spun on, with or without her love life.

At the aquarium, everything hushed. The only sound was the steady churn of filtered water and the low hum of the tanks. Blue light washed over her as she stood before a floor-to-ceiling wall of glass.

Silver fish moved like liquid metal, folding and unfolding around each other. A sea turtle drifted past, slow and ancient, its shadow sliding over Emily's face.

She pressed her palm gently against the cool glass and let the bubbles rise, watching them burst against the surface. The ache she kept buried—the one shaped like her father—rose slowly. But it wasn't piercing this time. Just a quiet, familiar feeling. She imagined him beside her, pointing out the hammerhead sharks, laughing when she flinched as one swam too close.

Lunch was a table for one at a casual place near the docks—a Mexican restaurant with open windows and mismatched chairs that looked trendy, not sloppy. She ate spicy shrimp tacos with lime crema. The soft tortilla was warm in her hands, and the glass of horchata dripped beads of condensation onto the tabletop.

Boats swayed lazily in the harbor, birds squabbled over crumbs, and a couple argued gently about which beach to visit. Emily watched it all without feeling left out. Being alone didn't bother her. Today, it felt like breathing room.

After she finished eating, she wandered into a used bookstore squeezed between a surf shop and a jewelry boutique. The place smelled like old paper and espresso from the shiny machine tucked beside the register. Palm-leaf ceiling fans turned lazily above, barely stirring the warm air. Sunlight slanted through the high windows, lighting up the stacks in thin, golden columns.

She drifted down the aisles—travel guides, beat-up romance novels, thrillers with cracked spines. It felt good to disappear into other people's stories for a while. But her mind, as always, involuntarily drifted back to her own.

Way back.

Back to Ryan. Her high school sweetheart. A wannabe musician who wrote lyrics in the margins of his notebooks and smoked cigarettes behind the practice field. The kind of boy you fall for at fifteen because his angst feels profound, and his attention feels like water in the Sahara.

They dated through high school and college. When he broke it off unexpectedly just before graduation, she braced herself for heartbreak—the kind that splits you wide open. It never came. He had been all wrong for her, and once the shock of the break-up wore off, she saw it clearly.

Then came Ash.

Where Ryan's silence had been heavy, Ash's had dimension. He didn't sulk exactly, he *felt*. And he didn't perform the way Ryan did. Ash simply existed—solid, thoughtful, unknowable—and somehow that made her want him more. He could say more with a look than Ryan ever could in a thousand songs.

Sure, he wasn't her type on paper—country music, boots, a pick-up truck—but he'd gotten under her skin in a way she couldn't shake. It was as if one month on Haven Island had done more damage than all those years of blind teenage devotion.

She picked up an espresso from the counter and retreated to a small seat near the window. Her notebook sat heavy in her lap. She flipped it open and wrote:

My birthday's this weekend. Turning 22 on July 4. It feels like nothing.

Her mom had wanted to throw a 'small but elegant' dinner at the clubhouse. Emily shut that down immediately. Twenty-two didn't feel worth celebrating, and certainly not with crystal centerpieces and a signature cocktail.

Her pen tapped against the page before she wrote again:

Lately, I feel untethered. Like I'm floating somewhere between the girl I was before Haven Island and whoever I'm becoming.

She hesitated, then let the next thought land on the paper:

If I could wish for anything this year, it wouldn't be a party. It would be for Ash to figure it out. To realize he's not meant for her. To show up and tell me I'm not imagining it.

Seeing it in ink made her feel childish.

"God, I shouldn't have written that," she whispered.

She tore the page out, ripped it into small strips, and dropped them into the remains of her espresso. There they floated like soggy confetti.

She crumpled the cup, tossed it in the trash, and slung her bag over her shoulder. The bell above the door chimed softly as she stepped back into the warm air. The light was lower now, lavender fading softly into gold across the horizon.

Emily jogged toward the docks, bag thumping against her hip, the scent of saltwater pushing closer with every step. Her notebook felt lighter, missing exactly one secret she'd admitted to, but only long enough to destroy it.

Chapter fourteen

The first week of July hit Haven Island like a hurricane. The sleepy streets transformed overnight into a patriotic carnival—golf carts draped in streamers, kids running barefoot with melting snow cones, couples in matching flag T-shirts weaving through crowds with plastic cups of beer sloshing in their hands. Music blasted from the balconies of beach houses. Springsteen, Gwen Stefani, whatever the local radio could spit out, layered over laughter, shouting, and the occasional snap of a rogue firecracker exploding somewhere down the beach.

The parade floated down Main Street, locals tossing candy from the backs of pick-up trucks while sunburned tourists waved from folding chairs. Later, the flotilla rolled through the marina—boats strung with lights and flags, their reflections shimmering across the water in red, white, and blue. The sunlight faded slowly, painting the horizon in sherbert colors while coastal humidity turned the air thick as syrup.

Every bar on the island was slammed for days, but High Tide? The place had entered a different realm. Live music vibrating the walls. People yelling drink orders three at a time. Jeanne barking instructions with an unlit cigarette clamped between her teeth. It was weeklong holiday madness.

When the Fourth arrived that Saturday, Emily was running on fumes. Her feet throbbed, her ponytail had wilted in the heat, and she smelled faintly of fried food and sugary cocktail syrup. Still, there was something intoxicating about it—this wild, electric mid-summer energy made everyone a little reckless.

When they locked the doors that night, Emily leaned against the bar, ready to melt into the floor. The kitchen doors suddenly swung open. Joel emerged holding a tiny chocolate cake topped with sparklers and candles shaped like a crooked 22. Kenzie followed closely behind him, her disposable camera flash popping in the dim bar.

"Surprise!" they screamed as the sparklers hissed and crackled.

Emily blinked at them, stunned. "Wait—how did you even know it was my birthday?"

Kenzie smirked. "Girl, please. You accepted my friend request on Facebook like three days ago. Did you think I wasn't gonna stalk your entire profile? You're a Cancer, by the way. Emotional, loyal, and slightly deranged—basically my favorite kind of human. I'm a Pisces, so we vibe."

Emily laughed, feeling her face go warm. "You're ridiculous."

"We're *ridiculously thoughtful,*" Joel corrected, already slicing the cake with a plastic knife. "Now eat this frosting before it liquefies, it's a thousand degrees in here. Happy birthday, Miss Em. You only turn twenty-two once."

Kenzie handed her a paper plate and added, "Oh, and you might want to change your shirt. We're going out."

Emily narrowed her eyes immediately. "Out where?"

"There's a Fourth of July party down the beach," Joel said, licking a smear of icing off his finger. "At Stool Pigeons."

Emily paused mid-bite. "What is Stool Pigeons?"

"It's… kind of a club," Joel said, though his tone made that sound aspirational at best.

"They have clubs here?" Emily snorted.

Kenzie shrugged. "More like a beach bar that *wants* to be a club. But they've got a DJ tonight and fireworks off the pier. It'll be fun. And you're coming."

Emily groaned. "Y'all, I look disgusting."

"Please," Joel said, waving her off dramatically. "You could walk in wearing a Hefty bag, and people would still break their necks staring."

Without warning, Kenzie lifted her chin toward the bar where Ash was restocking bottles. "Hey, Ash—you coming?"

Emily's heart stopped cold.

Ash glanced up, towel over his shoulder, brows lifting. "Coming where?"

"Stool Pigeons," Kenzie said brightly. "We're taking the birthday girl out!"

Emily waited for the automatic refusal. For his usual *nah, I'm good.* For him to say he was tired, or he had plans, or he was heading home.

Instead, he paused—barely a second—and a slow smirk curved at the corner of his mouth.

"Yeah," he said. "Why not? It's America's birthday, and apparently Emily's too. I'm in."

Joel shot Emily a look over his shoulder, the wide-eyed, scandalized, delighted kind. A look that said, *Oh my God, did that just happen*?

After Jeanne locked up the bar and set the alarm, she waved the four of them off with a lit cigarette between her fingers and a "don't do anything stupid tonight" rasp.

The night air was thick with humidity and the acrid smell of gunpowder drifting from the beach. Fireworks exploded nonstop—rogue roman candles, bottle rockets, sparklers—lighting the sky in bursts of illegal glory. No one enforced the fireworks ban here. Haven Island practically encouraged mischief on holidays.

Traffic crawled bumper-to-bumper down the island's main road, headlights stretching out like a ribbon of ants marching toward the boardwalk. Music pulsed from open car windows—country from one side, club beats from another, something pop-rock blaring from a golf cart creeping past them. All of it blended into one gigantic joy-drunk hum.

Joel groaned dramatically, leaning against Kenzie's Jeep. "We're never getting down there tonight. It'll take an hour to find parking—*if* we find any at all."

Kenzie threw her head back. “You’d think people had never seen fireworks before.”

Ash was propped against his truck, arms crossed over his chest, watching them with that lazy half-smile he did without trying.

“I might have an idea,” he said, pulling his phone from his back pocket.

Emily lifted a brow. “Oh yeah? What kind of idea?”

“The kind that involves calling in a favor.”

Ash stepped away, voice low enough they couldn’t hear.

Before Emily could decide whether to be curious or terrified, the chirp of a siren split the street. A white Dodge Charger—official, glossy, and completely out of place—rolled to a stop at the curb.

Joel blinked. “You’ve got to be *kidding* me.”

The driver stepped out, grinning beneath the brim of his sheriff’s cap. He was built like a brick wall—a few inches shorter than Ash but wider through the chest and shoulders. His uniform was crisp and perfectly pressed. He had that ‘clean-shaven, former military, and could still flatten your ass in a bar fight’ look.

“Arch!” Ash called, grinning. “Appreciate it, man.”

Archer Bell—Ash’s older brother—clapped him on the shoulder. “You owe me for this. I passed a bunch of drunk tourists, two fights, and a guy trying to pee on a palmetto to get here.”

Ash shrugged like he hadn’t just summoned law enforcement as easily as a taxi service. “We just need a ride down to Stool Pigeons.”

Arch glanced at the group behind him. “Birthday crew?”

“Something like that,” Joel said brightly, sliding into the backseat. “You’re our hero, Officer Bell.”

“Deputy,” Arch corrected, amused but not enough to hide the pride.

Emily ended up squeezed in the middle between Joel and Kenzie, knees pressed together, shoulders tucked tight. A shotgun was mounted inches from her seat, and she tried to pretend she wasn't sitting next to a weapon capable of blowing a hole through the roof.

"Is this even legal?" she whispered as Ash and Arch bantered in the front.

"He's the law," Joel whispered back, eyes sparkling. "Ask him."

Kenzie leaned close, voice barely audible. "I have three joints in my purse. If he runs us past a K-9 unit, I'm done for."

Emily snorted, elbowing her. "Just hush and look innocent."

The cruiser merged into traffic, lights flicking on just enough for people to move aside like the Red Sea parting for Moses.

Joel stared out the window, shaking his head. "This is officially the weirdest cab I've ever taken."

Ash turned slightly in the passenger seat, glancing back at them—at *her*. The smirk tugged at his mouth again, like he couldn't stop it.

"You're welcome, birthday girl."

Emily felt it hit her like a warm spark under her ribs. She couldn't help it; she smiled back.

Chapter fifteen

Stool Pigeons was the purest form of a beach club—half dive bar, half nightclub. The main floor was dark except for the pulse of colored strobes and the gleam of neon signs offering cheap beer and *2-for-1 Fireball Shots*. A long bar stretched across the far wall; the mirror behind it was fogged from humidity, and the liquor bottles glowed under flickering blue light. The smell of coconut rum and sweat hung thick in the air, laced with cigarette smoke drifting in from the patio.

The garage doors at the front were rolled up, turning the bar into one open-air blur of sound and color. At the rear, the patio spilled onto the sand, where a cluster of tables leaned crookedly toward the surf, as if ready to give up. Fireworks cracked over the ocean, reflections skipping across the black water. A narrow staircase led to the rooftop, where bass shook the floorboards, and the DJ's lights cast everything below in rolling washes of violet and pink. You didn't so much *hear* the music as *feel* it beating inside your chest.

The crowd that night was a perfect Haven Island blend—locals still in their work shirts, vacationers already sunburned, college guys in popped collars, and girls in sparkly tops who would be holding each other's hair back later tonight. An older dude in a Hawaiian shirt strutted through the bar with two women half his age clinging to his arms, and no one batted an eye.

The bouncer at the door was built like a refrigerator with a round face, square shoulders, and crooked jaw. When he spotted Ash, he cracked into a grin that showed off gaps where he was missing teeth.

"Holy hell, AB! I thought you disappeared on us."

Ash clapped him on the shoulder. "Still around, Tank. You runnin' this circus now?"

Tank's deep laugh boomed over the music. "Just trying to keep it *legal*. We're at capacity. But for you? Get on in, and don't make me regret it."

Ash flashed a grin and ushered the group through.

Emily followed close behind him, her shoulder brushing his arm as he guided them through the crush of bodies. Energy buzzed under her skin—the sticky floors, the heavy bass, the neon haze—it was exactly the kind of messy, no-questions-asked night she hadn't thought she wanted, until the second she'd stepped inside.

Behind the bar, a girl with a jagged purple mohawk and glitter eyeliner poured shots with machine precision. Servers in crop tops and cutoff shorts threaded through the crowd carrying trays of Jell-O shots topped with tiny American flags, yelling specials that got swallowed by the music. It was sensory overload. The kind of place you didn't stand back and observe; you let it swallow you whole.

Ash leaned close, "First round's on me!"

Joel shot his hand in the air.

"Sex on the Beach," he announced. "Unironically."

"I'll take a beer!" Emily shouted, swiping sweat from her forehead.

The bartender—purple mohawk girl—slammed two empty tap handles together above her head. "We are now OUT of everything except Busch and Busch Light!"

A collective groan rolled through the bar.

Emily stared. "God help us. Fine, a tequila sunrise."

Kenzie leaned in. "Just a soda for me. Or kombucha, if by some miracle they have it. I'm not drinking. I actually want to function tomorrow."

Ash nodded once, disappearing into the crush of bodies toward the bar. Even in the swirling lights, his six-foot-four height made him easy to track, and Emily's eyes kept finding him whether she meant to or not.

When he returned, he held four sweating plastic cups and wore the cockiest grin she'd seen all night.

"Drinks," he announced, passing them out.

Emily took what he handed her and blinked at the dark liquid. "This is not orange. This is not remotely tequila sunrise adjacent."

"Crown and Coke," he said, tapping his cup to hers. "I blanked. Forgot your order. This felt… festive?"

"Absolutely not," Emily said, shoving the cup back at him. "I'm not drinking whiskey ever again. And you're a bartender. How exactly do you forget an order?"

Ash raised a brow, leaning closer so she could hear him. "First of all, tiger, you gotta put in a ticket if you want your order right. Second, what's the story with whiskey?"

She smirked. "College party. Tears. Taco Bell. Sleeping on the bathroom floor and vowing never again. End of story."

He let out a low laugh. "All right then. I'll drink both of these."

He did, tipping one back after the other while she watched, trying not to let it show how much the move made her nauseous.

A few minutes later, he muscled his way back through the crowd again, triumphant. This time, he carried a bright orange tequila sunrise in one hand and a tray of sticky shot glasses in the other.

"Redemption," he said, sliding the drink toward her with a flourish. "And a peace offering."

Joel's eyes lit up like fireworks. "Shots? NOW we're talking!"

Kenzie crossed her arms but couldn't hide her smile. "You're all gonna regret this tomorrow."

"Probably," Emily said, tapping her shot glass against Ash's. Their eyes caught—brief, pointed, charged—right over the rims. "But tonight? We're gonna party!"

They threw back the tequila, the burn hitting hard enough to make Emily cough-laugh as she sucked on her lime. Her cheeks flushed warm, her pulse felt quick and light.

"Come on!" Joel shouted, already shimmying toward the stairs. "I wanna go dance!"

"Go," Emily said. "I need at least one more drink in me before I brave that mosh pit."

Ash nodded, finishing whatever mystery whiskey he'd adopted. "Agreed. I'm not ready to drown in sweat, and Axe body spray just yet."

Kenzie leaned into Emily's ear, voice pitched over the bass. "I refuse to stay here and watch you two eye-fuck each other. I'm going with Joel."

Emily elbowed her, but Kenzie only smirked and disappeared into the crowd, her light hair catching the neon in waves.

Ash waved down a server and ordered another round, sliding a fresh drink toward Emily as the two of them settled at a tiny high-top near the staircase. The music thumped like a heartbeat under their conversation, pushing and pulling at the space around them.

"So," he said, leaning on his elbow, "you're a Clemson girl. Let me guess—die-hard SEC trash talker?"

Emily tipped her glass toward him, swirling the rapidly melting ice. "Normally, I don't waste my breath."

"Wow," he said, eyebrows lifting. "Just gonna insult my entire identity like that?"

She grinned. "The Gamecocks haven't beaten us since—what—2001? Trash talk feels redundant at this point."

He pressed a palm to his chest, feigning wounded pride. "You're not wrong. Painful, but not wrong."

The banter dissolved into laughter that was easy, unforced, the kind that settles into your bloodstream and makes everything feel a little softer at the edges.

"All right then, big football guy," she said, nudging his arm. "Who's your NFL team?"

“As a kid? Dolphins,” he said instantly. “Now? Panthers, obviously.”

“Bandwagon,” she teased.

“Survival,” he shot back. “I had to pick someone local, or my brother would never shut up.”

She laughed, taking another sip as fireworks crackled somewhere down the beach, the glow shimmering through the open garage doors of the bar.

It felt natural—just the two of them, talking, laughing, and moving closer than they should.

Emily slipped away to the restroom and returned with a mischievous glint in her eye.

“You ready to get your dance on, cowboy?”

“Ready as ever.” Ash smiled back.

They pushed through the crowd toward the stairs, the air heavy and stagnant, swamp-thick and reeking of spilled drinks. It was single file going up, drunk strangers gripping the rail and laughing as they stumbled their way down.

Emily was a few steps above Ash, her hair sticking to the back of her neck, her tank top clinging to her skin. She reached back without looking, and he took her hand immediately, his palm warmly enveloping hers.

On the roof, the night swallowed them whole—strobe lights flashing, bass shaking the wooden boards under their feet, heat radiating off every packed-in body. It wasn’t a rooftop anymore; it was a rave strapped onto a beach bar.

Emily turned toward Ash, still holding his hand, the red-and-blue lights catching in her eyes. "Pour Some Sugar on Me" blasted from the speakers, and the place erupted.

Kenzie was already spinning in euphoric circles with two sunburned frat boys who were seconds from face-planting. Joel had somehow infiltrated a bachelorette party, center-stage, shaking his ass like he was auditioning for a prize, glow-in-the-dark Jell-O shots waving all around him.

Emily threw her head back laughing and tugged Ash straight into the midst of it.

Ash didn't dance—everyone who knew him knew he didn't dance—but with her? He didn't care. Not tonight. Whiskey thrummed through his bloodstream, the lights strobed, and the crowd surged around them.

When Emily leaned back into him, he caught her hips automatically, and the world fell away. Music, noise, people, it all blurred. He moved with her, not thinking, not guarding, just calmly letting the beat drag all the reasons he shouldn't want her out to sea.

For one night, they were almost anonymous—just two people burning under the lights, moving toward something inevitable. There was nothing but Emily. The way she leaned in, laughing at something he barely heard. Her hair softly brushing his arm. Her curves pressed tightly against him.

He imagined leaning forward, tasting her smile, feeling her lips part under his mouth.

Jesus. Calm down.

Maybe it was the whiskey. Or maybe it was just her—Emily Kennedy—messy, glowing, irresistible.

Yeah. Definitely her.

A few songs later, Emily turned toward him, pressing a hand to his chest to steady herself, her breath warm against his ear as she leaned close.

"I think I'm gonna throw up," she shouted over the music. "It's too hot. And I haven't eaten much of anything since lunch."

His expression shifted instantly into concern.

"All right, c'mon," he murmured, steadying her with a firm hand around her waist. "There's a food truck down the beach. Best thing you're gonna find after midnight. We'll grab some water first."

He didn't give her room to protest, just guided her toward the stairs, his hand hovering at the small of her back—close enough to catch her if she tripped, far enough that it didn't look like he was holding on to someone he shouldn't.

They paused long enough to check on Joel and Kenzie. Joel was now on a chair, bachelorette tiara lopsided, hips moving like he was in a Vegas revue. Kenzie leaned on the railing, laughing with a dude in a beanie, the faint scent of marijuana lingering.

"I'm heading out!" Emily called to them. "You guys good getting home?"

Joel flung a hand in the air. "Don't do anything I wouldn't do!"

"That doesn't narrow it down!" Emily yelled back, earning a howl from the bachelorette party.

She and Ash slipped downstairs and out into the thick coastal night. The roar of Stool Pigeons faded behind them, replaced by the steady crash of waves and the intermittent crack of fireworks over the pier.

Emily slipped off her sandals, sand clinging to her feet as they walked, shoes dangling from her fingers, her breath evening out with each step. She sipped from her water bottle silently. Moonlight skimmed the ocean in silver strokes; the night felt warm and close around them.

"Feeling better?" Ash asked, glancing at her out of the corner of his eye.

"Yeah," she breathed, still hearing the ghost of bass thumping in her ears. "I think I just needed air."

"Good," he said. "Let's get you something to eat before you pass out on me."

Boardwalk lights stretched ahead in a loose glittering line, and in the distance, a food truck sign was dimly visible—*Gustavo's Arepas*, glowing in soft yellow. For the first time all night, everything felt calm. Just the two of them, the salt wind, the dark water, and the slow sweep of the Amber Isle lighthouse casting white, then green, then white again across the horizon.

Emily devoured her arepa like she hadn't eaten in days, the crispy corn shell giving beneath her teeth, melted cheese stretching, spicy pulled pork, and avocado dripping down her fingers.

"Oh my God," she said around a mouthful, wiping her chin with a napkin. "This is literally the best thing I've ever eaten in my life."

Ash laughed, watching her with a soft, low smile she didn't just see, she felt. "Told you. Gustavo's never misses."

When she finished, they carried their waters down to a dark, quiet stretch of beach. The sky still glowed faintly from the last bursts of fireworks, smoke drifting across the stars like wisps of torn cotton.

Ash dropped onto the sand, stretching out on his back, hands folded behind his head. Emily hesitated for half a heartbeat, then sank beside him, easing closer until her head found his chest. He didn't move. Didn't stiffen. Just let out one slow breath and stayed exactly where he was.

The world felt fuzzy, softer around the edges—the tequila, the night, the distant music from the bar drifting over the dunes. Emily's fingertips wandered without thinking, tracing the lines of ink on his skin, the curve of a letter, then the faint scar disappearing beneath his sleeve. Ash's breath caught. Barely. But enough that she noticed.

"Do you have any tattoos?" he asked, the tease warm in his voice. "Maybe a tramp stamp? Something tribal? 'Live, Laugh, Love' on your ribcage?"

Emily snorted, nudging him with her shoulder. "I don't. I love tattoos, but I've never found something I want permanently on me. Ya know?"

"No," he murmured. "I don't know."

Ash's heart thudded under Emily's cheek—steady, loud, and absolutely at war with itself.

What are you doing? She's off-limits. She's young and drunk and looking at you like you hung the damn moon. You know better.

She didn't move.

He didn't either.

Somehow, this didn't feel like a mistake. The truth was quieter, stranger: they didn't make sense, not on paper. A girl from the suburbs and a guy from the coast. She grew up on SAT prep and track meets; he grew up on backroads, with a family name that carried more weight than he ever asked for. She listened to pop punk. He swore heartbreak only sounded right when it came from George Jones. Different worlds. And still they fit.

He wanted to bottle up this memory and save it. The way her hair smelled faintly of… Licorice? Maybe. He couldn't place it. How small she felt tucked against him. The tingling sensation of her fingers tracing his arm, making every uncertain thing inside him go quiet.

For once, he wasn't performing, or apologizing, or bracing. He just… existed. Breathing in and out. *With her*, not just beside her.

Emily felt it too—something happening she couldn't fully explain through the tequila-infused haze.

Her thoughts tangled, drunk and honest: *Don't move. Don't ruin this. He probably thinks I'm wasted. I'm definitely wasted. I can't even blink without getting the spins. When will I ever learn? I should sit up. Make a joke. Change the subject. Oh God, if I sit up, I might puke. Just… stay still. Stay right here.*

His chest rose under her cheek, steady and warm, and her body refused to move.

Why does this feel like we've known each other longer than a few weeks? Why does this feel so simple but still like something I'll never forget?

For a few suspended minutes, they weren't breaking rules or balancing on the edge of disaster. They were just two people lying on an empty beach. The full moon cast a sliver of silver across the ocean, the only witness to a moment neither of them could explain—let alone admit to wanting.

Eventually, Ash stood, brushing sand from his jeans. He offered her a hand. She slid her fingers into his palm, and he pulled her up slowly, like he wasn't quite ready to let the moment go.

"C'mon. I'll walk you home."

She blinked blearily. "How far is that?"

He laughed softly, the sound blending into the hush of the waves. "Look where we are, Em. We're north of the pier. You live in Haven Lakes, right? Ten minutes max, even if you're slow, drunk walking."

She squinted toward the street, trying to get her bearings. The world felt distorted—whether from the alcohol, exhaustion, or him, she couldn't tell.

"I can have my mom or Greg take me to get my car tomorrow," she mumbled.

"Good plan," he said.

"Shit." She winced. "I forgot they went out of town for the weekend."

He shot her a sideways look, amused. "Ah."

An embarrassed panic prickled across her skin.

"Not that I'm—I'm not saying that in a… like… 'come over' way." Her words tripped over each other, mortified. "I just meant—they're gone. I can run to the car tomorrow. You don't have to walk me all the way or… whatever."

He smiled. "Relax, Em. No expectations. I just want you home safe. It's your birthday."

She checked the time on her phone.

2:45 a.m.

"To be technical," she muttered, "it's not my birthday anymore. It's July fifth now."

They walked in silence for a few minutes, sand brushing their ankles, the soft roll of waves filling the space between them.

"How are *you* getting home?" she asked.

He shrugged. "I'm probably not. I've got a friend or two on the island I can crash with."

"Mandy?" she blurted before she could stop herself, sounding too snarky, too jealous.

He looked at her, face unreadable. "No. She's in Charleston with her parents."

"Oh," Emily said softly. Then, with a sharper edge she couldn't swallow back: "So that explains why you came out tonight. You're off the leash."

Ash smirked, glancing sideways at her. "What can I say? I really like fireworks, shitty old beach bars… and cute birthday girls."

A strange, shimmering warmth unfurled through her body—hope, maybe, or something even harder to define. As they turned for the road, Emily listened to the ocean's roar fading and tried not to stare at trouble in Wranglers walking quietly along beside her.

Chapter sixteen

By mid-July, Haven Island had traded its usual golden haze for gray skies and seemingly endless rain. Ash's twenty-seventh birthday had passed quietly—split cleanly between his two lives.

The first celebration was at his mama's. The kitchen was small, warm, and familiar. Cindy baked the same chocolate cake she made every year; it was leaning a little to one side and slathered in icing and love. Ryker blew out the candles before Ash could even inhale. Arch joked back and forth with him. For a moment, he'd felt sixteen again.

The second was in Savannah. Mandy had planned the entire weekend down to the minute: champagne on arrival, matching hotel robes, couple's massages, and dinner reservations at places with menu items he couldn't pronounce. She documented everything with her digital camera—every rooftop toast, every fancy meal, every posed smile: perfect couple, perfect weekend, perfect proof for all her friends.

At night, after too many cocktails, they collapsed into the satin sheets—breathless, tangled-up, and trying to pretend the chemistry wasn't thinning by the hour.

But the thing Ash thought about most—the thing that his mind kept tugging at like a loose thread—happened two evenings before they left for the weekend.

The sky over the marina had been the color of steel wool, the wind picking up off the water. When he pulled into the lot, Emily sat in her driver's seat with the door open, legs swinging, a bag of Twizzlers beside her.

When she spotted him, she waved and hopped out, stuffing the candy into her backpack. "Oh, hey Ash! I have something for you."

He frowned, confused. "For what?"

"Umm… Your birthday." She said it like she wasn't sure she should. Like she wasn't sure if this crossed a line.

Before he could argue, she rummaged in her bag and pulled out a package wrapped in brightly colored paper, secured with a neon pink hair tie.

He had to laugh. "Is this your professional wrapping job?"

"Rude to insult someone who's giving you a gift." She smiled. "Hush up and open it."

Inside was a Dan Marino jersey—teal, soft from age but in perfect condition. The kind he used to have as a kid, the one he'd mentioned when they were sitting on the beach the night of the Fourth, half drunk on fireworks and cheap liquor drinks. He barely remembered saying it, but she had.

“I found it at a consignment shop,” she said, cheeks going pink. “They had it in the window, and I remembered, after Stool Pigeons, you said he was your favorite? I don’t know if it’s the right size, but… yeah. If it’s dumb, you don’t have to—”

“Emily.” He said her name too quietly, too truthfully.

He ran his thumb over the stitched numbers, and something warm and grateful punched straight through him. No one had ever gotten him something like this. Not something expensive—Mandy excelled at expensive. Not something useful—his mama handled that.

This wasn’t really about the gift. It was about what she said with it: *I heard you. I remembered. It mattered to me because it mattered to you.*

He swallowed hard, still staring at the jersey. “Thanks, Emily… this is—hell, this is perfect.”

She smiled like she didn’t know what she’d just done to him.

In the Savannah hotel room—satin sheets, skyline views, Mandy sleeping beside him—he found himself thinking not about champagne or oysters or perfect photos. He thought about teal fabric. Cheap paper wrapping. A neon hair tie. And a girl who wasn’t his, but who seemed to get him.

For her part, Emily never brought up the Fourth of July to anyone. Joel and Kenzie tried to pry, of course. Three nights later, they’d shown up at her house with beauty masks, gossip magazines, and a bottle of pinot grigio they claimed was “for emergency self-care". Emily suspected it was an ambush in disguise.

Joel leaned against her headboard.

"Sooo," he said, swirling his wine like a villain in a soap opera. "You and our bartender friend disappeared after Stool Pigeons. Any notes? Highlights? Deleted scenes?"

Kenzie smeared a clay mask across her face, eyes glinting. "I saw how he was looking at you, Em. Spill."

Emily kept her focus trained on her nails, painting them a deep navy that reminded her of the ocean at night. "Nothing happened. We got food, talked, and he walked me home."

"Mm-hmm," Joel said, unimpressed. "I don't buy it."

Emily laughed, but she didn't explain. She couldn't. The truth felt too close to something that could break wide open. They didn't need to know she'd lain with him on the beach, her head on his chest, his fingers in her hair. They didn't need to know how her fingertips still remembered the heat of his skin or how her heartbeat had synced to his under the July moon. They definitely didn't need to know she'd bought him a birthday present.

She still felt mildly ridiculous about it. She'd stood in the consignment shop, staring at that old jersey like it was some omen. She'd known him for—what? Weeks? A month and change? Not nearly long enough to justify the way her fingers shook as she picked it up. It was too personal. But something in her chest had whispered, *he'll love this,* and she listened.

Her friends, she assumed, would have teased her endlessly. For going out on a limb. For caring too much. For noticing what no one else noticed. So, she kept it all to herself—the night on the beach, the jersey, the way she felt like she'd found someone she was meant to understand. Someone she was meant to collide with, even if the timing was wrong and the circumstances were worse. She wasn't naïve; she knew he belonged to someone else. But knowing didn't fix the way her soul stirred when he looked at her, or the way it felt like they'd known each other in another life.

At work, she was flawless—polite smiles, fast service, not a single slip-up in her routine. If anyone asked, the Fourth was just another night. Nothing more. She made sure of it. But every time she walked past Ash, every time he brushed by her, every time she felt his attention drift toward her like a reflex, something pulled tight and hot inside her. A temptation she felt in her bones. It terrified her. It thrilled her. And it already felt a little too late to turn back now.

Chapter seventeen

As the summer marched on and July slid toward a close, storms continued to roll in off the Atlantic every few days. Stubborn squalls that rattled windows and turned streets into rivers. The bar filled and emptied early now—just a few tourists and regulars chasing shelter while thunder rolled out over the water.

One Thursday night, the rain had just begun to pick up, hammering the tin roof while Emily finished wiping the last table. High Tide was empty now—chairs flipped, floors still damp from mopping, the whole place echoing with that strange hush that comes after a long shift.

Jeanne had left an hour earlier, muttering about her bad hip. Kenzie and Joel had vanished into the storm, hoods up, laughing. One by one, the rest of the staff trickled out until it was only Emily and Ash. He was counting the register when thunder cracked hard enough to rattle the windows. She jumped, laughing nervously as the lights flickered.

"Guess we'd better make a run for it," Ash said, snapping the cash box closed and slinging his keys.

They stepped off the porch as the sky split open. Rain came down in sheets, blinding, cold, and relentless. They sprinted through the gravel lot, soaked to the bone by the time they reached their cars.

Emily slid behind the wheel, tried the ignition, and nothing. Grinding. Clicking. Dead.

"You have got to be kidding me," she groaned, slapping the wheel right into the horn. "Not tonight!"

Ash pulled up beside her, his truck idling, window rolled halfway down despite the downpour. Rain was dripping off the brim of his ball cap.

She clumsily cranked her window down a few inches.

"You good?" he called, voice half-laughing, half-deep and rough.

"My car is dead! I was about to call my mom."

He leaned over the passenger seat and shoved the door open. "Get in before you drown. I'll drive you home."

Thunder cracked again, and Emily didn't think—she just ran. She climbed in, water sliding down her spine, her clothes plastered to her skin.

The cab was dark and warm, thick with the feel of the storm closing in from all sides. Her fingers shook as she reached for her seatbelt, and Ash's hand brushed hers. The air changed as their eyes met. Rain clung to her lashes as she watched his gaze drag down to her mouth, slow and deliberate. Neither of them spoke.

Softly, Ash reached across the bench seat to brush a wet strand of hair off her cheek. His fingers grazed her jaw, strikingly warm against her damp skin.

Emily's resolve slipped. The seatbelt fell from her fingers. She leaned in and pressed her palm carefully against his wet t-shirt. The scent of him—rain, soap, cologne—caught her up. He didn't look away. Didn't stop her. Their lips met like the break of a storm. Weeks of tension snapped open, desperate and unrestrained.

Ash's breath hitched, his hand found the back of her neck, holding her against his mouth like he'd been waiting for this. The rain pounded the roof. Lightning lit around them like flashbulbs. For one reckless moment, nothing else existed. Not consequences. Not guilt. Just this kiss, the storm outside, and the overwhelming relief of *finally*.

When they pulled apart, breathless, Emily heard her own voice come out in a whisper she hardly recognized. "Do you know somewhere we can go?"

Ash inhaled sharply. For a second, he didn't answer. He was fighting himself or trying to. Then he nodded once, slowly.

"Yeah," he said. "My cousin's place. Up near the Point. Renters left early this week 'cause of the weather. I've got the keys."

Her throat tightened. "Are you sure?"

He met her eyes with a look that was conflicted, yet wanting. "I'm sure." He shifted the truck into drive. "You cold?"

Emily shook her head, even though goosebumps raced across her skin.

He turned up the heat anyway, the pads of his fingers lingering on the dial just long enough for her to see that his hands were shaking.

The storm hammered the windshield as they pulled onto the road, wipers useless against the sheets of rain. The headlights carved out brief tunnels in the dark, guiding two people down a road that felt less like an escape and more like a trespass.

By the time they reached the beach house, the storm had swallowed the island whole. Wind whipped the palmettos sideways. Rain lashed the dunes so hard the sand looked alive. The two-story cottage rose out of the dark, perched on stilts, porch light dead.

"The power's out," Ash muttered, killing the engine. "Figures." He removed his hat and ran a hand through his rain-soaked hair. "House is hurricane-prepped—they've got lanterns and flashlights. There's a generator too, but I'm not firing that thing up unless we're stranded for days."

They sprinted up the stairs, storm pelting them from every direction. By the time Ash unlocked the door, they were drenched—hair plastered, clothes clinging, breathing hard from the shock of the cold, soaking rain.

Inside, the silence was thick—no hum of AC, no appliances. Just the low roar of the wind through the walls. It was already warm, the kind of sticky coastal heat that settles on your skin the minute the electricity goes out.

In the thin beam of Ash's phone light, Emily caught the rough outlines of the space: big open living room, dark furniture hulking like shapes underwater, framed photos of the coastline glowing faintly each time lightning cracked.

At the far end, the entire wall was glass—floor-to-ceiling windows looking out toward the storm-blackened beach. Lightning flared again, lighting the whole room in one wicked crack. She crossed the room, threw the curtains aside, and slid the balcony door open just enough to let cool, rain-heavy air sweep in.

Ash disappeared into a hall closet, rummaging through a plastic tote. "Got a lamp and some flashlights," he called out over the thunder.

He came back into the room carrying a small camping lantern and a couple of heavy Maglites.

The lantern cast a soft circle of gold around them, just enough for Emily to see the soaked shirt clinging to every line of his body, and the rain droplets sliding down the curve of his throat. She stood barefoot on the wooden floor, soaked through, hair dripping onto her shoulders. Her shirt clung to her like a second skin.

Ash's eyes moved over her like he knew he shouldn't look and couldn't stop himself.

"Come here," he said. Not a command. Not a question. Just his voice, low and steady, unraveling her with two words.

She stepped toward him, slowly, deliberately, the storm shaking the windows with every gust. When she was within arm's reach, he tipped her chin up with the gentlest touch, like he wanted her to know she could still walk away.

"This storm's bad," he murmured, eyes flicking to the window.

"Yeah, it is," she whispered, but she wasn't looking outside.

The next second, his mouth found hers, rough and searching, and she met him with equal force. Her hands fisted in his damp shirt, dragging him closer until there was no space left between them. The thunder cracked overhead, shaking the house, but neither of them stopped.

They stumbled back toward the couch. Ash pulled his shirt off over his head. Emily's soft laugh broke between kisses. He cupped her face softly, his thumb brushing her lower lip before slipping into her mouth, his breath shuddering as she closed her lips around it.

"Tell me to stop," he whispered, the words shaking more than the windows.

Her answer was barely a sound. "Don't."

She pulled her shirt over her head, and his breath left him in one shivering exhale. His hands skimmed her sides, slow at first, like he was asking permission with every inch. She arched into the touch, wanting more, wanting him. He unhooked her bra and closed his mouth around one of her breasts, flicking her nipple with his tongue as she moaned softly into his ear.

The storm raged harder outside—the sound of rain like static in the background—but all Emily could hear was their breathing and the pounding of her own heartbeat. For once, there was no overthinking anything.

"Do you have protection?" Emily asked, breaking away from a kiss.

"You're sure?" he breathed. "We can just kiss, Emily, we don't have to..."

In the dimness, he could see her eyes—hungry, almost begging.

"I need you," she whispered.

It was all she needed to say.

He stood, undid his belt, and slipped out of his wet jeans and boxers. Emily watched him undress, her eyes sliding over his body slowly, starting with his face, then all the way down. Her brain exploded into a stream of curse words and thoughts so erotic she could feel her face start to burn.

She was almost naked now, wearing nothing but thong panties. He knelt in front of her and slipped them off, kissing her thighs, spreading her legs wide, and circling his tongue where he knew she would like it. She moaned and writhed as he licked and sucked, her legs trembling as wetness dripped down her thighs.

"Fuck me," she breathed out quietly. Then louder, "Ash, fuck me."

He climbed up onto the couch, slid on a condom, and pulled her close. The fluid motion of it made her gasp for air. She moved down slowly onto him, partway, then deeper until she felt the length of him inside her. For a moment, she paused to revel in the sensation.

"Oh my God," she whined in his ear.

She rocked her hips back and forth, enjoying his moans as he held her tightly by the waist. She couldn't tell if the lightning was flashing outside the bungalow or inside her as rapture took over her body.

"Wrap your legs around me," he said softly.

She nodded and obeyed.

He stood up, still inside her, and gently lowered her down to the couch. She felt his weight on top of her, his breath in her ear. Inside of her, he was thrusting so deep she wanted to scream, but for some reason she couldn't.

The orgasm came like a sudden surge that took her over. It started between her legs, and then she felt her entire body contract in spasms.

"I'm coming, oh my God, Ash, I'm coming," she managed to breathe out in a throaty whisper.

She heard him groan and felt him thrust again deep. He let out his release as he kissed her, their mouths and tongues interlocking.

They lay still for a long time, the storm outside slipping from a violent roar into a steady, hypnotic rhythm. The thunder softened, the rain turned into a low drumbeat against the walls, and the lantern threw a warm, trembling glow over everything around them.

The couch pulled out into a bed. They found the blankets and sheets in the hall closet. At a point, somewhere between the thunder and the lamplight, the boundaries they'd both sworn to respect had slipped, then shattered. Not with a crash, but so quietly it almost went unnoticed.

Emily lay curled against Ash, her back fitted against his body as if she was meant for that space. His arm draped loosely around her, fingers drawing idle circles along her shoulder blade—slow, absent, like he wasn't even aware he was doing it. The dizzying, reckless urgency had cooled into something gentler. Neither of them spoke. Neither dared to.

What did we do?

What happens now?

Emily didn't want to think about any of it, not yet. Thinking meant consequences, and consequences meant facing reality.

A faint vibration broke the silence. Then another. Her phone was buzzing insistently from somewhere in her bag.

"Shit," she whispered, bolting upright, the blanket slipping. "My mom."

She scrambled across the dim living room, nearly tripping over the edge of the rug. Her fingers fumbled as she pulled the phone free, the screen lighting her face in stark white.

A flood of missed calls and messages:

Mom: *Where are you? Please call me.*

Mom: *The storm is getting worse, Emily.*

Greg: *You home? Check in with your mother, please.*

Her stomach dropped.

Behind her, Ash sat up slowly, his expression shadowed and unreadable in the low light.

"I—I need to call her back," she said, wrapping the blanket tightly around herself, embarrassment and panic fighting for space in her chest.

"Of course," he said softly. "Tell her you're safe."

Emily stepped toward the balcony door, turned her back, and pressed the phone to her ear. "Mom? Yeah—yeah, I'm okay. I'm fine, I promise. My car wouldn't start, and the storm hit, so I just… stayed with a friend. No, I'm safe. I swear. I'll come home when it clears. Mom, it's okay. I'm twenty-two now, remember?" She laughed weakly, even though her throat felt tight.

Marinda's voice came through frantic and scolding, relief tangled with fear.

Emily soothed her, apologized, reassured her again and again until her mother finally exhaled and let her go.

She lowered the phone as she looked toward the window. Her face floated there in the dark glass, caught between shadows and storm light. For a moment, she didn't recognize herself. The reflection that stared back was altered.

Ash's voice broke the quiet. "Everything okay?"

She turned, pulling the blanket closer around her bare shoulders. "She was just scared. I didn't mean to freak her out like that. I'm her only child."

Emily tried to smile.

"She's always been protective, especially after my dad died."

Ash's expression shifted in the faint light, softening, cracking a little at the edges. He knew that kind of loss. Too well. Something passed between them, unspoken and heavy. He reached out, brushing her wrist with just his fingertips.

"I get it," he said quietly.

Emily slumped down next to him, letting her head settle on his shoulder. It was too easy—too familiar—to occupy that space with him. She'd fallen into a moment, and she never wanted it to end.

"I'm starving," Ash said finally, breaking the silence. "But I don't think we're gonna find much here."

He rummaged through the kitchen, cabinets banging softly, and returned with a pathetic assortment: a half-empty case of Miller Lite sweating heavily, a box of chocolate Pop-Tarts, and a bright orange plastic tote labeled **HURRICANE SURVIVAL KIT**.

"Well," he announced, dropping everything onto the coffee table with a thud, "gourmet dining, coastal storm edition."

Emily laughed, pushing her damp hair back with both hands. "Honestly? I'm hungry enough that I don't even care."

"There's, uh…" He pried open the tote and read the labels like he was mentally preparing to be disgusted, "self-heating meals. Beef stew, chicken curry, and something called pasta primavera, which I don't trust for one second."

"Sounds *delicious*," she teased, eyebrow raised.

He cracked a grin and pulled one out, pressing the heating tab. It hissed violently, as if offended at being woken up.

"I'll warn you," he said, handing it over, "these taste like hot cardboard."

She took it anyway, setting it on her lap and balancing a Pop-Tart beside it. "Reminds me of eating MREs."

Ash's head jerked up, eyebrows shooting high. "Wait—*you've* eaten MREs?"

"ROTC," she said through a bite. "Weekend drills and survival training. I still have nightmares about those powdered eggs."

His laugh was loud and genuine, one of those rare sounds he didn't hold back.

"You? In ROTC? Damn, I didn't see that coming."

"Why's that?"

He gave her a slow once-over. "You strike me as someone much too stubborn to take orders."

She lifted her beer can and clinked it against his. "I like to surprise."

The storm beat against the windows, wind howling through the dunes, but inside it felt soft—warm, almost domestic. The lantern light shimmered across their faces as they ate cross-legged on the floor, trading stories, teasing each other, pretending the world outside this bubble didn't exist. Pretending that none of this was complicated or borrowed.

When the food was gone, and the rain eased into something gentler, Emily leaned back against the couch, watching Ash. The way the shadows played against his face. The quiet focus in his eyes. The softening she'd only ever glimpsed in fleeting moments until tonight.

He's nothing like I thought he'd be. He's more.

That night, she tucked herself naked against him on the pull-out as his arm came around to hold her without even thinking. Rain whispered against the windows. Everything felt warm, suspended.

A line drifted through Emily's mind—one she'd underlined a dozen times in a dog-eared paperback she kept on her nightstand.

"Whatever our souls are made of, his and mine are the same."

She fell asleep with that thought burning through her, soft as a secret—a secret she wasn't sure she could keep.

Chapter eighteen

The morning light was silent and pale as it spilled through the expansive, salt-washed windows facing the sea. The storm had finally broken, leaving the air threaded with the scent of wet sand.

Emily stood by the door, barefoot, her damp jean shorts clinging to her thighs and sneakers dangling from her hand. The house was still; the oven lights flashed 12:00. Proof that the power was back. Ash slept on the pull-out couch, one arm flung over his face, sheet tangled low around his hips. In the early light, he looked different, younger somehow, as if the storm had stripped away every layer he usually wore like armor.

For a moment, she let herself look. She half considered climbing back in beside him. Then her guilt got loud.

You can't stay here. You can't wake up beside him like this.

In the kitchen drawer, she found a scrap of paper, the back of an old Harris Teeter grocery list, and a Sharpie that wrote in fits.

Her hand shook as she scrawled:

Ash—I can't

She set it on the coffee table beside the empty beer cans and the extinguished lantern. Then she slipped out the front door, careful not to let it slam behind her.

Outside, the island was slowly waking up—streets steaming as sunlight baked the rain puddles off the pavement. Emily started running, shoes slapping wet ground, her lungs burning. She didn't stop, not even when her shins screamed, and the wet clothes chafed against her skin. She only slowed the pace when the pillars of the Haven Lakes entrance rose into view.

Now, in the sobering clarity of daylight, shame hit hard—a hangover with no alcohol needed. By the time she reached her room, she was trembling. Somewhere in the back of her mind, a quiet fear stirred, one that said she was no longer interested in playing by the rules.

She shut the door, turned the lock, and pressed her forehead to the cool wood.

"Shit," she whispered. "What did I do?"

Her phone buzzed.

Not him.

Of course not, just Jeanne asking about her car.

She tried to tell herself it didn't matter—it was just a hook-up, one night, no strings. She didn't need reassurance. Didn't need him. But that tiny sting in her chest said otherwise.

In the bathroom mirror, the disheveled mess looking back made her feel frightfully obvious. Tangled hair. Swollen lips. A faint bruise on her shoulder in the shape of a thumb, already turning blue. A souvenir. A secret. She didn't know whether she wanted to cover it or trace it.

She twisted the knob on the claw-foot tub until hot water roared out, steaming. Her reflection blurred in the fog as she undressed and stepped in, the heat stinging her skin. Her thoughts replayed the night in vivid, traitorous flashes.

You should forget this. Just move on. Get your mind right.

But the truth wouldn't let her go.

I want more. And that's the problem. If I'm going to be that girl, then at least I need to be smart. Start taking birth control again, for Christ's sake.

She sank deeper into the rising steam, breath shuddering, and let the water swallow her whole.

Trying to be responsible this morning only made last night feel more reckless, but somehow, more right. She'd acted on instinct, on want, on something she'd tried to starve until it devoured her whole. Beneath her practical reasoning, something darker and more pervasive pulsed.

I'd do it again. Fuck, I want him again.

She slid her fingers between her legs, moaning and pressing circles gently. When the orgasm finally crested through her, she gasped, whispering his name, soft but desperate, a confession to the empty room.

When Ash woke, the room felt wrong. It was too quiet, too still.

"Emily?" he murmured, voice hoarse.

No answer.

He pushed up onto his elbows. The lantern on the floor was cold. The bed beside him was empty. And on the coffee table, beside a couple of warm beers, sat a torn scrap of paper.

Ash—I can't

He stared at it, thumb dragging over the shaky lettering like maybe if he touched it enough, it would explain itself. But it didn't. It just sat there, heavy as a verdict.

He closed his eyes, exhaling slowly. This wasn't who he wanted to be—a man split in two, dragging everybody along with him. He had been walking a line so thin it was killing him. Last night, he'd crossed it. There was no pretending otherwise. For the first time in months, he knew exactly what he needed to do. No half-truths. No hiding. No "maybe later." If he wanted Emily—not just her body, but to truly hold her love—he needed to stop living a double life.

By midmorning, he found himself pacing Mandy's parents' kitchen, phone in hand, stomach twisted in knots. He'd rehearsed a dozen versions of what he needed to say. All of them sounded like bullshit.

Eventually, he just hit *call*.

She answered on the second ring, voice brisk. "Ash, I'm at work. What's going on?"

He swallowed hard. "Hey, Mandy. We… we should talk."

A long pause.

"About what?" she asked carefully.

"Not over the phone," he said. "Can you meet me at your parents' house?"

An exasperated breath fizzled on the line.

"Now?"

"Yeah."

Another pause—a shorter one.

"Fine. Twenty minutes."

When her Lexus finally rolled into the driveway, the rain had returned in a thin gray drizzle that felt more like judgment than weather.

Mandy stepped out looking incredible despite the storm: a stylish blazer, a tailored skirt, her high heels confident on the wet pavement. Not a hair out of place. Lip gloss unsmudged. She was every inch the woman she'd built herself into—ambitious and composed. Ash suddenly felt as if he were dragging mud across the spotless floors.

She crossed her arms the moment she stepped inside. The kitchen gleamed behind her—marble counters, candle burning, lilies arranged just so. A life curated. A life he would never fit into.

"Ash," Mandy said, voice tight. "What's this about?"

He rested both palms on the counter to steady himself. "There's something I need to tell you."

Her eyes narrowed. "You're scaring me."

He took a breath. There was no good way forward—only the truth.

"I slept with someone."

The silence seemed to crack like thin ice under pressure. Mandy blinked once. Twice. Her mouth parted, but no sound came out, her composure fissuring at the edges.

"I'm sorry," he said quietly.

Her voice finally found itself—unsteady and incredulous: "You… you *did what?*"

There it was: the moment everything broke open, and everything would have to be rebuilt or left behind from here.

"I didn't plan it," he said, voice low. "It just… happened. And it's not an excuse, but—"

"Oh my God." Mandy laughed, a biting, humorless sound. "You didn't plan it. That's supposed to make me feel better?"

"Mandy—"

"Don't." Her eyes flashed, that perfect ice blue turning glacial. "Who is she?"

Ash hesitated—half a second, no more, but it was enough to give him away.

"Don't you dare say it's that girl from the bar."

"It's not what you think—"

She slammed her palm against the counter, the snap echoing off the marble. "It *is* her! The *college girl*? The one who looks like she shops at thrift stores? That little whore?"

He straightened. "Enough."

"Oh, now you have principles?" she snapped. "You cheat on me, but God forbid I insult your bar fling!"

Mandy hurled her clutch straight at his chest.

Ash caught it easily, one-handed, which only seemed to infuriate her more.

"It's not—" he tried, the words choking halfway out. "It's not what you think."

"Oh, it's exactly what I think." Her voice dropped lower, more dangerous. "I was trying to help you. Pushing you to apply to MBA programs, introducing you to people who could actually do something for your career, trying to get my dad to hire you, while this whole time you were sneaking around with her."

He rubbed his face, exhausted from more than lack of sleep. "You don't understand—"

"Don't I?" she cut in. "I see this perfectly. You wanted something exciting. Some little nobody who made you feel like a big deal again."

"That's not it," he said, as his voice cracked, betraying him. "She's not—she's not like anyone I've ever met."

That stopped her cold. She stared at him like he was speaking in a riddle. Then she laughed, a sound that came out brittle, splintering at the edges.

"God. You actually mean that." She spat out.

"I do."

Her fingers trembled as she snatched her purse back out of his hand. Her voice shook now, not with hurt, but with fury barely caged. "You know what, Ash? You can have her. Hell, go fuck every small-town barmaid in the county. I'm done with this *redneck bullshit*."

"Mandy—"

Her veneer cracked wide open. She was incandescent. Ready to drop a bomb.

"You know what?" she said, chin lifting. "Since we're confessing sins, the rumors are true. I cheated on you, too. That guy Brad, the corporate lawyer? I slept with him after the company party in Charleston."

Ash's jaw clenched as the hit landed clean.

"At least," she hissed, "I had the decency to fuck a *man* with a yacht instead of a literal *child*."

"Really, Mandy? After all this time..." He wasn't sure if he was hurt or humiliated.

"Oh, don't you even." She paced, heels clacking sharply against tile. "You think you're the only one who felt trapped? I've been bored out of my damn mind waiting for you to grow up. You spend every night in a bar with people who never leave this town and seem totally fine with it. And now—what? Some little college waitress bats her lashes, and suddenly you've 'found yourself'?"

He didn't answer. The silence was answer enough.

"You didn't have to drag me into it," he said finally. "You could have just left me, Mandy."

"You didn't have to drag *her* into it," Mandy shot back. "But here we are. You have never appreciated or deserved me, Asher. You can say whatever you want, but you know it's the truth."

She spun on her heel, heading toward the front door, but stopped short—her eyes flicking around the immaculate kitchen: the lilies, the candles, the curated perfection she'd built around them. A hollow laugh punched out of her throat.

"What the hell am *I* doing?" Her gaze cut back to him, cold and resolute. "This is *my* house. Get out."

Ash lifted both hands in surrender. "Fine. I'm going."

He took one last look at her—all steel, all fury, all heartbreak buried under control—then walked out into the rain.

Mandy stood there alone, tears streaming, chest heaving, mascara smudged in gray shadows beneath her eyes. She slammed both fists onto the counter hard. The flowers trembled from the vibration, a few petals drifting across the marble like pieces of something broken.

The front door slammed somewhere behind her. Ash was gone. For a long moment, she didn't move. She just stood there, feeling the silence close in. Every truth, every lie, every ugly secret between them lay in the open now, throbbing like a toothache.

Her breath came quick and shallow. The room felt too bright, too white, too clean for the devastation ripping through her. Her heartbeat thudded in her ears. She gripped the counter to steady herself, but the edges tilted, the floor angling away under her heels.

Get a grip. You're fine. You're fine.

She wasn't. The air spun. Her stomach swooped. A cold sweat broke out across her hairline. Her vision tunneled.

Suddenly, the side door opened.

"Miss Mandy? Dios mio! Sit down, sweetheart!" The housekeeper, Ynes, stood frozen in the doorway, grocery bags sagging in her arms.

Mandy tried to speak, but her tongue felt thick and dry. The room blurred, then dropped out from under her. Voices swam through the fog: Ynes shouting, the clattering of heels on tile, her mother's panicked gasp.

When she came to, she was on the couch, feet propped on a throw pillow, a cold cloth pressed to her forehead.

Her mother hovered above her, pale and frantic. "Darling, we're getting Dr. Leslie. He lives two doors down. Ynes went to fetch him. You fainted."

Mandy swallowed, her throat tight. "No… no, don't do that. I just forgot to eat breakfast. I'm fine."

But her voice trembled. She was not fine. Her world had been cracking, but now it felt like it had finally split open. The breakup, the shouting, the guilt, the awful silence afterward. She'd managed to hold herself together through all of it, piece by rigid piece. Now her body had humbled her.

Her mother adjusted the cloth, fussing, whispering soothing things she barely absorbed. All Mandy could hear was the roaring in her own ears—her period was late. Not just a little late. She had brushed it off—too many workouts, too much stress, a few skipped pills here and there. She'd always been regular. Always responsible. Always *together.* Except… maybe she hadn't been, not recently.

Lying there, Mandy finally let herself do the math. The suspicion slid over her like ice water—cold, absolute, terrifying.

Oh God. Please not this. Not now. Not without Ash.

She squeezed her eyes shut and felt something inside her crumble, the part that had always been composed, controlled, perfect. The part that had built color-coded planners, lived by schedules, and made decisions logically. That part flickered. Then went dark. Suddenly, nothing was simple.

When she was able to stand, she excused herself to the bathroom. Her hand shook as she dug through her clutch for her phone. All she wanted—with a desperation that scared her—was to call Ash. To hear his voice. To have him tell her it would be okay. To tell him she hadn't meant the words "get out" and "you never deserved me." But she couldn't. She half hated him and half loved him, but she still had some self-respect. She couldn't stomach the thought of him hearing her panic, or worse, seeing her cry.

She pressed her trembling finger to the keypad. She didn't dial him. She dialed her doctor's office. The only rational thing… right?

Her voice cracked when the receptionist answered: "Hey, um—hey, I need to… I need to schedule an appointment. As soon as possible, please."

When she hung up, Mandy pressed both hands to her face. She wasn't sure what scared her more—that she might be pregnant, or that she had just lost the only person she wanted to tell.

Chapter nineteen

By the time Emily's mom dropped her off at work that Friday afternoon, the humidity was thick enough to chew, and the bar was already buzzing. Jeanne was fussing at a beer distributor near the walk-in, Kenzie was bent over the cooler restocking seltzers, and Joel was leaning against the bar casually sipping an iced latte that positively didn't come from High Tide.

"Good afternoon, sunshine," he crooned, sing-song sweet.

"Hey, babe," she said, tying on her apron and reaching for the napkin holders.

Joel let her get exactly thirty seconds of work done before pouncing.

"Sooo," he said, slyly, "how was he?"

Emily froze with a stack of cocktail napkins in her hand. "Who?"

Joel lifted a single judgmental brow. "Please don't insult me. You and Ash closed last night. Somehow your car 'mysteriously' died. And—shocker—it's still in the parking lot. Greg's having it towed, by the way."

"He told you that?" Emily asked in surprise.

"He told Jeanne, who told Kenzie, who told me," Joel said blandly. "This island is one big game of telephone."

Emily dropped her head into her hands. "Oh my God."

Joel leaned over the counter, eyes glittering. "It was storming like a mother. I know you didn't walk home."

He paused for dramatic effect.

"Sooo," he repeated, slower. "How. Was. He."

She tried to glare, but the corner of her mouth betrayed her. "You're insufferable."

"I'm persistent," he corrected proudly.

Emily exhaled, voice dropping low: "It just… happened. And—" she met his eyes, cheeks flaming, "it was amazing."

Joel slapped a hand over his heart. "Don't tell me the hot, tortured, ex-football player is a god in bed. That is so unfair to the rest of us. He probably has a huge—"

"Joel!" she hissed, smacking him with the napkin stack and laughing despite herself.

Kenzie popped up at the perfect moment. "What are we talking about?"

"Oh," Joel sang, "just Miss Em here getting folded up like a lawn chair last night by Bartender McSexy and trying to keep it a secret!"

"NO FUCKING WAY!" Kenzie screeched, loud enough that half the bar turned.

“Okay, enough,” Emily said, face somewhere between mortification and breaking into hysterical laughter.

“What the hell is going on out here?” Jeanne barked, stomping toward them. “If anyone’s shouting and cursing, it’s gonna be me. Now move! We’ve got a bar to run—look around!”

Joel cleared his throat innocently. “Yes, ma’am.”

Kenzie spun around, snorting behind her hand.

Emily ducked her head, biting back a smile she couldn’t stop if she tried. Underneath the laughter, her body still hummed with the memory of the storm—the rain, the heat, the way it had all felt so right. She could joke about it with her friends, play it off like nothing, but deep down, she knew she didn’t want whatever happened to be over.

When she closed her eyes, she could still feel him—the scrape of his stubble against her skin, the weight of him, the way his hands moved like they already knew her. Every shiver and every breath was burned into her. It kept replaying, no matter how hard she tried to shut it off.

Then the other side of her brain took over. God, what had she done? She’d made a conscious choice, no matter how much she blamed the thunder and the dark. He had a girlfriend—practically a fiancée, if the gossip was true. A whole life that wasn’t hers to touch. And yet, the memory of the way he’d said her name—low, rough, reverent—sent another rush through her, shame and want twisted together in equal measure.

By the time the dinner crowd thinned, and Joel was counting tips at the bar, the guilt and uncertainty had blended into something like an emotional whirlwind. Emily tried to busy herself—wiping tables that were already clean, stacking glasses that didn't need stacking—but her eyes kept flicking to the door.

Ash never came in. He always worked Fridays. At first, she told herself maybe Jeanne had given him the day off, but his name was clearly printed on the schedule. Maybe he'd gone fishing and lost track of time, maybe he was sleeping off their long night. But as the hours dragged on, that hollow space inside her began to ache like something bottomless.

She checked her phone—nothing.

Had he gone back to Mandy? Like nothing happened? She could see it too clearly—Mandy with her perfect hair and smile, opening the door, Ash meeting her with a kiss, like last night was a bad dream he'd already forgotten. The image made her feel cheap—disposable.

Yes, she had left a note and run out… but he wasn't going to talk to her about it? She'd started to hope last night had meant something—that the storm, and the way he'd looked at her, wasn't just impulse. Maybe she was just a mistake he didn't want to admit to. That thought hurt more than just her pride.

She stayed later than usual, pretending to scrub counters that already gleamed. She checked her phone every two minutes, waiting for a message that never came. When she finally hung up her apron and stepped out the back door, the night air wrapped around her like a wet blanket.

The parking lot was nearly empty. Her sneakers crunched on gravel as she crossed toward Kenzie's Jeep, the sound too loud in the stillness.

Kenzie glanced over as Emily climbed into the passenger's seat, one eyebrow raised. "You good?"

Emily forced a smile that didn't reach her eyes.

Kenzie didn't press. She just turned the volume up; some mindless dance beat filled the silence.

Emily's mind was a million miles away.

If Ash thinks he can pretend last night didn't happen, he's got another thing coming.

She could picture it already—him behind the bar, that easy grin, acting like everything was fine. Not this time. She wasn't some naive college girl who'd fall apart over good dick and bad timing. If he showed up tomorrow, she'd look him dead in the eye—in front of everyone, Jeanne, Kenzie, Joel, whoever—and tell him exactly what a piece of shit he was. Maybe even throw something at him, just to see his smug face flinch.

Her hands trembled in her lap. Not from fear. From fury. Because under it all, she still *ached* for him. And that made her hate herself almost as much as she hated the situation. She'd never wanted messy or complicated. She'd spent most of her life avoiding anything that could veer off-script. She knew who she was supposed to be. Or she thought she did. But Haven County had done something to her. Or maybe Ash had. Now the train had completely jumped the tracks, and she was watching the wreckage in slow motion, helpless, horrified, and unable to look away.

What scared her most wasn't hooking up. It was realizing she wasn't the girl who'd stepped onto this island in May. That version of herself would've run by now—clean break, clean conscience, clean hands. This Emily was different. This Emily was tangled and coming alive more than she wanted to admit. She didn't know how to go back.

Kenzie's Jeep rumbled as it pulled up the curved drive, headlights sweeping across the perfect rows of palm trees. The rain had stopped hours ago, but the air still carried the heavy scent of wet pavement.

"Thanks for the ride," Emily said, unclipping her seatbelt.

"Anytime, babe." Kenzie leaned over the console, eyes soft. "You sure you're okay?"

"Yeah," Emily lied, managing a quick smile. "Just tired."

She pushed open the door and jumped out. Kenzie honked once before her taillights disappeared down the dark street, their glow fading into the trees.

As Emily turned toward the house, the porch lights flickered on, and she jumped, not expecting to see anyone waiting there.

Ash was sitting on the top step. Elbows on his knees, head bowed, like he'd been there for hours. A grocery-store bouquet dangled loosely from his hand, sunflowers and daisies, bright and messy, like he'd grabbed them in a hurry. For a moment, she thought she was imagining him: the dark outline of his shoulders, the curve of his hair damp with mist.

He lifted his head.

"Emily," he said quietly.

Emily crossed her arms, bracing herself. "What are you doing here?"

Ash exhaled, rubbing a hand over the back of his neck. “I needed to see you.”

She almost spat out the words, anger and longing mixed. “You disappeared. Didn’t show up to work. Didn’t text. What the hell?”

“I know,” he said. “I messed up.”

“Yeah,” she snapped, voice cracking. “You did.”

He stood, taking one small step toward her.

“But,” he added carefully, “you ran out on me this morning. Left a note, didn’t say anything.”

Emily looked away, blood rushing to her cheeks.

“You wrote *I can’t*,” he said quietly. “How was I supposed to know what that meant?”

Her pulse pounded.

“Ash, I—” She broke off, dragging in a breath. “I wasn’t saying I didn’t want to be with you. But I couldn’t stay there and pretend last night was something it wasn't.”

“I told Mandy everything.” His voice was rough but level. “I’m done hiding. I’m done pretending I don’t feel what I feel when I’m with you.”

Emily’s breath caught as she lifted her gaze back to him. “You didn’t have to—”

“Yes, I did.” He took a step forward, eyes never leaving hers. “I want to do this right. No secrets. No more pretending we’re just two people who work together.”

He stopped in front of her, close enough to touch.

“I want you.”

She looked down at the flowers, her throat tightening. “Ash, I’m leaving at the end of August. It’s only a few weeks—”

"I don't care," he said, voice quiet but sure. "I don't care if it's three weeks or three days. I don't want to waste any more time pretending."

Emily's eyes burned; tears she hadn't expected stinging hot at the edges. Under the rush of emotions, a quiet question throbbed, a lingering one she couldn't outrun. What was she losing herself to?

"You don't make this easy," she whispered.

He smiled, small and crooked. "You don't either."

For a moment, neither of them moved. Then she stepped forward, closing the space between them. And when she finally kissed him again—it wasn't the dizzy rush of the storm. It lingered. A promise this time.

The kiss deepened, slow but sure, until she felt his thumb brushing away a tear she hadn't realized had fallen.

"Come inside," she whispered.

For a second, he hesitated, not out of doubt, but because he wanted to remember the way she said it, soft and trembling. Then he nodded.

The house was dark except for the soft glow of a lamp left on in the living room. Emily closed the door behind them, clicking like punctuation in the quiet. Ash set the flowers down on the entry table quickly, a few petals floating to the floor.

"You sure this is okay?" he asked, his voice barely above a whisper.

She hesitated for half a second, glancing toward the dark hallway. Somewhere deeper in the house, she could hear the low hum of the television. Her mom and Greg were still up.

"We can't stay down here," she whispered.

Ash's brow furrowed, but he caught her meaning, and the corner of his mouth curved into that familiar, dangerous half-smile.

"Lead the way."

They barely made it halfway up the stairs before Emily's heart was pounding in her chest. The house was so still it felt like the world had shrunk to the creak of the steps beneath them.

In her room, the air smelled like lavender and fresh linens. She turned to face him, cheeks flushed.

"Are you sure—" he started.

She cut him off with a kiss. He smiled against her mouth, hands slipping around her waist. She tugged off her shirt, half laughing, half trembling, when—*knock, knock—creak.*

"Sweetheart, do you want me to—oh!"

Emily froze, one arm tangled in her shirt, the other still clutching Ash's belt. Her mother stood in the doorway, wide-eyed, holding a basket of folded towels like a shield.

"Mom! What the hell!" Emily yelped, trying to cover herself with the shirt.

Marinda's face went red. "I knocked!"

"Yeah—once!"

From downstairs came Greg's voice, full of concern: "I heard yelling! Everything okay up there?"

Emily and Marinda both shouted in unison, "YES!"

There was a pause before Greg muttered something about "women losing their minds," and the TV hum resumed.

Marinda's mortified expression finally cracked into a small smile. "All right, well… I'll, uh, just—leave these towels right here."

She set them on the dresser and backed out so fast she nearly tripped over the doorframe.

When the door clicked shut, silence settled over them again. Emily was still red-faced, clutching her t-shirt to her chest. Ash was trying not to laugh but failing miserably.

She threw a pillow at him. “Don’t you dare laugh.”

“I’m not,” he said with a shit-eating grin. “I’m terrified.”

Emily rolled her eyes, but she was laughing too now, quiet, breathless laughter that dissolved the tension into something softer.

Ash brushed a strand of hair from her face. “Guess I should head out before your stepdad comes up here with a shotgun.”

“Greg? With a gun?”

The mental image was so absurd that Emily laughed again, louder this time.

He kissed her once more, slowly, then whispered, “Goodnight, Em.”

She smiled, voice low. “Goodnight, Ash.”

She walked him out, and when he left, she locked the front door and leaned against it, smiling like a perfect idiot.

Chapter twenty

The next morning, the kitchen smelled like coffee and cinnamon toast. Sunlight streamed through the windows, weightless and warm, unlike the anxiety building in Emily's chest.

Marinda stood at the counter, still in her robe, humming as she loaded the dishwasher.

"Morning, sweetheart," she said, just a little too pleasantly.

Emily hesitated in the doorway. "Morning."

Marinda glanced over her shoulder. "You were um, up late last night."

Emily froze halfway to the coffee pot. "Really, Mom?"

"Do you want to talk about it?" Marinda turned, crossing her arms.

Emily's stomach dropped. "Mom—"

"I knocked," Marinda said quickly. "But maybe lock the door next time."

Emily groaned and buried her face in her hands. "Oh my God."

Marinda bit back a smile. "He's very… muscular."

"Please stop."

"I'm just saying! I didn't realize you two were—whatever you two are."

"We're not anything exactly," Emily said too fast, fumbling with her mug. "I mean… I think we're dating? Kind of. It all just happened."

Marinda tilted her head. "Does Mandy know?"

Emily blinked as heat rushed to her cheeks. "What?"

"I saw them together at the Greens' dinner party," Marinda said gently, watching her daughter's reaction. "Sweet girl. Her parents said she and Asher had been together nearly ten years. They mentioned an engagement was coming soon."

Emily busied herself buttering toast she didn't want. "They… were together."

Marinda's tone softened, catching the guilt radiating off her. "Oh, honey."

Emily shook her head, voice trembling. "It's not what you think—or maybe it is. I don't know."

Marinda sighed and set a hand on her shoulder. "You can't build something on top of someone else's heartbreak, baby. No matter how good it feels right now, someone always ends up buried underneath."

Emily swallowed hard. "I didn't plan this."

"I know." Marinda smiled sadly. "But that doesn't mean people won't get hurt."

Silence settled between them, broken only by the soft hiss of the dishwasher.

Finally, Marinda exhaled. "I love you, Emily. I don't want to see this blow up in your face."

Emily nodded, eyes glassy. "It's okay, Mom. Ash is different. I don't know how to explain it, but I *know* this is meant to be."

Marinda gave her a reluctant look. "You're an adult. It's your life. I won't try to stop you. Just—be careful, okay? I'm always here if you need me."

She hugged Emily tight before heading upstairs. The house fell quiet again—the kind of quiet that made every thought amplify.

Emily rinsed her plate in the sink, watching crumbs swirl away. Her mother's words echoed in her head: *You can't build something on top of someone else's heartbreak.*

She knew it was true. And still, she couldn't stop thinking about the way Ash's breath had caught when she'd whispered his name, the feel of his hands against her skin. It wasn't just physical attraction; it was stronger than that. Every time she swore she'd pull back, something pushed her closer instead.

She leaned against the counter, staring out at the yard where her mom's hydrangeas were in bloom—pale blue, just like Mandy's eyes.

Emily took a deep breath, set down her mug, and whispered to the empty room, "I don't owe anyone an explanation. We're meant to be. You can't break apart gravity."

Ash woke to sunlight slicing through his room, cutting across the faded paneling and the quilt Cindy had knitted years ago. The air smelled faintly of coffee. His mama must've put the pot on before she left for work, same as always.

The double-wide wasn't falling apart, but it carried that lived-in comfort of a place patched up more times than anyone could count. His room hadn't changed much since high school: trophies lined the shelf above the desk, a cracked Miami Dolphins poster hung beside a faded Braves pennant. A few shirts were tossed over the recliner in the corner, and his boots sat by the door where he'd kicked them off last night. The curtains fluttered in the breeze from the rattling box fan. On his nightstand, a photo of him and Arch on a fishing trip leaned crooked in its frame.

For a long moment, he just lay there, staring at the ceiling, listening to the low hum of the TV in the next room. Everything about the night before still clung to him—Emily's voice, the way she'd looked at him. Morning light had a way of making even the best dreams complicated.

His phone buzzed on the nightstand.

Mandy: *We need to talk.*

"Of course we do," he muttered.

He could have ignored it. Pretended the text never came. But that wasn't who he was.

After a long pause, he hit the call button.

Her voice was soft, raw. "Hey, Ash."

"Hey," he said quietly.

For a moment, neither spoke—just the sound of breathing and silence. The kind that comes from both people knowing there's too much to say and no good way to start.

"I'm sorry," she finally said. "For the way I left things, for what I said. I was angry, but… You didn't deserve it."

He leaned back against the headboard. "You had every right to be angry, Mandy."

"I don't know if that's true," she whispered. "I did something too. I mean—with Brad. Just once. It was stupid, and I really hated myself for it. It didn't mean anything, but I should've told you before. I wanted to tell you." Her voice cracked. "You were always so good to me, and I just… I wasn't brave enough. I really admire your integrity, the way you took responsibility for what you did."

Ash exhaled, breath heavy. "Mandy…"

"I know," she said quickly, cutting him off. "It's too late now, but I didn't want you thinking I had any right to judge you. I know I messed up, too."

Silence settled between them, not sharp but still cutting. They had finally stopped pretending the cracks weren't there all along.

After a moment, Mandy gave a small, trembling laugh. "Do you remember when we watched *The Notebook*? I always thought that was us. I thought you were my Noah, and I was your Allie."

Ash smiled faintly despite everything. "Guess I missed my cue to build you a house."

"Yeah, well," she sniffled, "I don't paint anyway."

Another long pause, then she sighed.

"There's something I have to talk to you about, but…" Her voice softened, fading. "Never mind. Forget it."

"Mandy—"

"No," she said, gentle but firm. "It's okay. I just needed to hear your voice one more time. Take care of yourself, Asher."

The line clicked dead.

Ash sat there a long time. He didn't feel relief, exactly, more like the strange calm that comes when you finally stop fighting the inevitable. But the ache beneath it… that was real.

Mandy had been a part of him. People assumed that he'd dated her because she was the blond bombshell, the girl every guy in the locker room talked about. That was never the reason. Hell, he hadn't even known how to talk to girls back then. He hadn't expected someone like her to notice him—the quiet kid from the wrong side of the bridge.

Somehow, she had noticed him. And when he got to know her, Mandy was so much more than the perfect dream girl everyone saw from the outside. She could be rigid, sure—she loved a plan, a schedule, a five-year roadmap. She was also funny in sudden, off-beat ways, cracking dry jokes when no one expected it. She went after everything in life with a kind of determined grace he could only stand aside and admire. She inspired him without ever meaning to, and she had been the person who believed he had a future before he even gave it a second thought.

He had loved her, for reasons that had nothing to do with how she looked, and everything to do with who she was. And he'd ended it, badly at that—blindly leaping toward something that felt dangerously right. It didn't happen the way Ash intended, but he had to face the facts: he and Mandy were over now.

He lay back on the bed, replaying their conversation too many times, wondering if what he'd done was bravery or just selfishness dressed up as honesty. Even as guilt gnawed at him, he couldn't deny that what he felt with Emily wasn't something he could have stopped.

It wasn’t a decision made logically. It was like the pull of an invisible force.

Outside, birds chattered in the sunlight, and the day carried on, unaware that something sacred had ended. As Ash's chest hollowed at the loss, a new fear lurked beneath it. It whispered that he might never stop missing Mandy Green, and that he already didn’t miss her enough. For the first time since he was a teenager, he was about to find out who he was without her.

Chapter twenty-one

August rolled in like honey—slow, golden, and heavy with the promise of endings nobody wanted to name yet. For a few perfect weeks, everything between Ash and Emily fell into an easy rhythm. Mornings stretched lazy and bright; nights drifted away wrapped in laughter. It was as if the island itself had been holding its breath, and finally, it exhaled.

Several times a week, they met for breakfast at the diner. Cindy always had their booth waiting: the corner seat by the window, sunlight spilling across the sticky tabletop, coffee already poured, and a plate of buttered toast between them.

Emily loved those mornings. She loved the easy, laid-back nature of them—the way Cindy teased Ash about always running late, the way her eyes crinkled when she smiled, how she called everyone sugar or baby as though it were their first name.

Cindy had a way of making even small talk feel like something bigger. She'd ask about classes Emily had taken, her mom and Greg, and what she liked to read. Before long, they'd fallen into a habit of talking about books they both loved—Jane Austen, the Brontë sisters—women who'd penned novels centuries ago, but somehow the topics still seemed relevant. Cindy spoke with that kind of soft wisdom—the kind you only earn by walking through fire. She was the sort of woman who'd learned her lessons the hard way but wore them lightly—like saltwater pearls she didn't need to show off to prove they were real.

By the second week, Cindy had invited Emily over for dinner. "Nothing fancy," she'd said. "Just fried chicken and a few stories about the dumb things Ash did as a kid. You'll get a kick out of it."

Emily had smiled, trying not to show how much it meant—that invitation into the part of Ash's world that had made him who he was. She was starting to feel like she belonged in his life—not just the girl he'd fallen for, but someone who mattered in the long run.

One evening, when the water lay glass-smooth and the sunset burned orange, fading to pink, Ash met Emily at the pier. He showed her how to bait a hook and how to cast without tangling the line. When she caught her first tiny flounder, she squealed so loudly the old men two pylons over clapped for her.

"Not bad, tiger," he teased.

“Not bad for a Gamecock’s coaching,” she shot back with a grin.

They stayed until the stars came out, the wind shifting cool, the tide whispering against the pilings. Somewhere between her laughter and the ocean’s soft infinitude, something in Ash loosened. He told her about summers there with his dad, how the pier lights made the world feel less scary.

She listened, soaking it all up, the stories, the pauses, the way he looked toward the horizon like it held every answer he didn’t have. For the first time, she could feel him letting her in. And she—wide open as the sky above them—ran straight toward it. No hesitation. No guardrails. Just her whole heart on the line.

That weekend, Emily and Ash had brunch with her mom and Greg. Emily had been nervous, but it turned out better than she could’ve imagined.

Her car had finally given out earlier that week—the beat-up red Oldsmobile Cutlass she’d nicknamed “Old Moe", the one that had carried her through high school, college, and every mile in between. When the mechanic said the engine was done, she’d sat in the lot with her hand on the steering wheel, fighting tears. It wasn’t just the car she hated to lose. It was the history it carried.

Emily hadn’t expected her parents to bring it up, but after the mimosas were poured, Greg slid a small black key fob across the table.

“What’s this?” she asked, confused.

Greg smiled. “Your mother wanted to surprise you. You’ll need something reliable for law school.”

Her heart skipped. "You didn't—"

"We did," Marinda said, eyes bright with excitement. "It's out front."

Emily didn't think—she ran.

They all hurried out behind her. Parked in the driveway was a brand-new steel-gray Toyota 4Runner, a giant red bow gleaming on top.

"I wanted to get you a Lexus or a BMW," Marinda said, "but Greg and Asher both insisted this was more your style."

Emily blinked, stunned. "You—Ash?"

Ash grinned, a little sheepish. "Yeah. Told them you'd want something you could hit a few curbs in without making a dent."

She swatted his arm, laughing through the shock.

He reached into his pocket and handed her an oval bumper sticker, white letters on black: **HIL** and in smaller print underneath: *Haven Island Life.*

"Figured you might want to remember us while you're down in Charleston," he said softly.

Her throat went tight. "Y'all, I don't even know what to say. Thank you. Thank you so much."

The rest of brunch flowed easily. To Emily's surprise, Greg turned out to be a walking encyclopedia of football stats. He and Ash slipped into an easy back-and-forth about quarterbacks, defensive formations, and bowl games.

Marinda laughed, poured another round of mimosas, and leaned close to her daughter. "He's handsome," she whispered. "And polite. I like him."

Emily's cheeks flushed pink, and she couldn't stop smiling.

After brunch, she held the key fob in her palm, still half-convinced it wasn't real.

"Wanna take it for a spin?" she asked, grinning at Ash.

He smirked. "Thought you'd never ask."

They drove aimlessly for a while, windows down, summer air spilling through the cabin. The new-car smell clung to the seats, hinting at all the memories still waiting to be made. They glided around the teardrop-shaped island, past the marina and dunes, until the road ended at a quiet overlook near the old, decommissioned lighthouse.

Emily shifted into park. The world outside was still, gulls swooping overhead, the ocean glittering in golden shades under the afternoon sun.

Ash turned toward her, eyes soft. "You know," he said, voice low, "I think we ought to break the new car in properly."

She laughed, half nervous, half thrilled. "You mean… test the seat recline?"

He grinned. "Something like that."

What happened next wasn't rushed like the storm. It was slower, sweeter, gentle kisses, sunlight spilling through the windows, her fingertips dragging softly across his back. It felt both new and familiar, like something that had been waiting for them all along.

Afterward, they sat curled together in the back seat, the windows fogged, the world hushed except for waves brushing against the rocks.

Emily rested her head on Ash's shoulder, smiling as he lightly kissed her forehead and ran his fingers through her hair. She felt like the luckiest girl in the world, or at least the happiest.

At High Tide, everyone knew by now. Joel and Kenzie teased Emily mercilessly, but wore matching conspiratorial grins.

Jeanne just laughed one afternoon when she caught Ash stealing a kiss behind the prep counter.

"Well," she said, waving her ledger in mock disapproval, "I'm glad somebody's getting laid around here. Just stay the hell away from my supply closet."

Joel nearly dropped a tray laughing.

Work felt easier. The days felt shorter. The storms had passed, leaving the island sun-washed and bright, the air thick with possibilities. Ash's truck became a fixture on the curb outside her house. And for the first time in years, Emily stopped counting the days. She wasn't running to or from anything. She was exactly where she wanted to be.

Chapter twenty-two

The exam room smelled like antiseptic and hand soap, that same odd, sterile-clean mix Mandy had breathed in a dozen times over the years. Today, it turned her stomach before her doctor even opened the door.

Everything about the room should have felt familiar. She'd been coming here since she was fifteen for annual checkups, birth control refills, quick, reassuring chats about cramps or stress or nothing at all. Now the pale-green walls seemed too bright. The poster about folic acid felt like it was staring directly at her. Even the crinkle of the exam table paper sounded sharp enough to cut.

Dr. Carver stepped in with her usual steady stride, a chart in one hand and a pen tucked behind her ear—a woman in her early forties with warm brown eyes and the kind of no-nonsense expression that could calm you or call you out in equal measure.

She wore her hair in long braids pulled neatly back, no makeup beyond lip balm, her only jewelry a wedding band. Friendly, yes. But she had never been the type to sugarcoat.

"Hey, Amanda," she said, offering a small smile as she closed the door behind her. "You hanging in there? You look a little pale."

She asked the question with genuine care, but it hit differently today. Mandy pulled her cardigan tighter around her, with cold fingers.

"I'm okay," she lied.

Dr. Carver didn't push. She crossed the room with practiced ease and sat at the small desk, flipping open the chart.

Outside the window, the oak tree in the parking lot swayed in the breeze, its branches tapping softly against the glass. The HVAC hummed. The clock ticked. Everything normal. Everything ordinary. But Mandy's heartbeat felt too fast. Her hands wouldn't stay still. This place—this woman, this room—had always been safe. Now it felt like the surface of another planet.

Dr. Carver looked up, her expression shifting into one of those small, careful smiles Mandy had seen a hundred times. The kind that eased nerves without pretending.

"All right," she said gently, "let's talk about this. There's no doubt. You're pregnant."

Mandy felt the world move under her as gently as an earthquake. The word was too big for the tiny exam room. It pressed at her chest, lodged in her throat, made her swallow twice before she could manage a small, polite nod. She kept her face composed the way she'd practiced—chin high, eyes dry, voice steady.

"Based on your last period and lab results, I'd say around six or seven weeks." Dr. Carver went on. "Are you feeling dizzy? Any nausea?"

"Just tired," Mandy murmured. "And sometimes dizzy."

"That's normal," her doctor said with an encouraging smile.

Dr. Carver's voice blurred after that. Mandy tried to focus, tried to listen, but the word *pregnant* echoed inside her skull, drowning everything else out.

When the appointment wrapped up, Dr. Carver paused in the doorway and gave her one last sympathetic look. "And remember you have options—whatever you choose, I'll support you."

Mandy nodded, thanked her, took the pamphlets along with the folder of medical information, and walked out with the grace of someone determined to hold herself together by sheer force of will.

She didn't fall apart in the parking lot. Or in the car. Or on the drive home. She held it all in—every shaking breath, every tremor—until she made it upstairs and turned the lock on her bedroom door. She slid onto the bed, pressing a hand tight over her mouth as sobs ripped through her—the kind that left a metallic taste in her throat, the kind that hurt.

The facts ran through her mind on repeat: she was pregnant, Ash didn't want her anymore—he had someone else, and she was utterly, terrifyingly alone.

A soft knock came at her door, followed by her mother's voice: "Mandy? Honey?"

"I'll be down in a bit," Mandy called, wiping at her face until her skin stung.

Her mother lingered. Mandy could feel it—the hand hovering near the knob, the instinct to push inside. Instead, Elizabeth's footsteps retreated slowly.

When she was sure she was alone, Mandy grabbed her phone and dialed the one person she knew she could break in front of—her Delta Zeta little, her best friend, her ride-or-die from bid day to formals to every late-night Waffle House run: Jennifer Hayes.

Jenn picked up on the second ring, voice bright as always. "Hey, Mama M, you okay? I was just thinking about you. I swear, if that man puts you through one more—"

"I'm pregnant." It came out shredded, like something tore her throat open and spilled the words out.

Silence first, then the horrified exhale of, "Oh my God."

Mandy could picture her perfectly, like they were still college kids: Jenn sitting cross-legged on her dorm bed in a garnet DZ mixer T-shirt, eyeliner smudged from the night before, auburn hair in that messy bun she insisted wasn't intentional—soft heart, smart mouth—the girl who took nothing seriously except the people she loved.

"Mand," she whispered, "are you… Are you okay?"

Mandy shook her head as if Jenn could see it. She pressed her palm to her forehead like she could physically keep the panic inside.

"Ash isn't coming back," she said, voice cracking. "It's over. And now this… and I don't know what to do."

Jenn hissed out a breath, fierce and protective. "He's such an absolute bastard. I will key his truck. I want to punch him right in his stupid face. I swear I'm gonna—"

"Jenn."

"Okay. Okay." A slow breath. "It's going to be fine. You know I've been exactly where you are."

Mandy closed her eyes. She remembered—junior year, Jenn sobbing in her lap, Mandy driving her all the way to the clinic in North Carolina, hand glued to hers the whole time.

"You don't have to have his baby," Jenn said softly. "Not after what he did. You have a whole life ahead of you. Not one tied to… that."

The words were heavy—a little too real.

"You think I should get an abortion," Mandy whispered.

"I think you should do what's right for you. If you're asking what *I would do*? Yes. I think you should end this pregnancy. Give yourself a clean start. You don't deserve to carry his consequences."

Mandy let herself fall back on her duvet, staring at the ceiling like it might have answers.

"Okay," she said hollowly. "I'll call."

"I'll come down there," Jenn said instantly. "I don't care about work. My boss already hates me. I can skip—"

"No," Mandy whispered. "I just… I need to deal with this myself."

Jenn reassured her again and again that it would all be fine. Jenn had been through it and come out on the other side—married to a doting husband, living the white-picket-fence life. Mandy would, too, someday; she would see.

When they hung up, Mandy sat up straight, swallowed her tears, and dialed her doctor's office back.

"Hello," she said, forcing her voice steady. "I… I need to schedule a follow-up appointment."

They gave her a date. She wrote it down. She thanked them. She hung up. Then she stared at the ink—her own handwriting—and felt dread wash over her. She'd made a choice. But it didn't feel like relief. It felt like stepping off a cliff. Was this right? Wrong? What would Ash say if he knew? What would *she* say if he asked her not to?

Mandy curled onto her side, clutching her pillow. Silent tears soaked into the fabric. She had a date on the calendar. She had a plan. But was it one she could live with?

Deep down—in the quietest, most secret part of herself—Mandy wanted this baby. Not planned. Not perfect. Not how she ever imagined it. But still… wanted.

She rested a hand over her stomach, stunned by the tenderness of the instinct. Another life was now tied to hers, tiny and fragile.

She picked up her phone and scrolled to Ash's name, staring until her eyes burned. She hated him. She loved him. She wanted him back. She never wanted to see him again. Beneath all that tangled mess lay a single unbearable truth: If he knew, he wouldn't let her go through this alone.

Chapter twenty-three

The Bells' small house smelled like banana pudding and fried chicken, the kind of scent that wrapped around you like a hug. The table was already set when Emily and Ash walked in. Complete with mismatched plates and a vase of wildflowers from the yard.

"Y'all made it!" Cindy called from the kitchen, wiping her hands on a dish towel. "Asher, grab the tea pitcher, would you?"

Then she turned to Emily with open arms.

"Hey, sweetheart," she said, pulling her in for a warm, flour-dusted hug that smelled faintly of vanilla extract and hand lotion. "You look just beautiful, baby."

Emily blushed. "Thank you for having me."

Dinner was cozy and easy—fried okra, chicken, biscuits that melted in your mouth. Cindy was a natural storyteller, teasing Ash about his terrible handwriting and the time he tried to build a go-kart out of lawnmower parts.

Halfway through dessert, Emily's gaze wandered to a framed photo on the wall. It showed a much younger Cindy, slender and blond in a simple satin gown, standing beside a tall man with dark hair and a 1970's mustache, his grin identical to Ash's.

Cindy caught her looking and chuckled. "Lord, I was skinny back then. Hard to believe that body went on to birth two ten-pound boys."

She paused before continuing.

"There was no man on this earth like Jesse Bell," she said softly, eyes glinting. "Not for me, anyway."

Emily understood perfectly. What lived behind those words wasn't just love—it was devotion. A steady warmth that filled the little house as surely as the smell of fried chicken.

Cindy clapped her hands once. "Now, y'all wanna see something embarrassing?"

"Oh, no," Ash groaned, sinking lower in his chair as Cindy reappeared with a floral box stuffed full of photo albums.

The next hour passed in laughter. There were pictures of Ash missing his front teeth in a baseball uniform, holding a puppy half his size, standing knee-deep in a pond with Arch, Jesse crouched between them, proud and sunburned.

Cindy told stories: the time the boys set a bird loose in their grandma's house, the time they nearly burned down the church house trying to light all the Christmas Eve candles. By the end of the night, Emily's stomach hurt from laughing. She couldn't help but notice the quiet pride in Ash's eyes as his mother flipped through the pages of his childhood.

When they stood to leave, Cindy pressed leftovers into Emily's hands. "You're welcome here anytime, sugar," she said.

Outside, the air was thick with the scent of marsh grass. Crickets sang loudly beneath a dark, wide sky; the moon was hanging low like a silver thumbnail.

Ash smiled, a little sheepish. "Sorry about the photo album ambush."

"Are you kidding?" Emily said, smiling back. "It was perfect… and hilarious."

Behind the house, the old pole barn loomed, its tin roof catching the moonlight.

"Come on, I wanna show you something," he said, taking her hand and leading her toward the building.

He slid open the heavy door. The interior was pitch dark until he reached up and pulled a chain, the hanging bulb flickering to life. Amid the dust and clutter sat a beat-up fishing boat—paint peeling, engine half apart, a pile of tools scattered on the floor.

"She's seen better days," Ash admitted, running his hand over the faded hull. "But I've been working on her—slowly. I wanna get her running again someday."

Emily smiled. "You will. I know it."

The name on the side read "*Chrissy's Smile*".

"Ohhh, who's Chrissy?" Emily teased.

Ash chuckled. "No idea. My dad bought her off some guy years ago. She needs a new name—it just hasn't come to me yet."

He turned toward her then, close enough that she could see the smudge of grease on his wrist and the softness in his eyes. The air seemed to go still around them. She stepped closer, resting a hand against his chest. The kiss started soft and hesitant, tasting of promise, sawdust, and summer. Then it deepened and slowed, as the rest of the world fell away.

Somewhere between the smell of motor oil and the night closing in, they ended up in the old boat, sound muffled beneath the whisper of wind through the rafters. As they lay wrapped together beneath the half-fixed canopy, everything around them felt suspended, as if this was always meant to be.

"Guess I really should finish fixing her up," Ash murmured against her hair.

Emily smiled into his chest.

"Yeah," she whispered. "I think she's worth saving."

The nights started to cool, the air soft with that bittersweet edge that always came when summer was almost over. One evening, instead of heading toward the beach, Ash drove across to the mainland and turned down a narrow two-lane road lined with moss-draped oaks. The pavement gave way to gravel, then to a dirt trail swallowed by weeds. A faded **NO TRESPASSING** sign hung crooked on a rusted post.

"Uh, I don't think we're supposed to be here," Emily said, eyeing the sign as the truck bumped along the overgrown path.

"It's fine," Ash said, easing the wheel. "This used to be my family's land; it's been in the Bell name since right after the Revolution. William Bell built the first house here. His grandson turned it into a full working plantation—Rosefield Hall, they called it."

Emily frowned. “Plantation? As in…”

He nodded grimly. “Yeah. Slaves. It’s ugly history, but it’s what it was. After my dad died, there wasn’t enough money to keep the taxes up. We sold most of the land, some to the state, the rest, the house and outbuildings, went to the Haven County Historical Society. They were supposed to restore it, but… those things take time.”

They rounded a bend, and the ruins of Rosefield Hall appeared through the trees. The old Georgian manor rose out of the wild grass like a ghost, its once-perfect symmetry fractured by time and neglect. Columns leaned at odd angles, their capitals crumbling beneath tangles of ivy. The roof sagged in the center, beams bleached silver by years of rain and sun.

Once grand—the regal gem of the county—it now stood heartbreakingly human in its ruin. Roots cracked the front steps, moss spilling over the stone like green lace, and shuttered windows hung askew, the broken glass gaping hollow as eyes.

Emily’s voice dropped to a whisper. “It must’ve been beautiful once,” she said. “In a sad kind of way.”

Ash’s gaze lingered on the broken façade.

“Yeah,” he said quietly. “That’s about right.”

“Why not just level it?” Emily asked gently. “Wipe it clean. Maybe the world doesn’t need another monument to pain.”

Ash turned to her, expression unreadable but steady. “I asked my dad that once. He said if we erase it, we forget it. And if we forget it, we run the risk of repeating it.”

She didn’t answer, but something in her face shifted, a quiet understanding that didn’t need words.

Ash killed the engine.

"Come on," he said, tossing her a can of bug spray.

The air was thick and humming with mosquitoes. The ground squelched underfoot, the scent of earth rising with every step. They walked through tall grass and what had once been gardens, following the path toward a narrow stream. On its bank sat a small fenced-in plot surrounded by wrought-iron gates, the grass inside was freshly mowed, oddly neat amid the wilderness.

Emily frowned. "Someone still takes care of it?"

Ash nodded. "Yeah. The county keeps it up now."

He pushed the gate open with a metallic groan. "Bell family cemetery. The newer graves are up front—my grandparents, my uncle, a few of Daddy's cousins. The old ones in the back… You can barely read those anymore."

For a moment, neither spoke. The wind stirred through the trees, carrying the soft rush of the stream and the low drone of cicadas. Emily slipped her hand into Ash's, and he didn't let go.

They stopped before a simple gray headstone, a small vase of daisies set at its base.

Jesse Archer Bell

August 26, 1958 – January 21, 2000

Husband. Father. Friend.

Ash crouched, brushing a few stray leaves from the stone.

"It's always strange seeing his full name," he said quietly. "Everyone just called him J."

Emily knelt beside him. "It sounds like he was a good man."

"He was," Ash said, his voice rough but steady. "Big heart. Fast temper sometimes, but he loved hard. Worked his ass off for us." He smiled faintly. "I think he would have liked you."

Emily smiled softly, hoping he was right.

When they left the little cemetery, the light was fading fast, the last streaks of sun slipping through the moss-hung oaks. They walked back through the overgrown pasture and past what was left of the gardens—crumbling fountains, weeds, and wildflowers tangled together, fireflies blinking in and out like tiny lanterns.

The truck waited near the ruins of Rosefield Hall, ivy curling up the brick like slow reclamation. Emily tried to picture the plantation as it once was—horse-drawn carriages lined along the drive, women in hoop skirts gliding across the porch.

Out of the corner of her eye, she thought she saw something move, and she grabbed for Ash's arm.

"Sorry," she squeaked, forcing a laugh. "I think it was just a squirrel."

Still, a chill crawled up her spine. The place felt eerie, like the air itself had a memory.

Ash glanced back toward the house.

"Hard to believe people used to live here," he said quietly.

"Hard to believe they bought and sold other human beings and thought that was okay," Emily said, her voice taut with conviction.

"Yeah," he said, eyes still fixed on the ruins. "That part's terrible. My dad knew all the stories—the whole Bell line. The historical society interviewed him before he passed. I figure I'll learn them someday, but…" He exhaled slowly, shaking his head. "For now, they're just in the wind. Maybe when I have a kid, I'll take the time to learn more. Pass it down."

Her chest squeezed at that. It was too soon for talk of rings and babies—they had only been dating a few weeks, and they'd known each other less than three months. But Emily's brain didn't care about timelines. It was already sketching out a future like some lovesick teenager—doodling *Emily Kennedy Bell* in the corner of a notebook and pretending it meant nothing.

By the time they reached the truck, the sky was streaked in peach and gold. They climbed onto the tailgate, their legs swinging as twilight closed in. For a while, neither spoke.

"So," Emily said finally, nudging his arm with her elbow. "You're really taking the coaching job?"

Ash nodded, eyes on the horizon. "Yeah. USC wants me in Columbia on the first of the month. Honestly, they wanted me weeks ago, but I told them I had some things to finish here first."

She smiled. "I'm proud of you. You're gonna be amazing. Look how much my fishing skills have improved. You're already a great coach."

He laughed softly.

"The only way this works is if you visit," he said. "Two hours isn't bad. You drive up some weekends, and after the season, I'll drive down."

Emily grinned. "That's exactly what I was thinking. Law school's gonna chew me up and spit me out. I'll need an excuse to escape the library."

"Perfect," he said, voice warm. "We'll trade exhaustion stories and eat terrible takeout until we feel human again."

They both laughed, the sound carrying into the quiet evening. It felt right, simple, and real.

Ash reached for her hand, his thumb brushing slow circles against her skin.

"You know," he said, voice low, "visiting my dad, and seeing this place… it reminds me not to waste time. Daddy thought he had more of it. We all do."

Emily was silent for a moment, her gaze drifting toward the silhouette of the house against the dimming sky.

"My dad died in a car accident," she said finally. "On his way home from work. It was just… a normal day."

Ash's hand tightened around hers.

"I was seven," she continued softly. "He was only thirty. My mom said he probably didn't even see it coming. One minute he was driving, and the next…" She trailed off. "It's strange how fast everything can change. I don't even remember the last thing I said to him. I hope it was 'I love you,' but I don't know."

Ash swallowed hard. "God, Em. I'm so sorry."

She nodded, blinking quickly. "I still think about him a lot. Especially lately. I wonder what he'd say about the choices I've made—if he'd be proud of me."

"I'm sure he would be," Ash said, voice rough. "He'd have to be. You're incredible."

He looked back at the ruins, his voice low.

"When my dad got cancer, I was angry for a long time. Watching him go from this big, solid guy—stronger than anyone I knew—to barely being able to stand… it broke something in me. But at least I got to say goodbye. To tell him I'd see him again someday. I think that's what hurts most, knowing you didn't get that chance."

Emily leaned her head on his shoulder. "We have to promise each other we won't waste time."

He kissed her temple, soft and sure. "I don't want to waste anything. I don't want this to be just a summer thing, Em. I want more than that."

She turned toward him, her voice barely above a breath. "Then we'll make it more."

The light faded until only the fireflies remained, twinkling like stray embers in the dark. The world around them fell away, leaving just the two of them—sitting on the edge of the past, making promises to the future, both quietly aware of how easily time could take everything away.

Chapter twenty-four

Ash was wiping down the bar when his phone started buzzing.

Mandy.

He almost ignored it. They hadn't spoken in weeks, and whatever she wanted now couldn't be good.

Maybe she was drunk, maybe it was another relapse into nostalgia—a make-up booty call she'd regret by morning. But something in his gut told him otherwise. The way she'd sounded the last time they'd talked… off. Fragile even.

"Hey," he answered cautiously, wiping his hands on a bar towel.

Her voice was shaky, a little thin around the edges. "Can you come over? Please. I just… I really need you to come."

Mandy never sounded like that. She was the kind of woman who looked perfect crying at a funeral. This wasn't about attention—it was a collapse.

"Yeah," he said quietly. "I'll be there in ten."

The sky was turning from blue to purple when he pulled up to her house. Her Lexus sat crooked in the driveway. The front door was unlocked, so he let himself in. The living room was dim, with only one lamp on in the corner.

Mandy was sitting on the edge of the couch in a t-shirt and sweatpants, hair in a messy up-do, eyes swollen. Tissues were scattered across the coffee table, beside an empty wine glass and a bottle still waiting to be uncorked. He'd never seen her like this—not once in nine years.

"Mandy, what happened?" he asked, moving closer, every muscle tensed.

She looked up, mascara smudged beneath her eyes.

"I'm pregnant."

The words landed like a body blow. For a second, Ash just stood there, the room silent except for the sound of rain starting to drip off the eaves outside.

"You're sure?" he finally managed.

Mandy's eyes flashed. "Of course I'm sure."

She handed him a folder from the medical center.

"Based on what my doctor said, I'm about eight weeks now. It happened in July, probably when we were in Savannah."

His stomach dropped.

"I had an appointment today," she went on, voice breaking. "To end it… But I cancelled. I couldn't—"

She pressed a hand to her mouth to stop a sob.

"I couldn't decide something like that without telling you. You have the right to know."

Ash sank into the chair opposite her, burying his head in his hands. A thousand thoughts raced through his mind—Emily, the coaching job, what his mama would say, everything that had just started to feel right. He pushed it down quickly because this wasn't about him.

All he could manage to say was, "Okay. We'll figure this out."

When he looked up and read Mandy's face, he saw that she wasn't angry—she was scared. Frantic. She looked like she was drowning, desperately reaching for something that might keep her above the surface.

Down the street at her parents' house, Emily rechecked the clock.

7:43 p.m.

Ash was supposed to have picked her up at seven. Dinner first, then a movie at the old drive-in by the marina—the kind of night that had *normal* written all over it. They'd talked about it for days. She'd even curled her hair, put on mascara and a little eyeliner—small touches that suddenly felt stupid now.

Her phone sat on the counter, stubbornly silent except for her little bubbles of unanswered texts:

You on your way?

Everything okay?

Are you standing me up????

Ash?

???????

Nothing.

She tried calling. It rang, then went to voicemail. She waited five minutes and called again. This time, straight to voicemail.

Something twisted in her gut. Ash was always running late, but he also always called.

By eight-thirty, she'd already called Jeanne. He wasn't at the bar; he'd left hours ago. Then she tried Cindy, who said she hadn't seen him since breakfast. She sounded calm, but Emily could hear the worry tightening her voice.

By nine, Emily was pacing the kitchen, chewing her thumbnail, scrolling through her contacts. She wanted to call 911, but forced herself to breathe, to think. She walked to the corkboard by the fridge where the emergency numbers hung, tracing the list until she found Haven County Sheriff's Department.

She hesitated, then dialed.

"Haven County Sheriff's Department, how can I help you?" a woman with a syrupy Southern drawl answered.

"Hi, um… I was looking for Deputy Bell. Is he working tonight? I'm his brother's girlfriend, and I just had a question."

"Oh, hey, honey! This is Sherri. How are you?" The voice was friendly, like she'd known Emily forever, even though they'd never met.

"I'm good, thanks, Sherri. Is Arch there, or how can I reach him?"

"Oh, he's not in the office, sweetheart, but I can try him on the radio. Hold one minute, baby."

Sherri must've set the phone down instead of hitting hold, because Emily could faintly hear her in the background—static, a few muffled voices, the crackle of the radio.

"Hey, honey, thanks for holding," Sherri said, coming back on the line. "I'm gonna give you his cell. You ready for the number?"

Emily scribbled the digits on a Post-it, murmured her thanks, and dialed as soon as she hung up.

Arch picked up on the second ring. "This is Deputy Bell."

"Hey, Arch—it's Emily Kennedy," she stammered.

His tone softened immediately, though surprise flickered slightly in it. "Hey, Emily. Everything all right?"

"I don't know," she said, trying to steady her voice. "Have you seen Ash tonight? We had plans, but I can't get ahold of him. His phone's off or dead or something."

A pause, the faint rumble of an engine, a police scanner crackling in the background.

"He hasn't responded to me either," Arch admitted. "I'll drive around, see what I can find. Don't panic yet, okay?"

"Arch, I'm trying not to, but I'm really worried. This isn't like him."

"I know. I'll call you as soon as I know something."

The line went dead, and the silence inside the house pressed in, heavy and suffocating. Outside the window, rain drizzled, and lightning flashed in the distance.

Emily tried not to picture the worst, but her mind went wild anyway: a car accident, getting lost in the marsh, drowning in the ocean. She drifted toward the front door, praying to see his truck pull up. Her reflection caught in the hallway mirror—hair still curled, makeup perfect, heart slowly breaking. Something was wrong. She could feel it all over.

Chapter twenty-five

The rain dripped outside—soft, steady, tapping against the windows like sand in an hourglass running out of time. Curled under a blanket in her bed, Mandy's head rested on Ash's chest.

Her eyes were swollen, her voice small: "I… I can't do it, Ash. I can't have the abortion. I thought I could, but today I started driving there and… I just can't."

Ash rubbed her back and smoothed the long blond hair that was damp with tears.

"It's okay," he murmured. "You don't have to do anything you don't want to. I'm here, okay? Whatever you need, whatever this means, I'm here."

She looked up at him, eyes searching. "Even if it ruins everything for you?"

The question hit like an unexpected jab to the ribs. He didn't answer. He just pulled her closer, resting his chin against her hair as he stared out the window.

Outside, faint flashes of heat lightning pulsed through the heavy black sky. Reality was sinking in slowly.

I'm having a baby with Mandy. But I'm in love with Emily.

A knock echoed from downstairs—loud, sharp, impatient.

Mandy flinched. "Who the hell is that?"

Ash gently eased her against the pillows and hurried downstairs, barefoot, heart pounding. Through the glass, he caught a flash of blue and the sheriff's decal on the car parked in the drive.

He opened the door. "Arch?"

Arch stood there on the porch, hat and jacket dripping from the rain, his expression drawn.

"You've got people worried sick, man," he said, clearly agitated. "Emily's been calling everyone. She thought something happened to you."

Ash exhaled, dragging a hand through his hair. "It's not what it looks like, Arch, I swear."

He hesitated, voice breaking under the weight of it.

"Mandy's pregnant. Eight weeks. She just told me."

Arch's face shifted to confusion, then pity. "Jesus, Ash."

Ash nodded, the words spilling fast now. "She said she was going to end it, but she changed her mind. She was falling apart tonight. I couldn't just leave her here alone. But Emily—"

He stopped, shaking his head.

"Emily doesn't know yet."

Arch let out a slow breath, glancing toward the rain-dark yard. "Well, you'd better tell her before she hears it from anyone else."

Ash swallowed hard. The rain pattered against the porch roof, thunder rumbling far off.

"Yeah," he said finally, voice low. "I have to tell her."

Arch nodded once, eyes heavy with something that looked like understanding. "Then go now."

Emily's porch light cut through the darkness like a spotlight as Ash pulled up. He wanted to puke. Every step toward the house felt like a slow walk to the firing squad—no blindfold, no mercy, just the knowledge he'd earned what was coming.

She opened the door before he could even knock, rushing out under the porte-cochere.

"Where the hell have you been?" she demanded, voice trembling.

Ash choked out the words. "Em, I need to tell you something. Let's go inside."

She knew it was bad. She could see it in the way he held his face perfectly still, like he was wearing a mask.

Her voice lowered, barely above a whisper. "Just tell me."

"Mandy's pregnant."

The sentence stunned her more than a slap would have. For a moment, Emily just stood there, her mind scrambling to catch up, as if the words refused to shape themselves into meaning.

You fucking asshole! She screamed inside her head, but the only sound that came out was a weak, "What?"

He rubbed the back of his neck, unable to meet her eyes. "She showed me everything—the paperwork, the due date. It happened back in July."

"So, you're sure it's yours?" The words came out harsher than she meant, but she couldn't stop them.

He cringed. "That's not fair, Emily. Yeah, I'm sure. She didn't make this up."

"She did this to you," Emily spat, her voice cracking. "She planned this."

Ash shook his head. "No. She was devastated, Em. She told me she thought about… not having it. But she couldn't. Said I needed to know, and she's right about that."

Hot tears welled in Emily's eyes. "So, what, you're just gonna marry her now? Play house? Pretend this—whatever we have—never happened?"

He stepped toward her, voice low, "I'm not pretending anything. But I'm not the kind of guy who walks out on his kid."

She looked at him like she didn't recognize him anymore. "People have babies every day, Ash. You can still be a father and not be with her. You don't owe her the rest of your life!"

His voice broke. "I owe that baby a life. Two parents. Stability. The least I can do is try."

Emily's chest heaved, her voice trembling. "You owe me something, too."

Silence—the kind that stretches until it hurts.

In the light of the dim gas lamps, Ash could see a slow red blush creep up Emily's neck to reach her cheeks.

"Oh my God, just say it to my face," she finally snapped, her voice trembling, her tone somewhere between rage and heartbreak. "You *want* to be with her. You were just bored and fooling around with me this summer, weren't you?"

She shoved him—hard—but he stood in place like he was made of stone, and that only made her angrier. She looked like she might hit him again, with her fists this time, or break down and cry.

Ash could hardly bear to watch her—the fire in her eyes, the pain he'd caused.

"Emily…" he started, but the words stuck while she glared at him, green eyes piercing his soul. Finally, he managed, "You deserve better than a half-version of me. You deserve someone who doesn't have to choose."

Her lip trembled, but she lifted her chin anyway, defiant through the tears. "I feel like you already made your choice a long time ago."

She turned toward the house.

"I hope you enjoyed your summer fling," she yelled bitterly. "Because now I know that's all I ever was to you."

He took a step forward. "Em—"

"*Fuck you*!" she screamed as loud as she could, running up the steps and slamming the front door before he could say another word.

The sound echoed through the night, leaving him standing alone in the dark, her words burning through him like poisoned arrows.

When Ash climbed into his truck, the rain picked up again—hushed this time, almost tender, like the world couldn't even bother to fall apart with him.

He couldn't get Mandy's face out of his head. Pale. Scared. Her hands gripping his shirt like she might disappear if she let go. She looked so small. So breakable. For the first time that summer, he didn't see the woman he had outgrown; he saw the girl he used to love. The one he'd once promised never to let down. And now she was carrying his child. *His*. That meant something. It had to.

Then there was Emily.

Christ, Emily.

An unbound beauty and all the things he didn't know he needed until she smiled at him from across the bar. Loving her felt like breathing again after years underwater. She made him feel weightless. Seen. Whole. But Emily was strong, he told himself—too strong to fracture. She'd find a way through this, even if it wounded her for a while. She'd survive alone. Mandy wouldn't. His baby wouldn't.

That's what gutted him—he could love one woman with every part of himself and still have to walk away from her to do what was right. Sitting there in the dark, he could have sworn he felt every seam rip as his heart broke clean down the middle. Finally, he turned the key.

Chapter twenty-six

Inside the white stucco beach house, Emily was shaking. She'd kept it together just long enough to slam the door behind her when her knees gave out, and she fell onto the couch face-first.

"Emily?"

Her mother's voice floated from the kitchen.

When Marinda appeared in the doorway, her hair was perfectly smoothed, a glass of white wine still in her hand. She took one look at her daughter's face, and the color drained from her cheeks. "Oh, honey."

Emily tried to speak, but the words splintered. A sob tore through her chest, violent and uncontrollable, ready to break free. She covered her face, choking on the sound, and Marinda was across the room in an instant, arms wrapping tight around her.

"It's okay," her mother whispered, her voice gentler than Emily had heard it in years. "It's okay, baby. Just breathe."

Emily shook her head, words tumbling out between gasps. "He—he got her pregnant, Mom. Mandy. He—Ash—he said he has to be there for her and the baby, and I can't even hate him because he's doing the right thing."

Marinda just held her tighter, stroking her hair. "Oh, sweetheart…"

"I love him," Emily sobbed, voice breaking. "And I finally thought maybe someone saw me. Loved me. It was so perfect. It felt so good, Mom. So right. And now it's just… gone."

Her mother was quiet for a long time, just breathing with her, letting the sobs come.

After a few minutes, she broke in softly, "You know what I think? I think you found something rare. And sometimes those things don't last the way we want them to. But they can change us forever and for the better if we let them."

Emily sniffled, voice small. "Why does it feel like I'm dying?"

"Because your heart's breaking," Marinda said, brushing the damp hair from her face. "And that hurts like hell. But you'll survive it. You're stronger than you think you are, Em. You always have been."

For once, Emily didn't argue. She let herself cry until she had nothing left.

When she finally lifted her head, her mother handed her a tissue and said softly, "Tomorrow, we'll get up. We'll have some coffee and make some breakfast. Then you can start figuring out what's next."

Emily nodded. "I'm not going back to the bar," she choked out the words. "I was supposed to finish out my last two shifts, but I just can't."

Marinda smiled softly. "I'll have Greg talk to Jeanne. I'm sure she will understand."

Emily practically crawled up the stairs. She stood in the shower, staring into space for what felt like an eternity, letting the water run over her, trying to wash the ugly reality away.

When she fell into bed, she was still in her bathrobe and didn't bother to run a brush through her hair. All she could do was lie there. The anger toward Ash had dulled into something heavier—self-loathing.

For weeks, she'd told herself she was Elizabeth Bennet—clever, principled, impossible to overlook. Asher was her Mr. Darcy—brooding, misunderstood, and worth the wait once pride and circumstance fell away.

Now the truth crept painfully closer. She wasn't Elizabeth at all. She was Marianne Dashwood—the foolish romantic who mistook passion for permanence, who believed every glance, every sweet word, meant forever. And Asher? He wasn't Darcy. He was Willoughby—charming, magnetic, and utterly wrong for her in every way that mattered.

She had read the stories a hundred times, knew exactly how they ended, and somehow managed to cast herself as the heroine who would be chosen in the end. Only now, in her own story, there was no happy conclusion; there was only a lesson.

Morning crept in quietly, but Emily didn't feel rested. Her eyes were swollen, her throat sore, her body heavy with the kind of exhaustion that comes only after you've cried yourself empty. Last night had wrecked her in a way she still couldn't quite name.

"Mom?" she rasped, her voice weak as she padded barefoot down the stairs toward the kitchen, following the smell of something burning like someone moving through a fever dream.

Marinda stood at the stove in her silk robe, flipping what appeared to be a blackened piece of French toast with a sigh.

"Don't look at me like that," she said. "I forgot how fast this burner heats up."

Emily tried to smile. "You're lucky you're pretty."

"Sit," her mother ordered, pouring something foamy into a mug. "Cappuccino. Don't ask how I made it."

It wasn't terrible—sweet and strong, with a hint of too much froth on top. The French toast, however, was limp in the middle and burnt around the edges.

Emily ate it anyway. It was the first thing she'd eaten since the afternoon before.

Marinda sat across from her, eyes soft.

"You get exactly one day to sit around moping," she said. "Tomorrow we're going to Charleston. We'll stay one night and check out your new apartment. Maybe we can shop for a few pieces of nice furniture to make it feel like home."

Emily nodded. "I got the lease signed. I need to go pick up the keys."

"Tomorrow, you start moving forward," Marinda said with a gentle smile.

Emily stared down at her plate, pushing the last bite through a puddle of syrup. "You really think I can just… forget him?"

"No," her mother said gently. "But you can start building a life that doesn't revolve around him. And trust me, sweetheart, that's the first step."

Emily swallowed hard, blinking back the sting in her eyes.

"Okay," she whispered. "Charleston."

"To Charleston," Marinda repeated, raising her mug in a toast. "And better food."

They clinked cups, and Emily laughed—small and tired, but genuine.

Charleston was everything Marinda had promised—horse-drawn carriages clip-clopping down cobblestone streets, pastel houses draped in ferns, the feeling that history still lived and breathed around every corner.

They stayed at a little bed-and-breakfast near the Battery, a creaky white house with wicker chairs on the porch and a French bulldog that followed guests like a concierge. Their room overlooked a magnolia courtyard, and every morning, the owner served lemon scones with coffee strong enough to wake the dead.

For the first time in what felt like forever, Emily and Marinda were just *them* again—mother and daughter. They wandered the City Market for hours, trying on sun hats they'd never wear, admiring handmade baskets and jewelry. At lunch, they sat by the water sharing lobster rolls.

That evening, they found a little French bistro tucked off King Street. Marinda ordered a bottle of wine and insisted they split a dessert. They laughed so hard over crème brûlée that the waiter joined in. Afterward, they wandered into an old general store near their inn and bought a bag of saltwater taffy they were too full to eat.

Sitting on a bench outside, the streetlamp haloing them in gold, Marinda leaned back on her elbows.

"You know," she said softly, "I've missed this. Just us. Together. Having an adventure."

Emily smiled faintly. "Me too."

Her phone buzzed.

The screen lit up—**Ash** (11:09 p.m.): *Please, Em. Just tell me you're okay.*

She tossed the phone into her purse, watching the glow fade. He hadn't called—just text after text. And though she hadn't answered a single one, she'd read every word.

The ache that tore through her wasn't simple anymore. It used to be a clean, sharp wanting. Now it came tangled with something she didn't have a name for. Sitting there with her mom, the night warm and safe around them, a quiet truth rose in her. One she hadn't let herself look at directly.

Maybe part of me is mourning who I was when I was with him.

It hurt because she *liked* that version of herself. She liked the way Ash had seen her—braver, bolder, a little daring in a way she hadn't known she could be. For a while, she'd tried to live up to the girl reflected in his eyes. But when was she going to be just Emily? Not the Emily he needed. Not the Emily she became around him—just… *her*.

The realization didn't crush her. It was a little painful, yes. But honest. And honesty, she realized, was something she could build from.

As they walked back to the B&B, the cobblestones slick beneath their sandals, Emily looped her arm through her mother's. She felt lighter, not healed, not yet, but strong enough to start.

Chapter twenty-seven

By the last day of August, Haven Island had begun to shrink. The crowds thinned, the golf carts and beachgoers slowly disappearing from the streets. The air was still warm, but softer now. Shops that had blared music all summer turned quiet, their chalkboard signs fading in the heat.

Out on the water, boats drifted lazily, their wakes carving through the glassy sea green water. The sun sank faster each evening, the shadows stretching long and reluctant over the horizon—as if the island itself wasn't quite ready to let go of summer.

For Emily's farewell party, Jeanne had done something unheard of—she closed High Tide for the night.

"Don't get used to it," she'd barked when Joel got teary. "But damn it, that girl's a special case. She earned a proper send-off."

When Emily walked in, the bar looked transformed. Colorful paper lanterns hung from the ceiling, the jukebox hummed her favorite playlist, and a banner above the bar read:

GOODBYE, EM — GOOD LUCK IN CHARLESTON!

Kenzie ran up and hugged her tight. “You’d better stay in touch, law-school girl,” she whispered.

Joel brought glittery cupcakes and insisted on giving a speech that made half the room cry and the other half laugh. Even Jeanne needed a cigarette after that.

Later, when the party noise settled into something softer, Emily dug into her tote bag.

“I have something to give y'all,” she said.

She handed Joel a wrapped box first. He peeled back the tissue paper and froze.

“Em… is this—?”

“The Lafayette 148 blazer,” she said, cheeks warming. “You’ve been talking about it all summer. I want you to have it.”

Joel covered his mouth, eyes immediately glossy. “Em, I swear to God if you’re trying to make me bawl—”

Kenzie snorted. “Oh, please, you were already halfway there.”

Emily turned to her, pulling out a small fabric pouch covered in faded florals—something she’d found in her favorite thrift store. “I saw this and immediately thought of you.”

Kenzie opened it and gasped.

Inside was a delicate vintage ring—a thin gold band, a tiny turquoise stone, imperfect and sun-worn in a way that made it more beautiful.

“Emily…” Kenzie’s voice cracked. “This is so perfect.”

"I'm glad you like it," Emily said softly.

Kenzie didn't hesitate; she threw her arms around Emily, squeezing tight.

"You're coming back here someday," she said into Emily's shoulder. "I'm not accepting any alternate timelines."

For the last song, Joel, Kenzie, and Emily swayed together in a big group hug, belting out every word to "Closing Time" by Semisonic as if it were an anthem. People began to drift out to the porch slowly, the evening sea breeze was rolling in, and the sun was almost gone, hidden behind boats in the marina.

Making her way outside slowly, Emily leaned against the railing, trying to memorize everything—the sticky air, the laughter, the glow of the lights. Her gaze drifted to Ash, who was standing a few feet away. He hadn't said anything all night, but he'd been there helping Jeanne clean glasses, carrying chairs, pretending to blend into the background.

Mandy came toward the end of the night to pick him up, sipping a La Croix at the bar, quiet and composed. Emily caught her glance once—cool, assessing—but not cruel. She wanted to hate her, but she couldn't. Not really. Mandy hadn't cheated or schemed; she'd won by default.

As the party dwindled, Mandy touched Ash's arm and murmured something. He nodded, and she gave him a small, understanding smile before grabbing her purse.

"I'll wait in the car," she said softly.

That was how Emily knew the war was over. Mandy understood this moment needed to happen—a truce of sorts.

One by one, the others drifted off until only Emily and Ash remained, bathed in the hazy glow of the porch light, the tide creeping closer, whispering against the sand.

"I didn't think you'd come," Emily said quietly.

"I almost didn't." He laughed once, low and tired. "Didn't know if I had the right to."

"You didn't," she said, her voice trembling. "But I'm glad you're here."

For a long moment, they just looked at each other—the tension, the love, the regret—all the things that would never fit neatly into words.

"I wanted to tell you…" Ash started, then stopped to take a breath. "I never wanted it to end like this."

"Me either." Her throat felt raw. "But maybe it's supposed to. Written in the sand, not in the stars. Isn't that how the saying goes?"

He nodded, eyes unreadable in the dim light. "Something like that. You changed me, Em. You made me remember what it feels like to *want* something. Not because it's expected, but because it's real."

Her tears came silently. "Then don't forget it. Not even when you think you have to."

He reached for her, hand brushing her cheek, lingering. "I won't. Not ever."

She wanted to kiss him, but she didn't. They both knew this was goodbye.

Emily turned, blinking back tears.

"I know we can't ever be just friends," Ash said, his voice low and uneven as she started to walk away. "But can we at least talk sometimes? I don't think I can lose you forever. Not completely."

She paused, her back still to him. Something in his tone—so desperate, so sincere—pulled her halfway around. The porch light caught the tears in her eyes.

At first, shutting him out had felt necessary. A way to cauterize a wound that wouldn't stop bleeding. She told herself it was closure. Letting him back in again felt like undoing that work.

She did it anyway.

"Yeah," she whispered. "I promise I'll always be there for you. If you text or call… I'll answer. Always."

Ash nodded, swallowing hard. "Then I promise the same," he said. "If you ever need me—if you ever reach out—I'll answer. Forever, okay?"

For a long moment, neither of them moved. The soft breeze felt thick, heavy with everything that promise meant and everything it couldn't fix.

Emily turned and walked to her SUV, her footsteps crunching softly against the gravel. The door shut with a dull thud. In the rearview mirror, he was still standing on the porch, hands shoved deep in his pockets.

The realization came too late: she hadn't gotten away clean. Whatever she'd just promised Ash felt like an anchor—tethering her to something she feared would drag her back into an old mess. One that might cost her more next time.

The morning Emily left Haven Island, the sky was a pale watercolor blue. The air smelled clean, the ocean's scent still lingering in the breeze. For once, she didn't feel the weight of leaving—just a quiet calm she hadn't known she could carry.

Her new 4Runner gleamed in the driveway, sunlight glinting off the hood. It still felt strange seeing it there instead of "Old Moe," but when she climbed inside and turned the key, she couldn't help smiling.

The engine purred to life eagerly, and she took the long way through town—past the marina, the diner, the boardwalk, and High Tide. The neon sign still flickered faintly in the daylight, the pier slick from the morning rain, the air thick with that familiar mix of salt and grease that now smelled like home. Not a home she was born to, but one that had claimed her.

The bridge came into view. The same one that had terrified her that first day—rising high over the inlet, shimmering in the early light. Once, she'd gripped the wheel white-knuckled, heart pounding, breath shallow. Now, she just turned up the radio. The tires hummed against the asphalt as she climbed, the island shrinking smaller and smaller in the rearview. At the top, she slowed—just a little—and let her gaze sweep across the vast stretch of water below.

She'd come to the island unsure of everything—who she was, what she wanted, where she belonged. Somehow, she'd found more than she ever expected. She'd met friends who didn't make her audition for their affection. Who let her be loud, flawed, and unfinished.

She'd loved a man—fully, without calculation—and she'd survived him choosing someone else. She'd gone all in without realizing she was gambling, and she'd lost the hand. But maybe not the game.

The pain was still there—heavy, unfinished, sharp around the edges. So was the risk she'd taken. So was the love she hadn't held back.

Grief and gratitude sat side by side in her chest, neither willing to move.

The bridge leveled out, the mainland stretched wide and waiting. Sunlight danced across her windshield like a promise. Emily let herself smile through the tears, but she didn't look back. Not even once.

Part Two

Chapter twenty-eight

The months that followed August blended into a blur of money and decisions. Ash and Mandy bought a townhouse off the island, but close by. It was halfway between her parents' gated neighborhood in Haven Lakes and downtown Bellefontaine. Modern, sleek, and far too posh for Ash's taste—white walls, marble counters, and furniture that looked like it belonged in a catalog—but Mandy loved it. He joked with her, saying he was going to add some deer heads to the walls. She rolled her eyes, knowing better. The baby's room was still a blank slate for now.

Ash sold his old truck, the one everyone knew him by, and traded it for a brand-new Tahoe. The guys at the weight room roasted him mercilessly, calling it "the dad-mobile," but he didn't care. He had a baby on the way and, for the first time, something that almost looked like a plan. Turned out, the years of saving cash tips and bartending double shifts had left him with a surprising amount of cushion in his bank account.

Even Mandy had been shocked when he told her how much he'd put away. She had almost lost her mind when he got down on one knee and held up a Tiffany blue box one night in mid-September as they walked along the beach.

"You're full of surprises, Asher Bell," she'd said with a beaming smile, kissing his cheek and holding up her left hand to show off the two-carat brilliant round solitaire she had always said she wanted.

By October, he'd been accepted into an online MBA program and started chipping away at coursework in the evenings. Mandy's father had pulled a few strings, landing him a steady job as a logistics manager for a recycling company. It wasn't glamorous, but it was reliable—nine to five, benefits, a title he could put on paper.

As autumn rolled on and the hastily planned but still expensive wedding crept closer, everything looked like Mandy's version of perfect. On paper, anyway.

At the 20-week ultrasound appointment, Elizabeth perched on the little stool beside the table, her designer tote tucked neatly at her feet. She'd been the one who wanted to find out the gender, already planning a "surprise" reveal for later.

For Mandy, the baby wasn't an abstract idea. She'd been living with the reality for weeks: the nausea, the cravings, the mood swings. Ash had seen her pale and shaky, running for the bathroom to vomit. All he could do was bring ginger ale and crackers, rub her back, and tell her it would pass. It made him feel helpless—like no matter how much he wanted to fix things, there was nothing he could do but watch.

Sitting in that dim little room, the steady *whir* of the machine filling the silence, his world turned upside down. The screen flickered, black and gray and strange, and then the technician turned a knob and pointed with a gloved finger.

"There," she said. "That's your baby."

Ash leaned forward, elbows on his knees, staring at the fuzzy image. The baby was so small—barely more than a ripple of movement—but it was *real.* A heartbeat filled the room, fast and fluttering, like the wings of a trapped bird. That sound hit him harder than anything else had.

Mandy smiled weakly from the table, tears sliding into her hairline. Elizabeth squeezed her hand, cooing softly, but Ash couldn't speak. This was it. *His*. Not a mistake or an accident or a consequence—*a life.* Something he helped create.

He reached for Mandy's other hand, squeezing gently. She squeezed back. He didn't know what he was supposed to feel. He just knew everything had changed.

Law school wasn't easy, but Emily loved it in a way she didn't expect to. The reading was relentless, the competition cutthroat, but she found herself thriving in the routine of the fall semester—the early mornings, the long nights, the way her mind stretched in new directions.

David Jordan was her first friend at Charleston College of Law. He had sat down beside her that first week in torts and offered her an extra pen when hers ran out of ink. Somehow, they'd never stopped talking.

He was a little nerdy—the kind of guy who actually read the footnotes in their casebooks—but there was a quiet steadiness about him, a calm that made her feel safe when everything else in her life still felt uncertain.

David was lanky, lean, with a runner's body, the kind built from dawn miles and discipline. His frame was wiry but strong, every movement efficient, unhurried. His skin was a warm, smooth, amber-brown. His light brown eyes, framed by dark lashes and black-rimmed glasses, always seemed to be studying something more profound than what was said. His curls were just loose enough to fall over his forehead, no matter how often he pushed them back, and his voice carried that deep, low, easy calm that could make even law books sound like poetry.

Like her, David had gone to Clemson. He'd run cross country and track, and when she mentioned she still tried to run a few mornings a week, he'd invited her along. He was faster, of course, but he always slowed his pace, matching her stride perfectly. They talked about almost everything—professors, favorite restaurants, people they both knew. Emily always managed to steer the conversation safely away from the past summer. She gave him the highlights but glazed over most of the details, especially the details about Ash.

They studied together in the library until it closed, their notes spread out between empty coffee cups. On Saturday afternoons, they went to mass together, sitting side by side in the same pew each week. It felt peaceful. Different from the heart-wrenching passion she'd once known.

When her parents visited for brunch, David fit in seamlessly. Greg liked his sharp mind and easy manners, and her mom looked relieved. As if she finally believed Emily might have found someone stable.

Sometimes, Emily stayed over at David's apartment after movie nights—Hitchcock marathons and old black-and-white films they both loved. They'd kissed, soft and slow, but hadn't gone further. It wasn't that she didn't want to. She just wasn't ready. She was still learning herself again, still figuring out who she wanted to be—not just who she was when someone else was looking at her. David seemed to understand, without her having to say a word.

It wasn't wild, and it wasn't reckless. With David, everything felt calm—predictable in the best way. He never made her feel off balance or uncertain. There were no mixed signals, no wild rushes of adrenaline that left her dizzy afterward. Where Ash had been fire—spark and heat and lightning—David was rhythm and steadiness. He didn't pull her outside of herself; he reminded her that love didn't always have to be ferocious to be real. When he smiled at her across a library table or matched his pace to hers on a run, Emily wondered if this was what happiness was supposed to feel like. It wasn't dramatic. It didn't rip her in half. But maybe that was the point.

Still, some nights, when Emily lay awake in David's bed, she thought about how some loves burn so brightly they leave a mark. The kind that is seared into your bones, so that no matter how much time passes, you still feel the warmth beneath your skin.

Maybe the best kind of love wasn't meant to last forever. Maybe the extraordinary loves are the ones that change you, and stay, quietly, even long after they are gone.

It was late on a cold November night when Emily's phone buzzed on the nightstand. She was staying at David's place and almost ignored it, assuming it was someone from her study group cramming for finals.

Then she saw the name—**Ash.**

The messages came in bursts. He'd been drinking. She could tell.

You up?

I'm at Stool Pigeons lol

Bachelor party... weird right?

Out on the beach now.

Can you call me?

Her palms went slick. The phone trembled slightly in her hand. Every rational part of her said *don't.* But her heart? Her heart had never listened to reason where Asher Bell was concerned.

She slipped quietly out of the bedroom and pressed *call* before she could stop herself.

"Hey," his voice came through low and rough, threaded with coastal wind.

"You shouldn't be texting me like that," she whispered, trying to sound calm.

"I know." A pause. "But I can't stop thinking about you. I've tried, Em. I really have."

"You're getting married next weekend." The words came out sharper than she meant, half a hiss, half a plea.

"I know that, too."

The ocean, on Ash's end, filled the line with the sound of waves crashing softly.

He exhaled, long and heavy. “I’m sitting in the same spot we were that night. Your birthday. July fourth. You said the arepa was the best thing you’d ever eaten. Then you put your head on my chest.”

Despite herself, she half-smiled. “I remember.”

“I thought if I came out here tonight, it might make me feel different. Like I could finally put it behind me.” He gave a short, dry laugh. “But all I can think about is you. All I ever do is think about you, Emily.”

She pressed her hand to her forehead, her breath catching. “Ash, you can’t do this. You can’t call me and say things like that and then still marry her.”

“I know.” His voice broke, fragile as the wind. “I just… don’t know how to stop loving you.”

Neither spoke; there was just the surf and static and everything they didn’t have words for.

“Ash…” she whispered, but the moment was already unraveling.

“I should go,” he said at last, though his tone made it sound like he didn’t want to. “Goodnight, Em.”

She hesitated.

“Goodbye, Ash.”

Emily sat there in the dark, the glow of the streetlight spilling through the window, the city humming softly beyond. David’s cat, Booger, brushed against her legs, meowing up at her with round amber eyes. For the first time since she’d left Haven Island, she let the tears fall.

Chapter twenty-nine

The bridal suite in the church annex smelled faintly of perfume and hairspray and buzzed with that subtle mix of excitement and nerves. Mandy sat at the vanity while the stylist fussed with the last few pins in her hair. Her veil lay draped across the back of a chair, shimmering like spun sugar in the early December light.

Behind her, her bridesmaids were in full party mode, with Jenn taking the lead. Mandy had been Jenn's maid of honor last year, and now the roles were reversed. Jenn was determined to keep her calm, handing Mandy "water shots" while the rest of the girls threw back champagne and shrieked.

They were trying to keep the energy high and light, but when Mandy caught her own reflection in the mirror, her breath snagged.

Wedding jitters and pregnancy hormones were one hell of a combination.

Elizabeth appeared, holding a mimosa in one hand and a box of tissues in the other, still in her silk robe, pearls already clasped around her neck.

"You look beautiful, baby," she said, as her eyes moistened.

Mandy turned slightly. "Don't cry, Mama. You'll ruin your makeup."

Elizabeth smiled faintly, sitting on the edge of the vanity table.

"Who me? I'm not crying," she said, dabbing her eyes with a tissue before taking a sip and setting the glass flute down carefully. "You know, you don't have to do this just because you're pregnant. I know your father spent a small fortune. There are people out there waiting, and the papers are ready to be signed, but—" she paused, choosing her words. "Sweetheart, marriage isn't something you walk into because you feel like you should. It's something you do because you can't imagine not doing it."

Mandy blinked faster, the tightness in her chest surprising her, not from doubt, but from the weight of how much she wanted this.

"I love him, Mama," she said, and she meant it.

Mandy had known what she wanted since the first time she'd seen Ash. Maybe the order of things wasn't what she'd pictured, but her life was still moving exactly where she'd always hoped it would go. A marriage. A baby. A family. He was the father of her child and the man she had built her future around long before today. For her, that was more than enough.

Elizabeth reached out and patted her hand.

"I know you do. But you're still so young...." Her voice trailed off as she teared up again.

Mandy forced a smile, looking down at the crisp folds in her dress. "It's fine, Mama. It's all going to be fine."

Her mother kissed the top of her head and stood, smoothing her robe. "If you're sure, baby, then that's all that matters."

When the door closed behind her, Mandy exhaled slowly. Her hand drifted to the faint curve of her stomach.

It's going to be fine.

She internally repeated it as a mantra. Not out of doubt, but because the moment was enormous. The words sounded confident. She knew what she wanted. She wasn't backing out.

Down the hall, in a small side room off the vestry, Ash stood in front of a mirror in which he barely recognized himself. The suit fit perfectly—a black tuxedo with a crisp white shirt and a bow tie Mandy had picked out. His hands felt too big for the delicate fabric. He tugged at his collar once, twice, then gave up. It wasn't the clothes that were choking him.

Arch leaned in the doorway, hands shoved into his pockets, a lazy half-smile on his face.

"You look like a grown-up, little brother," he said.

Ash sighed. "Feels weird."

Arch shrugged. "It's supposed to." Then, with a conspiratorial glance, he reached into his jacket and pulled out a battered silver flask.

"Here," he said, unscrewing the cap. "For your nerves."

Ash hesitated. “You sure this is a good idea?”

“Better than puking on your shoes halfway down the aisle. Take a sip.”

Ash tipped back the flask and instantly regretted it. The liquid hit like sweet gasoline—fire and sugar all at once. He gagged, coughing so hard his eyes watered.

“What the hell is that?” he rasped, wiping his mouth.

Arch grinned, the corners of his eyes crinkling. “Homemade peach moonshine. You'd better man up. Can’t have my little brother looking like such a pussy before he says I do.”

Ash groaned, still coughing. “I think it just stripped the lining off my throat.”

“Good,” Arch said, clapping him on the shoulder hard enough to jolt him. “Now you’ll sound like a real man when you say your vows.”

Despite himself, Ash laughed, a sharp bark of relief that cut through the tension. For a few seconds, it was just the two of them: brothers, idiots, troublemakers, joking around like teenagers before things got serious.

Arch handed him the flask again. “One more for luck.”

Ash shook his head. “Not a chance.”

Arch’s laugh still echoed down the hall as he disappeared toward the front of the church, leaving behind the faint bite of peach moonshine in the air.

Ash leaned against the wall for a moment. His stomach still burned, but the jagged edge of his nerves had dulled slightly.

“That boy is just like his daddy,” came a familiar voice behind him.

He turned, already smiling. “Hey, Mama.”

Cindy Bell stood in the doorway, short and sturdy, her diner uniform traded for a pale blue dress that matched her eyes. Her light hair was pinned up neatly, but a few curls had escaped, softening her face. She looked beautiful in her own unpretentious way.

"Arch been feedin' you that rotgut again?" she asked, hands on her hips.

"Moonshine," he admitted with a grin.

Cindy chuckled, shaking her head. "Men never do grow out of bein' fools." Then her expression softened as she looked at him. "You sure you're okay, Asher?"

He nodded automatically. "Yeah, I'm good."

She didn't buy it—mamas know their children.

Cindy crossed the room and fixed his boutonniere, her hands steady. "You know, I was a lot younger than you and Mandy when I married your daddy. Seventeen, scared to death, already pregnant with Arch." Her voice wavered just slightly. "I loved him, don't you think I didn't. He was wild as a buck, but Lord knows, I loved him."

Ash listened quietly.

She kept going, eyes distant. "Still, sometimes I wonder what it would've been like if I'd gone to college, or traveled, or just… figured out who I was before I became somebody's wife and somebody's mama. Not regret exactly—just curiosity, I guess."

Ash swallowed. "You think I'm making a mistake?"

Cindy smiled faintly, thumb brushing the lapel of his jacket. "Don't put words in my mouth, now. I'm not saying that. What I'm saying is—it's been the privilege of my life to be your mama and your daddy's wife. But I know what it feels like to wonder what else might've been."

She met his eyes.

"You ever heard the saying, 'love whispers, it doesn't shout?'"

He nodded, throat tight.

Cindy rested her hand on her son's arm, eyes soft but steady. "Sometimes, love, the real kind, doesn't come in loud or sweep you off your feet. It sneaks up quietly. It's in the small things—the showing up, the staying, the forgiving." She paused, smiling a little. "I know what you had with Emily, baby. And I don't ever want you to think it wasn't real. It was real. Just like a summer storm. Beautiful, wild, and over too soon."

Ash looked down, holding back tears.

His mama kept going, her voice gentle. "But what you've got with Mandy… that's something different. Maybe not as fiery, but steady. She's a good woman. Not perfect, none of us are, but I see the way she cares for you, how she fights for you, pushes you to do better. That's what love looks like when it lasts."

She gave his arm a squeeze.

"Don't spend your whole life chasing what might've been, Asher. You deserve a chance to build what *can* be."

They were both crying now and not even trying to hide it.

She gave him a quick, fierce hug, her voice muffled against his shoulder. "Now go get married before Arch gets any more of that shine in him."

Ash laughed—low and grateful—and when she left, the laughter faded into a quiet resolve. The doubts weren't gone. But for the first time all morning, he could keep them quiet.

The string quartet began to play softly from the loft, “Canon in D,” slow and reverent. As the procession began, Mandy took her father’s arm and inhaled deeply, steadying herself. But before she could take her first step, a strange flutter rippled low in her stomach.

For one startling second, she thought she might be sick right there, in front of everyone. Her hand tightened around her bouquet.

Then it hit her—not nausea.

Movement. The baby.

The heavy oak doors opened, bright winter sunlight spilling across the aisle through the stained glass. She could see Ash standing at the altar beside the pastor and Arch, tall and still, his expression unreadable from where she stood.

Her breath caught. Tears welled instantly. The first baby kicks. Right now, of all times.

Her father glanced down, mistaking her face for nerves. “You okay, honey?”

She nodded quickly, unable to speak around the lump in her throat.

As they began down the aisle, the flutters came again—faint but discernible—tiny reminders of everything that had brought her here, and everything that was coming next. Tears streamed now, making her vision blurry. It wasn’t sadness. It was everything all at once.

Ash looked up as the doors opened and saw Mandy, glowing and graceful on her father's arm. Her dress shimmered ivory under the soft light—lace over silk, her veil trembling faintly with each step. She looked like something out of a bridal magazine—poised, luminous, so ethereal he almost forgot how to breathe.

Mandy swayed slightly as she walked, smiling through her tears. Later, she'd tell him about the baby kicking, the first flutters, faint but real. Now, he could only watch. He saw two versions of her coming together in that instant—the girl he'd fallen in love with years ago, and the woman who was about to be his wife.

The pews blurred at the edges. He thought of his mama's words: *Don't spend your whole life chasing what might've been.*

This was it. Game time. No more what-ifs. No more looking back.

When Mandy reached him, her hand trembled in his, and the music's final note lingered in the air. Ash caught her eye and smiled reassuringly. For the first time that day, the next step felt like a *choice*. The vows, the future, and whatever came next—they would choose to face it together.

The reception that night at The Palm was nothing short of opulent. Mandy's father had bought out the entire venue—chandeliers glowing gold, tables draped in cream linen, centerpieces of roses and eucalyptus perfuming the air with a clean, elegant scent. A live band played softly in the corner while servers floated through the room with trays of champagne, cocktail shrimp, and miniature crab cakes.

Ash moved through the motions—the toasts, the photos, the congratulations—feeling a little like a spectator. He smiled when people expected him to, laughed when they made jokes about "joining the family," but the world felt just a little strange now, a little too bright.

From across the room, he could feel the glances. The ones that said everything without saying a word. *She's glowing. She's definitely showing now. That explains the quick wedding.* They were too polite to gossip openly, but too Southern not to notice and take notes.

Mandy didn't seem to care. She was radiant, her hand brushing her stomach now and then with unconscious protectiveness. She didn't even bother pretending with a glass of champagne. Her blue eyes sparkled under the lights as she thanked guests and accepted compliments.

Ash started to believe he could be happy here. Maybe this version of life would be enough.

Elizabeth tapped a champagne glass, her voice slightly tipsy and rising above the crowd.

"If I could have everyone's attention!" she called, beaming. "As most of you know—or have guessed—our beautiful newlyweds have exciting news to share. Tonight, my daughter has given me permission to say it out loud, in public, for the very first time…" She paused for effect. "I'm going to be a grandma!"

Applause broke out, but Elizabeth wasn't done. She raised a hand to shush them. "But what Asher and Amanda don't know is that I've arranged a very special surprise for them. Come on up here, y'all—we need to cut this wedding cake!"

The lights dimmed as the staff wheeled out the cake: three tiers of white buttercream trimmed in gold leaf, a cascade of deep red roses tumbling down one side like a ribbon. A gold topper glimmered in the candlelight—*Forever to Thee.*

A hush fell as Mandy and Ash took the knife together.

"Three… two… one…" the crowd chanted playfully.

The knife slid cleanly through the frosting. When the first slice lifted, a shock of bright blue cake appeared inside. For a heartbeat, the room went silent. Then cheers erupted. Blue confetti cannons fired from the stage, raining sparkles through the candlelight.

Ash's heart stopped.

It's a boy.

Mandy's eyes filled with tears as she turned to him.

"You have a son," she whispered.

He laughed, kissing her forehead. "Guess I'd better start working on my spiral again."

He tried hard to believe it: a little life, half him, half her. The words felt surreal, barely solid enough to hold onto. Someone to toss a football with, to teach how to bait a hook, to hopefully be better than he ever was.

The cheers swelled, flashbulbs strobed, and he pulled Mandy into a kiss for the cameras. But even in that perfect frame—champagne bubbles, golden light, applause—another image broke through.

Emily Kennedy.

Barefoot in the sand, her laughter tangled in the wind. It pierced through, painful and unbidden. He shoved it down hard, the way he always did. Tonight wasn't about *what if.* It was about *what is.*

Emily stared at the calendar—December 4th. She told herself she should throw her phone in the ocean. She didn't. Her apartment was dark except for the faint orange glow of the streetlight seeping through the blinds. She'd been sitting there for hours, staring at her notes, barely absorbing the material. Her phone was resting heavily on her lap.

Every few minutes, she'd check to make sure it still had a dial tone, like maybe that would make it ring. Ash hadn't said he would call—of course he hadn't—but Emily found herself waiting anyway. Waiting beyond reason and pride, for one last conversation she knew better than to want.

The day had come and gone, and the silence stretched on. She kept glancing at the clock—5:17, 6:02, 7:40. Each hour that passed felt like another door closing. Somewhere out there, Ash was saying vows, slipping a ring on Mandy's hand, and building a life without Emily in it.

By the time the tears came, she didn't even bother wiping them away. It wasn't heartbreak anymore; it was something else. Grief, she realized, for what had burned so brightly but never really stood a chance.

Her phone buzzed obnoxiously—**Joel.**

She picked up, trying to sound normal. "Hey."

"Don't 'hey' me, bitch," Joel said, voice soft but still able to slice through the tight ball of sadness in her chest. "I saw your away messages. You sound like you should be in a padded room."

Despite herself, she gave a shaky laugh. "You're not completely wrong."

"I mean, for God's sake, are you eating? Drinking water? Wearing something other than that ratty Clemson hoodie?"

"Maybe," she lied.

"Uh-huh." A pause, then gentler. "Em, you've got to stop torturing yourself. You can't keep obsessing over the man. He has a whole-ass wife now and a kid on the way. It's not good for your mental health. You need to block, delete, *bye*. For your own sanity."

"I know," she whispered. "I just… want to talk to him. It's so stupid. I keep thinking he's going to call—even though saying that out loud sounds like insanity. It's almost like I can *feel* him sometimes. I think I'm losing my mind."

Joel sighed, the sound full of affection and exasperation. "Girl, if he does call, I'm changing his name in your phone to *Absolutely Fucking Not.*"

That made her laugh through her tears.

Joel launched into a story about his newest "situationship" with a muscle-bound barista from Barcelona named Mateo, who—according to Joel—made the best latte in Savannah and terrible life choices everywhere else.

Emily smiled weakly through her tears, letting him ramble about outfit crises, mismatched throw pillows, and how "love is a scam, but caffeine is forever." Her mind, however, wasn't entirely with Joel. It drifted to David. She owed him an explanation—at least that much. The past week, she'd been distant, dodging his instant messages and texts, skipping their morning runs, claiming she needed to study when really, she couldn't focus on anything but Ash and that phone call from the beach. David didn't push because that wasn't his way. He just told her that she knew where to find him.

Joel kept talking, light and funny, doing what he did best—filling the silence until she could breathe again. When they finally hung up, Emily sat for a long time in the dark. Somewhere on that island, the man she still loved was building a life she'd never be part of. She had to find a way to make peace with that.

She opened her contacts.

Ash.

Naturally near the top of the list.

Her finger hovered for a long moment over *Delete Contact.* Then she pressed it down.

She'd promised once that she'd always be there for him. But when had he ever truly been there for her? Not lately. And now everything was different. He had chosen someone else, and she needed to choose a life that wasn't built on getting attention from a man.

She wasn't sure when she'd stop missing him—maybe she never would. But she knew one thing with absolute clarity. If she was ever going to move forward, this had to be the first step.

Chapter thirty

The first weeks after the wedding fell into a strange, dreamy rhythm. Mandy kept waiting for something to go wrong. Waiting for that whisper in the back of her mind to be right. The one that said she would wake up from this.

Instead, December blurred into soft mornings at their new townhouse, Ash sleeping warm beside her, his palm always drifting to her slightly swollen belly before he even opened his eyes.

By January, the changes felt impossible to ignore. Her clothes wouldn't fit. Her breasts ached. She kept crying over commercials and then getting mad that she was crying at all. She'd always been in control of her body—impossibly thin, toned, disciplined. Now she felt like she was inflating by the day.

One morning, she stood in their bathroom, just out of the shower, staring at herself sideways, and moaned, "I look huge."

Ash walked by, paused, backed up, and leaned in the doorway with a smirk.

"You look pregnant," he said. "And your ass looks incredible. I'm serious. Like… distractingly incredible."

She rolled her eyes, but smiled as he stepped closer, leaning in for a kiss and softly running his hands over her body.

Ash thrived in the simplicity of their new life. The wedding had quieted something in him. He was going home every night to a wife—his wife—and a future he could see clearly for the first time in his life.

Emily crossed his mind from time to time, and he missed her, but he didn't text or call. He loved taking care of Mandy. Loved watching her belly grow. Loved the way she'd pretend to be annoyed when he knelt and talked to the baby like he could hear him already.

"We're gonna teach you to catch fish off the pier," he'd say to her stomach, and Mandy would sigh like he was impossible. Still, she smiled every time.

He surprised her by painting the nursery after work one day. She had cried happy tears, and he kissed them off her cheeks. They argued sometimes—about household chores, about the way she overthought everything, and about how he didn't always understand her moods. But the arguments didn't break them—it felt human, normal. Life was settling.

The baby shower in February was more elegant than Mandy ever would've planned for herself. Elizabeth and Jenn had insisted on hosting it at the Haven Lakes Clubhouse, and when Mandy walked in that afternoon, she teared up at the sight.

Soft floral arrangements spilled out of glass urns. Pale blue linens were draped over the tables. Velvet-blue ribbons accented the decor—subtle and stylish, the exact opposite of the tacky baby-boy stuff she'd dreaded.

Elizabeth had brought in a caterer, and the whole room smelled like chicken, warm rolls, and vanilla cupcakes with blueberry cream. The dessert spread looked like it had been prepared for a magazine.

Mandy felt swollen and tired, but also undeniably loved. Every woman she'd ever known seemed to be there—co-workers, neighbors, a childhood dance teacher she hadn't seen in ten years—hugging her, handing her tiny onesies, telling her she was glowing. She didn't believe that for a second, but she didn't correct them either.

By the time the party wrapped up, Mandy was parked in a chair near the fireplace, feet up, ankles swelling, watching Elizabeth box up leftover cupcakes. Jenn was nearby, trying to convince the bartender to give her his secret recipe for the mocktail they'd served. Cindy stopped to hug her tight, promising to stop by tomorrow with a casserole because "late pregnancy is not the time for pride," before she swept out the door.

Ash showed up just as the last guests were leaving. He kissed Mandy's forehead, exchanged polite hellos, and immediately started gathering up half the gift table in his arms like it was nothing.

Jenn drifted over, her whole energy shifting into something softer. "Okay," she said quietly, leaning in. "Don't cry until I'm done, because once you start, I'll start, and we'll both look insane."

Mandy frowned. "What is happening?"

Jenn grabbed both Mandy's hands; her eyes were already watering. "I'm pregnant."

Mandy's face broke open in a smile. "Jenn, are you serious?"

Jenn nodded, laughing as the first tear streaked her perfect winged liner. "We found out after New Year's. I didn't want to announce it in front of everyone because today is your day. You deserve the spotlight."

Mandy yanked her into a hug, and instantly they were sobbing—quiet, messy, ridiculous tears that neither of them tried to stop.

"I'm so happy for you," Mandy whispered into her friend's shoulder.

"I can't wait to do all this with you," Jenn said, voice shaking. "Even if I live three hours away. Playdates, holiday photos, matching swimsuits in the summer. Our kiddos are going to grow up like cousins."

Ash came back for the rest of the gifts and stopped short when he saw the girls wrapped around each other, crying and laughing at once. Something warm flashed in his eyes.

"You two good?" he asked with a smile.

Jenn waved him off. "We're fine. Female hormones and joy—it's a lot."

Mandy wiped her face, then reached for Ash's hand.

"You ready?" he asked.

She nodded, squeezing Jenn one last time.

"Yeah," she breathed. "I really am."

Ash helped her to her feet and guided her toward the doors, toward the Tahoe stacked with blue-wrapped gifts, and toward the next chapter she'd been a little afraid of but suddenly wasn't anymore.

Chapter thirty-one

After the dead of winter, Charleston was starting to stir again in the crisp March air. The sun was warm and bright, even though a chill lingered on the breeze. Patios began to slowly open, with tourists and college students sipping lattes outdoors again.

The tattoo studio was small, tucked between a bookstore and a coffee shop on Meeting Street. The air smelled faintly of antiseptic. Emily sat in the chair, watching in the mirror as the artist prepped her shoulder blade.

She'd gone back and forth for weeks—scrolling through quotes, sketches, symbols—trying to find something that said what she couldn't. In the end, she'd chosen five small words in delicate script: *Whatever our souls are made of...* The beginning of her favorite line from Wuthering Heights. The one that had always undone her.

She'd chosen the placement deliberately, because sometimes when she closed her eyes, she could still feel Ash's fingertips there. She remembered the exact way they'd moved over her skin that night. The storm raging outside, his touch slow and lingering; it was the softest she'd ever known him. A moment that would never belong to anyone else. By putting the words there—inked deep into her skin like a quiet ritual—she could finally lay that ghost to rest.

It wasn't just about Ash, though. Not really. It was about her—the girl who'd learned that love could wreck you and rebuild you. That you could be torn open and still stand, like the shoreline after a hurricane—changed, scarred, and ragged but still there.

When the needle buzzed to life and dragged across her skin, she didn't flinch.

Afterward, she walked along Waterfront Park, the air crisp and clean. The fresh tattoo burned faintly under her shirt, a secret reminder just for her. It made her feel alive again—restored, somehow.

She thought about David, how he'd be getting ready soon, probably choosing a vinyl record to play before their sushi date. He didn't know about the tattoo yet. She'd tell him over dinner. He'd smile softly, thoughtful as always, maybe quote a movie or something literary back to make her laugh.

They'd slept together for the first time last weekend. It wasn't fireworks exploding, but it was good—safe, tender, sincere. The kind of love that could grow roots. It felt different from anything before. Soft and unhurried, full of pauses and quiet laughter. There was no desperate rush, just two people finding a rhythm that made sense. It felt like security, the kind of hold that made her feel seen, not confined.

After, they'd lain in bed listening to the rain begin outside. Not a summer storm shaking the windows, but a soft, steady drizzle tapping against the glass. David's lips pressed against her forehead, Booger, a pudgy gray lump, purred at their feet, and Emily smiled into the dark.

She'd soaked in the warmth beside her, the cat's rumble, the quiet of the night. For the first time since summer, she hadn't felt haunted. Just present and whole.

David had asked her to move in with him when her lease was up, and she said she would think about it.

Tonight, I'll tell him yes. It feels like the next right step.

Her phone vibrated in her back pocket. She pulled it out, expecting a text from Joel or David. There was no name, just an 843 number.

Emily, please call me—Ash.

She stared at the screen for one long moment, listening to the tide pushing against the seawall below. The wind tugged at her hair. She didn't reply. Not yet. Maybe not ever.

Standing at her bathroom sink that evening, Emily twisted her hair into loose curls as mellow electronic music hummed from her desktop speakers. The apartment smelled faintly of hairspray and her new perfume.

Tonight was supposed to be simple—take-out sushi with David, a movie, maybe a walk down King Street afterward. He'd been patient all week, giving her space to think about his offer.

Move in with me when your lease is up, he'd said casually from across the library table. He hadn't pushed, but the question still lingered between them—a fork in the road.

Her phone buzzed once on the counter.

Then again.

Then again.

She glanced at it.

Arch: *Call me. Now.*

Arch: *It's Mandy.*

Arch: *She's in the hospital. It's not good.*

Emily's stomach dropped.

When she called, his voice was ragged, breathless. "Mandy, she had the baby. There were complications. She's being life-flighted to MUSC. Mama has to stay here with the baby. I'm not there yet. I'm driving down now. I can't get ahold of Ash. I think… I think he's losing it, Em. He asked for you."

Her hands trembled. "Is she—?"

"I don't know. They won't say. Just—please come."

Emily grabbed her keys and told Arch she was on the way.

David's text popped up just as she hit the door.

David: *Leaving now. You want spicy tuna or rainbow roll? Or both?*

Her thumbs flew over the tiny keyboard: *Can't. It's an emergency. I'll call you later.*

The drive to MUSC slipped past in wet reflections. Rain smeared across her windshield, traffic lights bleeding color into the dark. Storm clouds gathered low over the city, the kind of heavy sky that always tugged her mind back to the island, whether she wanted it to or not.

Emily fought to steady her breathing. She wasn't that girl anymore—the one from that impossible summer. She had grown past it, past *him.* She had built a new life these last six months with intention, with discipline, with a sense of self she'd fought hard to reclaim. So why was she here again? Why was she letting Ash pull her into a story she'd already survived? Once she'd told him—promised him—she would always be there. She'd just never imagined how much keeping her word might cost her.

By the time she reached the hospital, Arch was pacing the lobby, shoulders tight, eyes wide.

"She's still in surgery," he said. "They won't tell us much. The baby's in the NICU at Haven General, but he's okay. Healthy and strong, Mama said."

Emily touched his arm. "Where's Ash?"

Arch pointed down the hall. "Chapel."

Ash sat alone in the back pew, head bowed like he was praying, but Emily could see through it. He was trying not to fall apart.

When she sat beside him, he didn't look at her right away. His eyes were dark, and his face sallow, like all the life had drained out of him. Her heart broke as she shifted into being what he needed her to be, reflexive as breathing.

"She's been in surgery for hours," he said hoarsely. "They keep saying they're doing everything they can. I don't even know what that means anymore."

Emily didn't speak. She put her hand on his shoulder gently and just waited. Slowly, the words started to spill.

"Today keeps replaying," he said. "Like a movie I can't turn off. It was just a normal Saturday. Mandy slept in. She's been so tired the last few weeks. I went to the diner because she was craving chocolate chip pancakes—extra chocolate chips."

He swallowed hard and continued.

"Then she went upstairs to take a bath. I was cleaning up breakfast when I heard her scream my name."

Emily's heart pounded. "Ash…"

"She was standing in the hallway, barefoot, water everywhere. There was blood on her. She kept saying, 'This wasn't supposed to happen.' I called 911."

He took a breath.

"They had said the baby was breech. The doctor scheduled a C-section, but she went into labor early. She was in so much pain. I've seen guys blow out knees on the field, break bones—nothing like this. They rushed us to the OR. The baby came out crying loud. They handed him to me so she could see."

He stared at his shaking hands.

"He's got so much hair, Em. He's beautiful. Mandy was holding my hand, and then her face just… went pale. Her eyes rolled back. They grabbed the baby, started shouting. They pushed me out before I even knew what was happening."

He rubbed his eyes.

"I don't even remember driving here." He paused. "You know what the messed-up part is? I keep thinking about those pancakes. They're probably still sitting on the counter, cold and half-eaten. Mandy hates it when I leave dishes lying around."

Before Emily could formulate a response, the chapel doors creaked open. A doctor stepped in, still in scrubs, his expression grave.

"Asher Bell?"

Ash stood so fast the pew groaned. "That's me."

The doctor hesitated just long enough to tell Emily everything she needed to know.

"I'm sorry," he said quietly. "We did everything we could."

Ash staggered backward, shaking his head. "No. No, no, you—there has to be—" The words broke into a strangled sound, half scream, half sob.

Emily suddenly became aware that Arch was there, wrapping his arms around his brother just as Ash's knees gave out. She reached out, pressing a trembling hand to Ash's back.

"She's not gone," he rasped. "She can't be gone."

He didn't cry so much as *gasp*. Raw, broken sounds that happen when someone's world ends.

Emily wrapped her arms around him, resting her head on his back, because there was nothing else she could do.

When Emily walked into David's apartment late that night, the first thing she noticed was the smell—soy sauce and takeout rice. Some empty take-out boxes and her untouched sushi roll still sat on the coffee table. The lights were low. A movie was paused on the screen.

Booger, perched like a judgmental loaf on the arm of the couch, fixed his wide eyes on her, studying.

"Hey, you didn't answer your phone," David said softly, stirring. He didn't look angry—just tired.

She set her purse down. "I know. I'm sorry. It was—"

"An emergency," he finished for her. "You said that much."

David stood, hands shoved into the pockets of his sweatpants. His eyes searched her face, reading the exhaustion, the pain.

"Did something bad happen?" he asked.

Emily nodded, her voice shaky, "Yeah. Amanda Green, I mean Bell. She… she passed away."

David's expression softened instantly. "Oh, Em. I'm so sorry. She was the one from…"

"Haven Island. Yeah."

He exhaled. "God, that's awful. Was it sudden?"

"She had complications after having a baby," Emily said quietly. "They tried everything. They flew her here to MUSC, but there was nothing they could do."

He stepped closer, rubbing her back gently. "You went down to the hospital for that?"

She hesitated before the truth came out like a flood. "Arch called me. Said Ash was alone at the hospital, and he… he wasn't doing well."

David's hand froze. "You went for *him*?"

The silence that followed was long and uncomfortable.

"I had to, David," she whispered finally. "He was falling apart. He wanted me there… as a friend."

David looked down at his feet. "You could have told me. You should have."

"I didn't know how," she said, tears threatening. "You would've told me not to go."

He gave a quiet huff. "You're probably right. You're not family. It wasn't right of you to be there for that, Emily."

When he looked back at her, there wasn't anger in his eyes—just more hurt.

"I'm not trying to be that guy, Em. But I know when something's off. I know when I'm only getting part of the story."

Her posture stiffened. "You're not. I swear."

As the words left her mouth, sickening guilt pricked her nerves. She hated lying to him—hated the way it twisted in her stomach the second she did it—but she couldn't seem to stop.

David didn't believe her; she could see it. He didn't answer. He just nodded once—slowly—and turned off the TV.

Chapter thirty-two

The sky looked like it didn't have the decency to be sad. It was one of those perfect spring mornings—cloudless, warm, sunlight spilling gold over the dunes just beyond the churchyard. Azaleas were in bloom along the fence, their pink petals bright against the fresh-cut grass.

It should have been raining. Storming, even. But it was beautiful. Heartbreakingly beautiful.

Emily stood beside David near the church doors, her hand small and cold in his.

It's fitting.

The day was showing up the way Mandy always had—bright and impossible to ignore. The parking lot was already full; even the shoulders of the road were lined with cars.

Inside, the chapel overflowed. The air was thick with tissues rustling and quiet sniffles. Joel sat near the front, uncharacteristically still, a silk handkerchief pressed to his eyes, while Mateo wrapped an arm around him. Kenzie sat beside Jeanne, chin trembling. Even Jeanne—snappy, loud, unflappable Jeanne—was silent, her eyes red and puffy.

David squeezed Emily's hand. "You okay?" he whispered.

She nodded, eyes fixed on the white casket at the front. Sunlight streamed through stained glass, scattering in a kaleidoscope across the polished lid. If the sky couldn't cry, it would paint her in colors instead.

The organ began softly: "It Is Well With My Soul."

Emily closed her eyes.

Of course, it's sunny. Of course, it's beautiful. It's for Mandy—the most beautiful person I've ever seen.

She'd dreaded seeing Ash. Told herself she was there to pay respects, to be kind. But when she spotted him in the front row, slumped forward, fists clenched, something inside her ruptured all over again.

Ash sat with his mama and the Greens, hands clasped so tightly his knuckles ached. Across the row, Mandy's friend Jenn had folded herself into her husband's arms—sobbing so hard her breath came in shudders, and mascara was streaking down her cheeks. She looked the way Ash felt—gutted, miserable, utterly destroyed. But he couldn't cry with her. Not yet.

He hadn't spoken since they brought the casket in and set up the photograph beside it. A portrait of Mandy in pink, blue eyes bright, curls shining, that pageant smile eternal. It was the only smile in the room.

After the hymns and scripture, a slideshow of Mandy began—baby photos, laughing with her sorority sisters, tossing her hair in the summer sun, radiant in lace on their wedding day. Each picture landed like a fresh blow.

One from the past December flashed, both of them posed beside the world's most perfectly decorated tree.

Our first married Christmas. Our only married Christmas.

His mind reeled through their years—high school hallways, homecoming crowns, a wedding in this same church.

Now, this.

A photo, a coffin, a silence he couldn't fill. He didn't feel like a husband; he felt like a vampire, like he had drained the life from something beautiful and could only sit there numb.

Even in death, she'd left him something perfect: their son, Jesse Carter Bell. He'd been passed between Cindy and Elizabeth all morning, swaddled and cooing, oblivious to the grief around him.

Ash couldn't look. Every tiny sound from the baby made him flinch. How could something so innocent and brand new exist when everything else had ended?

The pastor's voice blended into the organ's hum. When the screen went dark, only muffled crying broke the hush.

Ash silently wished for one more minute with her. Just enough time to tell Mandy she'd been right that day in the kitchen, the day she'd said he didn't deserve her.

I never did.

From her pew, Emily watched the tension in Ash's shoulders that never loosened, his mother's hand hovering near but never touching. She could still hear him at the hospital. *She can't be gone.* Now he sat gasping for air in a room full of people.

Mandy had only been twenty-six years old—she should have been cradling her baby, not lying in a casket.

Why, God? Emily prayed silently. *Why this? Just when everything was falling into place, it had to break apart.*

When the service ended, people filed into the courtyard murmuring condolences. Joel and Kenzie hugged Emily tearfully before slipping away. She hesitated, then made her way toward Ash.

He stood at the front of the church, staring at Mandy's photo. Arch hovered nearby, warding off well-meaning church ladies. He gave her a quiet nod.

Ash eventually looked up, and his eyes darkened immediately.

"You shouldn't have come," he said abruptly.

Her stomach twisted. "Ash, I—"

He shook his head. "You don't get it. Everyone here thinks I killed her. Hell, maybe I did. I wasn't good enough for her. I wasn't what she needed. Now she's dead because of me."

Emily's eyes burned. "That's not fair! Nobody thinks that. You can't do this to yourself."

"Fair?" His laugh was bitter and cutting. "You think any of this is fair? Tell my son about fair, Emily."

He took a step closer, voice low.

"You show up like you have any right." His eyes drifted to the photo. "You being here just makes this worse."

"You're the one who texted me from the hospital. You told Arch you wanted me there," she said, voice quivering.

He looked at her, and she thought he might break. But his face hardened. "My mistake."

Emily winced.

He looked away before she could answer, as if even standing this close to her might split him open.

David appeared at her side, quiet and protective.

"Em," he murmured, "maybe we should give the family some space."

Ash's eyes flicked to David, then back to her, filled with recognition, jealousy, shame, and something she couldn't name. Whatever it was, it stung.

"Yeah, *Em*," he said roughly. "You should go."

She opened her mouth, but nothing came out.

Ash turned away, his shoulders heaving once before he disappeared into the crowd.

David guided her toward the doors in silence. When they reached the parking lot, he squeezed her hand.

"I get that you care about him," he said. "But that—what I saw in there—Emily, that's not just caring. That's something else."

And for the first time, she didn't have the strength to deny it. Tears slipped down her cheeks, catching sunlight like glass.

When they got back to Charleston, David dropped Emily off before heading to the library. He said he needed to study, but she knew he was giving her space—to grieve, to breathe, to untangle whatever *this* was.

She stood in the doorway for a long while after he left, the faint trace of his cologne still in the air. She wanted to feel grateful for him. But all she could see was Ash, hollow-eyed in that sunlit church, telling her she shouldn't have come.

She sat on the couch and stared at her hands. David was patient. Good and kind. She wanted to love him the way he deserved, to build something that could last. She'd already told him she'd move in that summer. But her feelings for Ash ran deep, tangled through her like roots she couldn't pull free from. The more she felt him slipping, the more she wanted to reach out, even if it meant free-falling along with him.

She leaned back, eyes closed.

"Get it together," she whispered to the empty room.

But even as she said it, she knew whatever gripped her wasn't something that would let go easily.

Chapter thirty-three

They held the graveside service a few days later. The drive down the coast to Savannah was long and silent. Clouds hung low over the highway, swollen with cold spring rain.

In the back of the hearse, Mandy's casket gleamed. It was too perfect for something so final.

Ash rode in the Tahoe behind, but he let Arch drive. The wipers beat a slow, hypnotic rhythm. Every mile felt like penance. Less than a year ago, he and Mandy had driven this same stretch for his birthday weekend, joking, laughing, bickering over who controlled the radio dial. Now she was in the back of a hearse, and he was too disoriented to even know what day it was.

I set this all in motion.

He'd been so head over heels for Emily that Fourth of July when everything between them still felt inescapable. He should've ended things with Mandy right then, before it got messy. If he had, she wouldn't have gotten pregnant, and she wouldn't be dead.

He stared out the window, thinking about the way he'd spoken to Emily at the funeral, the look on her face when he'd told her to leave. She hadn't deserved that. None of this was her fault. He was the one who'd texted her, who'd reached out, who'd wanted her there when his world was falling apart.

He wasn't really mad at her. He was mad at everything—the whispers, the pity, the weight of what he couldn't undo. Mad at God. Mad at himself most of all. He could only handle one emotion at a time right now. Anger was easier than grief.

I'll tell Emily I'm sorry.

He didn't know when or how, but he promised himself he would tell her.

They slowed as Bonaventure's iron gates came into view—ornate and somber against the gray sky. He could've insisted Mandy be buried in Haven County, near his father, in the Bell family plot. Legally, it was his right. But he couldn't. She didn't belong there. She belonged here beneath the Spanish moss, where the Carters and Greens slept under angels and marble crosses.

The centuries-old cemetery felt suspended in time—stone sculptures beneath oak limbs, the river glinting through the trees. Her parents had arranged everything: white roses, a small gathering, the pastor reading Psalms in an unfaltering tone.

Ash stood between his mother and Elizabeth, but he barely heard a word. Everything felt surreal—the soft hum of insects, the smell of wet grass, the dull ache of sleeplessness gnawing behind his eyes.

Before the pallbearers lowered the casket, the funeral director asked quietly if the family wanted a private goodbye.

Elizabeth nodded, already crying.

Ash told himself he wouldn't look. He didn't need to. He wanted to remember Mandy smiling, barefoot on the beach, fussing at him for something silly that didn't matter now.

When they opened the lid, his knees buckled.

Mandy looked small, so impossibly small. Her hair had been brushed smooth, a soft wave across her shoulder. Her hands folded over a single white rose. The makeup couldn't hide the pallor. It didn't look like her, not really. To him, she looked like a mannequin, a shell emptied of light.

Elizabeth's wail cracked the still air. "My baby… my baby girl."

Andrew caught her, holding her as she sobbed.

Ash looked down again, one last time, and something inside him broke loose. He bent over, pressing a trembling hand to the edge of the coffin.

"I'm sorry," he whispered, voice cracking. "Mandy, I'm so sorry."

He didn't know exactly why he was apologizing—for cheating on her, for the pregnancy, for every fight, for standing helpless as she bled out in front of him, or for never knowing how to love her enough.

When the lid closed for the last time, the casket sank slowly into the earth. One by one, the mourners drifted away until only Ash remained. The sun broke through then—pale and hesitant—glinting off the wet grass. Mosquitoes hovered in the damp air. Arch waited by the SUV, patient and silent.

Ash knelt beside the open grave, the smell of rain and fresh-turned soil heavy around him. He just stayed there, perfectly still, until something cut through the haze. Something small, strange, and unexpected.

Relief.

Not joy. Not peace. Just a soft easing.

What lay in that coffin wasn't Mandy—not really. It might have been her body, but it wasn't the woman who sang off-key in the car, who micromanaged everything, who rolled her eyes at his stupid jokes, and stole the covers every night. That lifeless form was just what she'd left behind. She was somewhere else now. Probably bossing around angels, straightening their halos, telling them how things ought to be done.

That realization cracked something open in Ash. And when he started to cry, it wasn't quiet. It came from somewhere deep—a sound that emptied him.

He wanted to make sense of this, to hold onto anything that might explain it, but all he could do was grasp fruitlessly at the cavernous space she'd left behind. The grief he had tried to avoid was starting to take him over—an aching emptiness waiting to swallow him whole.

Chapter thirty-four

David's apartment still didn't feel like home when she moved in that August. Emily told herself it just needed time—a few weeks, some framed photos, maybe new curtains that were more her style. But every night, as she brushed her teeth and glanced at the second toothbrush in the holder, she couldn't shake the feeling she was living someone else's life.

David was dependable. The kind of man who remembered her coffee order and cooked breakfast on Sundays. He left Post-it notes on the counter when he had to leave early, signed with little inside jokes. But he wasn't stupid. He noticed when she was only half there, when her eyes drifted toward her phone mid-conversation, or when she came home from the library with that faraway look.

The calls had become their quiet war.

Ash had called Emily to apologize a couple of weeks after the funeral. He kept in touch every few days, and sometimes he would text her late: *You up? Can't sleep.*

Emily, against her better judgment, would always answer. She told herself it was compassion, not weakness. He was grieving and broken. But each call dragged her a little deeper into the undertow. Back into the part of herself that still remembered the way he said her name. The part that hadn't stopped wondering.

Some nights they talked for hours. He'd ramble about the baby, about Mandy and his dad, about how time didn't feel real anymore. She'd listen until her phone burned hot in her hand. David didn't mention it at first; he just gave her knowing looks over his glasses. Now, in their one-bedroom apartment, she had nowhere to hide.

One night, Emily sat on the edge of the bed, laptop open, phone glowing beside her. David folded laundry in silence before he finally spoke.

"Who's calling tonight?" he asked quietly.

She flinched. "What?"

He didn't raise his voice. He didn't need to. "You think I don't know when it's him? You don't even try to hide it anymore, Em."

Her throat went dry. "David, it's not like that."

"Then what's it like?" His voice rose, just barely. "You run out of the library to talk to him for hours. You text him back before you even text me. You talk about how sorry you feel for him. Do you ever think about how that feels for me?"

She swallowed hard. "He lost his wife. He's not okay."

He nodded slowly. "Yeah. I get that. But you can't save him, and it's not your job to try."

Emily blinked back tears. “I can’t cut him off, David. You don’t understand—”

“You’re right,” he said firmly. “I don’t. Because if it were me—if I'd lost you—I’d never call another woman in the middle of the night. I wouldn't drag someone else into my grief.” He looked straight at her then, eyes soft but unwavering. “He *needs* a therapist. What he *wants* is your attention.”

Silence hung heavy between them for a moment.

Then he said it, quiet and final, “Either you’re with me, or you’re trying to fix him. But you can’t do both.”

The calm words hit her harder than a fist.

Silence settled again, and in that pause, something uncomfortable stirred inside Emily's chest—the realization that she’d started shaping her days around someone else again. Putting her own life to the side. Letting someone else’s crisis dictate her choices. She knew exactly where that led. And it wasn’t healthy. It wasn’t love. It was codependency masquerading as loyalty.

Finally, she nodded, voice small. “Okay. You’re right. I’ll talk to him.”

She called Ash the next day from the parking lot outside the law library.

He answered on the second ring, voice rough. “Hey, Em. Thought you forgot about me.”

She closed her eyes. “I didn’t forget. I just… can’t keep doing this.”

His laugh was short and bitter. “Doing what? Talking?”

“Trying to save you.”

The line went quiet.

Then his voice came low, wounded. “I didn’t ask you to save me.”

"No, but you expect me to pick up the phone every time you fall apart."

He exhaled hard. "You think this is easy for me? I'm trying, Em. I'm trying to keep my head above water."

"I know," she said softly. "But you're drowning me, too."

For a second, she thought he might understand. That he'd sigh and tell her she was right.

Instead, the words came angry and final, "You know what? Fuck you, Emily."

The line clicked, and silence rushed in.

Emily sat there, the phone heavy in her hand; she didn't quite know how to put it down.

Far off, the church bells of Charleston tolled the hour, slow and indifferent. She didn't cry. But somewhere deep inside, something fragile splintered, the first crack in everything she'd been holding together. It felt like breaking a promise. But if she couldn't choose herself now, when would she ever start?

Ash stared at his phone. The screen went black, reflecting a face he barely recognized—bloodshot eyes, weeks-old beard—the look of someone who hadn't been himself in a long time.

He threw the phone onto the couch and stood there, hands braced on his hips, breathing hard. He hadn't said *fuck you* to Emily because he hated her. He'd said it because the pain of her backing away was so stunning he needed to punch at something.

She was right. He *was* dragging her down. He knew it, hated it, couldn't stop it. Nothing had been able to stop the miserable agony he felt after losing Mandy, but somehow Emily's voice—that steady, familiar calm—always pulled him back from the edge of breaking down completely. She'd been a lifeline when everything else felt blown to hell. Now she was gone. Cut loose. Done trying to save him.

He paced once across the room, then again. The silence in the townhouse pressed down on him, heavy and suffocating. The baby's things were still stacked neatly in a corner—untouched since the last time Cindy had dropped Jesse off.

Ash willingly let his mama or the Greens keep Jesse most of the time. It wasn't that he didn't love him. God, he did. How could he not? But love felt too small against everything he didn't know how to do.

He'd tried in those first weeks after the funeral. Tried to feed the baby, to hold him right, to quiet his crying. Nothing about it came naturally. The guilt reached for him every time he passed that corner room—the empty crib, the unopened box of diapers. He told himself it was better this way, that Jesse was better off surrounded by people who knew what they were doing.

When Ash did see him, it was always in short bursts—an hour here, an afternoon there. Every time, it undid him a little more. A baby needed a mother. Needed her soft voice, the lullabies, the hands that knew instinctively what to do. Jesse didn't have that anymore, and Ash knew he'd never be enough to replace her.

On the kitchen counter sat a bottle of Wild Turkey he'd picked up a few days earlier—a brand he hadn't touched in years. He'd promised himself it was just for the bad nights. Lately, every night had qualified.

He twisted off the cap. The smell hit him, whiskey sharp, sweet, and familiar. Ash took a long pull straight from the bottle. No glass. No ice. The burn slid down his throat until it hit his chest and spread like a ring of fire.

He leaned against the countertop, eyes closed, bottle in hand. For a moment, he could almost hear her voice—Mandy's, soft and disappointed: *You're better than this, Asher.* But he wasn't. Not anymore. Not without her. Not without Emily.

He drank again, deeper this time.

Outside, thunder rolled somewhere over the marsh. Rain began tracing uneven lines down the window, the streetlights beyond blurring into gold streaks. He didn't move. He just stared, letting the whiskey do what it did best, numbing, dulling, pulling him under.

Somewhere deep in his mind, a sober voice whispered that this was how it all started coming apart. But the bottle was already half-empty, and he didn't care. He wasn't trying to forget Mandy's death anymore. Or the way Emily had walked away. He was trying to forget himself.

Chapter thirty-five

The bar was a few towns over. Far enough from Haven County that no one would recognize him, close enough that he could still find his way home blind drunk if it came to that.

The jukebox wheezed out an old 'done-me-wrong' song, matching Ash's melancholy mood perfectly. Mechanics and fishermen made small talk over bottles of Budweiser. The place smelled like cigarettes and stale beer. Nobody here asked too many questions, nobody cared. That was part of the appeal.

Ash had lost his job a few weeks after the funeral—not that it mattered. Mandy, being the meticulous planner she was, had life insurance. A will. A trust fund. She'd left him everything, even her car, her accounts, her savings. It was more money than he'd ever seen in one place. But it wasn't money he wanted. It felt like blood money, or a satirical form of charity.

He had called her parents, told them it didn't feel right, that it wasn't his to keep. But they said they couldn't take it, that he should hold onto it for Jesse. So, he did. He took some to live on, then put the rest into an investment account for Jesse.

With the unexpected windfall came something worse riding on top of his grief: idleness. It was strange not needing to work, not having a reason to get up, no shift to clock into, no routine except for numbing himself. That, he could manage. That, at least, was easy.

He'd halfway considered going back to High Tide, asking for a few shifts to keep him busy, but he couldn't even bring himself to drive over to the island most days. He was in no shape to face the memories that place dredged up.

He sat hunched over the counter, nursing his sixth bourbon. Or maybe his seventh. He and the bartender had stopped keeping count. Every sip burned less than the last. Every thought burned more—Mandy, Emily, Jesse. The house that didn't feel like home. All the things he'd lost and all the things he couldn't seem to hold on to.

Underneath everything else, anger still simmered, hot and ugly—at the circumstances, at the world, at the mess he kept making out of his life, and at Emily's voice echoing in his skull: *You're drowning me too.* She was right. He hated himself for doing it, and he hated her for saying it, because now he couldn't un-hear it.

The guy two stools down laughed too loudly at something. Ash's fingers tightened on the whiskey glass until it cracked, bourbon and blood spilling across his hand and the bar top.

"Hey, man, you good?" the bartender asked, wary.

Ash didn't answer. He just tossed down a handful of folded bills and staggered outside into the cool air.

The parking lot shimmered under a buzzing streetlight. His Tahoe sat near the edge. He told himself he was fine. He'd done this before—driven home after a few, no problem.

Tonight, the road felt darker, longer, and unfamiliar. The yellow lines started to blur. Headlights stretched into halos. Then a tight, twisting bend came up quickly, and so did a silvery-gray flash of guardrail. Tires screamed, and metal crunched. The SUV flipped once, twice, then kept rolling into the ditch like a toy tossed aside.

When he came to, everything was smoke and noise. Blood dripped into his eyes. His left leg was pinned. Pain throbbed through him like a hammer hitting an anvil. Somewhere, far away, sirens wailed—slow, muffled, like they were underwater.

Then—*nothing*.

Ash woke up disoriented, under neutral white hospital lights. His mouth was dry. His head felt like it had been split open. Voices and noise came and went in a haze of pain medication—nurses, machines, a clipboard clattering.

Then a man's voice: firm, official, "Mr. Asher Bell?"

A state trooper stood at the foot of his bed, arms crossed.

Ash blinked. "Yeah."

The trooper nodded. "Sir, you're under arrest for driving under the influence of alcohol. You're lucky you didn't kill yourself."

Then he read Ash his rights.

Lucky.

The word lingered, cruel and meaningless.

Later, his mama came. Eyes red, voice trembling. "You could've died, Asher. You could've left Jesse without either of his parents."

He couldn't look at her. Couldn't look at anyone.

Then Arch appeared, filling the doorway with that familiar, solid presence. He didn't say anything at first—just stared. Finally, he stepped closer, arms crossed tight over his chest.

"Dammit, Ash," he said, his voice low and shaking. "Do you have any idea how scared we all were? I thought you were dead. Mama thought you were dead."

Ash swallowed, throat raw. "I didn't mean—"

"I don't care what you *meant.*" Arch's deep voice cracked through the sterile air like a whip. "You've been circling this drain since Mandy died. I tried to give you space, man, I did. But this? You've got a kid. You don't get to destroy yourself anymore."

Ash flinched, staring at the blanket. "I know."

"No, you *don't.*" Arch leaned forward, eyes fierce. "You think this is rock bottom? It's not. You're lucky we aren't visiting you in the damn morgue."

Ash wanted to yell, to tell him to leave, but he couldn't. His brother was right.

After a long silence, Arch sighed and straightened. His voice softened, barely. "I'm not gonna pretend I know what you're going through. But I do know this—you either get your shit together, or you're gonna lose everything you've got left."

He turned to leave, then paused in the doorway.

"You want help getting a lawyer? Call me. But this is on you now, Ash. Nobody else."

Arch shut the door behind him, leaving only the steady hum of machines.

Some passage of time later, Elizabeth Green came. Grief had sharpened her features into something cold and merciless.

"I filed an emergency order for temporary custody of Jesse," she said flatly. "You're in no condition to raise a child right now. You'll have every other weekend when the judge says you're fit. Until then—"

She didn't finish.

Ash nodded, too ashamed to argue.

The next few weeks blurred together—hearings, fines, court-ordered therapy sessions, and the humiliation of a breathalyzer wired into his new truck. Weekends with Jesse were quiet. The baby didn't understand, but Ash felt like those bright blue eyes were looking straight through him.

His leg had healed enough for a soft cast, though it still throbbed when he moved wrong. Every morning, the ache in his head hurt worse. The doctor had told him to stay off his feet, keep the leg elevated, and *let the body heal.*

But his body wasn't the problem.

His phone barely rang anymore—not since Emily had told him to back off. That wasn't entirely true, though. People still called—he just stopped answering anyone he wasn't legally required to. Except his mama. And Arch.

The fridge held one photo—Jesse, about three months old, flashing a gummy grin. Every time Ash looked at it, something inside him twisted hard. He was doing what he was supposed to. He paid the fines. Appeared for the hearings. Sat through the therapy sessions. He'd even gotten a part-time job down at the marina to keep his hands busy.

Ash showed up sober. Acted polite. Smiled when he was supposed to. Then came home and poured another drink. It was a desperate pattern—one he couldn't seem to break. Every night ended the same: Jesse's photo staring back at him from the fridge, the sound of the bottle cap twisting loose, and the sting of loss filling the silence.

One night, after work, the darkness felt heavier and lonelier. It was the kind of night where the silence crowded in, and the self-hatred shouted a little too loudly. The new liter bottle from the liquor store sat half-empty on the counter, its amber contents catching the glow of the stove light.

Ash's head throbbed, his leg ached, and the world had shrunk to the phone in his hand. He didn't mean to call anyone. Not really. But for reasons he couldn't fully rationalize, he needed her.

"Hello?"

Emily, her voice was soft and low.

"Hey," he rasped. "It's me."

A pause, the kind that stretched.

"Ash? Are you okay?"

He gave a bitter laugh. "No. Not even close to okay."

He talked half in broken sentences, half in confessions. About the townhouse that felt too big. How the baby's cry made him feel helpless. How he woke up feeling broken, useless, and angry.

Emily didn't interrupt. She just listened quietly on the other end. She should've made an excuse and hung up. She knew it, but she couldn't.

"Ash," she whispered finally, "you sound awful. Where are you?"

Chapter thirty-six

By the time Ash gave Emily the address, she was already shoving books into her bag and hurrying out of the library. It was a 45-minute drive from downtown Charleston to his place near Bellefontaine. She drove fast, the 4Runner's headlights cutting through the dark stretch of highway.

She told herself she wasn't doing anything wrong. He just needed help, someone to check on him. But the minute she saw him—slumped on the couch, bottle at his feet, lost look in his eyes—she knew that was a lie.

"Ash," she breathed, kneeling beside him. "You shouldn't have called me."

"I know," he whispered. "But I wanted you anyway."

The room dissolved into silence—the kind that hangs between two people who can speak to each other without words. Then came the touch, his fingers on her lips, tentative at first, almost a question.

Emily didn't pull away. His hands found her waist, strong and urgent, drawing her against his body until she could feel every inch of him, hard in his jeans.

She'd forgotten how small she was beside him, how easily he could overpower her if he wanted to. The thought of his strength, his ability to control her, sent a rush of something dark and thrilling through her body. She pressed in closer, letting herself melt against him.

The air felt thick, charged with grief, guilt, and something dangerous weaving around them. When his mouth met hers, she could taste the faint burn of whiskey. It wasn't gentle. It wasn't sweet. It was desperate. Two bodies colliding, trying to feel something again. It wasn't love, not in the way it had been before—it was soul-shredding desire.

Upstairs, Emily didn't stop to look around. The bedroom was half-dark, lit only by a sliver of light from the hall. Her hands moved on instinct, shedding layers until there was nothing left between her and the mistake she had already committed to making.

I shouldn't be here. I shouldn't do this. But I don't care. I want him so badly. I don't think I'll ever stop wanting him. What the hell is wrong with me?

Ash kicked off his boots, undid his belt, let his jeans fall, and tossed his shirt across the room. In three long strides, he was on top of her, pinning her wrists to the bed. She struggled slightly beneath him, and he held on even tighter.

"I won't hurt you, Emily," he said, voice low. "I just want to remind you that right now, in my bed, you're mine."

She wrapped her legs around his waist submissively and audibly gasped as he roughly pushed into the soft, wet space between her thighs.

Emily bit his shoulder as he held her down and thrust deeply. The way he felt moving inside her was intoxicating. She squeezed her eyes together so tightly that light was flashing behind her lids.

“Look at me, Emily,” he breathed into her ear.

She blinked up at him, her vision adjusting slowly. She knew every line of his face by memory, but his eyes burned with something she’d never seen before. It wasn’t just passion; it was possession, need, and something else underneath it—something feral and instinctive.

His mouth hovered near hers, close enough that she could feel his breath, but he didn’t kiss her. He just stayed there close and suspended. Ruining her from the inside out.

“Say my name,” he ordered, sliding a hand onto her neck.

Emily didn’t say it; she screamed it loud enough to wake the neighborhood. Just then, she felt her body give in. All her senses were taken under in a wave, and there was nothing else, only her release.

Ash groaned into her ear, an uneven and guttural sound.

Emily felt his body tense, then relax and go still. He was so heavy resting on top of her that her lungs felt short of oxygen. With her free hand, she stroked the back of his neck gently, but she couldn’t stop the sting of tears building behind her eyes. The saw-toothed edge of regret tore through her body like a tornado, already replacing the euphoria.

Ash seemed to sense it. He pulled away, turned on his side with his back to her, and said nothing.

For a long time, Emily just lay there. Her heart slowly found its normal rhythm as hot, silent tears streamed down her face. She wasn't aware of how long she stayed that way, or of the moment her body gave in, surrendering her mind to a deep, dreamless sleep.

The following morning, sunlight spilled through the blinds—thin, sharp, and unforgiving. The kind of light that made everything about last night feel too real.

Emily sat on the edge of the bed, half-dressed, hair tangled, staring at the floor like she could will the moment to rewind. Ash stirred beside her, the sheets twisted around his ankles, the faint scent of whiskey still clinging to his skin. Every sound—the gulls outside, the ticking clock, his low exhale—felt too loud, too close. She'd meant to leave before he woke up. She'd never meant for last night to happen at all.

His voice came, rough and lazy. "Got some fresh ink, huh, Em?"

His fingers brushed her shoulder before she could stop him, tracing the dark line peeking out from below her bra strap. She'd forgotten the tattoo—the one in delicate script curling along her skin.

He leaned closer, squinting.

"'Whatever our souls are made of,'" he read, slow and deliberate. "What's that supposed to mean?"

"It's from a book," she said quietly, pulling her shirt over her shoulder.

Ash gave a low and mocking laugh. “Of course it is. Probably one of those quotes your fancy law-school boyfriend understands. Something the rest of us wouldn’t get.”

She turned, green eyes catching the light. “I never said that.”

“You didn’t have to.” His tone was cutting. “I’ve seen you with him. That skinny guy who looks so calm and put together. You’re actually sleeping with him?”

“He’s my boyfriend. What are you even trying to start right now?”

“I just wonder how he’d feel if he knew you fucked someone else last night. I bet he wouldn’t stay so polite.”

“Ash, what the hell? You think I planned this? You think this was easy for me?”

He sat up, meeting her eyes like he was about to speak. Anger rolled across his face with something raw underneath.

She spoke first, voice shaking. “Honestly, I don’t even know what this was. I shouldn’t have come.”

“Then why did you?” His voice was broken with too many emotions to track. “You keep showing up, Em. You keep coming back to me, and then you act like you don’t wanna be here.”

Her face burned from the anger and shame. “Because I don’t know how to stop caring about you. But I can’t keep doing this, Ash. I deserve more than just being your emotional crutch or a distraction when you’re lonely.”

He looked away.

“You’re right,” he said quietly. “You do deserve better. I just… don’t know how to give it to you. Not anymore.”

She stared at him—the man who still had an impossible hold over her. Shame twisted through her chest, but so did longing. If he'd said *stay*, she might've. But he didn't, and her pride wouldn't let her crawl.

"Then stop only calling me when you're hurt." She forced the words out. "Stop pretending I still mean something more to you."

He didn't answer. His eyes glazed over. Then, without looking at her, he muttered, "Just go, Emily. Get the fuck out."

For one long heartbeat, she waited—hoping for another word, a reason, *something*. But there was nothing. No apology. No softness. Just the flat sound of his voice telling her to fuck off and the unbearable quiet that followed.

She blinked hard, grabbed her jeans from the floor, and dressed without looking at him. When the door shut behind her, the sound echoed through the house—final and cruel.

Ash didn't move. He just lay there, staring at the wall. It felt like cheating all over again, like he'd betrayed Mandy twice over. Dead or not, he'd broken something sacred—brought another woman into their bed.

He'd promised himself he'd be better. Stronger. But he wasn't. The pain still burned, alive and merciless, no matter how much he drank to drown it. He shouldn't have called Emily. Shouldn't have let her come. Shouldn't have touched her, kissed her, fucked her. But he had—because the bottle made him reckless, and the loneliness made him weak. For a few hours, at least, it was easier to feel wanted than cursed.

By the time the sunlight shifted across the floor, his head was pounding, and his stomach was sour. By noon, the bottle was back in his hand.

When his mama came by to bring supper, the first thing she saw was the wreckage—the empty bottle, the leg brace tossed carelessly on the couch, her son half-lost behind reddened eyes.

She didn't yell. She just stood there, voice low but steady. "You're gonna lose everything, Asher," she said. "Not just your boy—yourself."

He didn't answer. His gaze stayed fixed on the floor, the words reaching something inside, but not deep enough to move him. There was nothing left to fight for, not really. The truth was, he'd already lost everything—including the man he used to be.

Chapter thirty-seven

Emily pulled into the parking lot just after 9 a.m. The autumn sun was already scorching and merciless over Charleston. Her head throbbed from lack of sleep, and her stomach had twisted in knots. She was still in yesterday's jeans and t-shirt, both wrinkled and smelling faintly of sweat and regret.

Her feet dragged on the stairs, and her key felt heavy in the lock. When the door opened, the smell of coffee and fried eggs hit her—cozy, domestic, undeserved. Booger sat on the windowsill, blinking slowly like an unimpressed spectator. David was in the kitchen, barefoot, brewing a pot of coffee.

"Hey," he said, surprise moving across his face and tightening his features. "You didn't come home last night."

Her throat went dry. “Yeah. I—uh—ended up staying at my parents’ place.”

A lie.

A fast, clumsy lie.

David knit his eyebrows. “Wow, all the way out there? You didn’t say anything. Couldn’t even call or shoot me a text?”

“I should’ve,” she murmured, setting down her purse and intentionally avoiding his eyes. “I’m sorry. It was late, and I didn’t want to wake you.”

He studied her—the tired eyes, the wrinkled clothes, the faint but noticeable bruises forming on her wrists. Something in his expression shifted. Not anger. Not yet. Just a slow, dawning unease.

“Are you okay?” he asked softly.

“I’m fine.”

Another lie.

Emily forced herself to sit at the table while he plated some eggs and toast, pretending to eat, pretending to listen as he talked about his early morning run and the professor who’d extended their midterm deadline. She couldn’t focus. Every sound felt distant, every word muffled under the reverberating echo of what she’d done.

David looked at her again, longer this time. “Em, you seem… off.”

She tried to smile. “Just tired.”

The silence stretched as he poured more coffee, his movements deliberate.

“Was it Ash?”

The fork stopped halfway to her mouth. “What?”

“You said you went back to Haven Island last night.” He didn’t phrase it as a question. “Please tell me I’m wrong about this, Emily.”

She swallowed hard. "He called me. He's—he's not okay, David. He had a pretty bad car accident a little while ago. I just went to check on him."

"Right," he said quietly. "And you couldn't just… call? Or let someone else handle it?"

"I felt like I had to go," she whispered, eyes stinging.

He nodded, voice gentle in a way that made her want to crumple from regret, like a soda can under pressure. "You keep saying that. That you have to save him. But what about us, Em? When do you save us?"

She opened her mouth, but nothing came out.

David pushed back from the table, coffee mug still in his hand.

"I'm not angry," he said finally. "I'm just tired of feeling like I'm competing. You know me. You know the man I am, and if that's not what you want, I don't know what I can say." He walked past her, quiet and slow, then calling over his shoulder, "Don't forget we have the boil tonight."

Emily started with surprise, "What?"

David turned, "The low country boil with my family. Come on, I told you weeks ago."

"Shit, yes, you did," she said, ashamed all over again, now for a different reason. "Let me go shower and get to the library so I can get some work done before we have to leave!"

In the shower, she stood under the much-too-hot water, letting it wash away the smell of Ash from her skin. When she finally stepped out, steam had fogged the mirror and filled the room until she could barely see her own reflection.

As she towel-dried her hair, her thoughts were still loud and jumbled. She wanted to call someone—her mom, Joel, Kenzie, anybody. Tell them what happened, confess the whole mess. But every time she picked up her phone, her hand shook violently.

The secret made her feel ill. It was a fever—cooking her alive.

Damn it, Emily. What are you doing?

It was bad enough that she was screwing up her own life over a man. She shouldn't drag David down with her. He deserved so much better than this.

At the library, she found David at their usual table and slid into the seat across from him. He smiled, that reassuring kind of smile that made her feel safe, and she tried to match it. She spread out her notes, opened her laptop, and pretended to focus. But her mind kept fracturing, her concentration breaking in little bursts.

For a fleeting moment, she thought about telling him everything—spilling her guts right there in the quiet sanctuary of the library. Maybe he'd be furious with her, maybe he'd even raise his voice. But she doubted it. His eyes were too soft, too kind. Telling him would have been like strangling a puppy. Instead, she smiled when he looked up, nodded when he asked about her outlines, and forced herself to breathe.

She was proud of herself for standing up to Ash, for finally saying he couldn't use her anymore. But beneath the pride, she was twisting herself into an emotional pretzel. She worried that she'd pushed him too far. Feared that he'd implode, and she'd somehow be the one to blame. Next came the scathing anger. At him for calling. At herself for going. Anger for fucking him, for still wanting to fuck him, for even thinking about him at all right now.

When the bells clanged the late afternoon hour outside the library windows, they packed up their books, and Emily told herself to shift gears. Tonight was the boil. A chance to breathe, to start again, to try and leave last night exactly where it belonged—behind her.

Chapter thirty-eight

The air in the country smelled like salt and spice—shrimp shells, Old Bay, sweet corn roasting in butter. The sound of laughter carried across the yard, mingling with the soft rush of the tide just beyond the trees. Picnic tables stretched beneath the oaks; strings of lights draped through the branches like fallen stars. The sun was sinking low, turning the marsh gold and painting the water in ribbons of copper and pink.

David's family knew how to throw a party. Women in sundresses moved between the tables with trays piled high—crab legs, sausage, cornbread, roasted potatoes slick with butter. David's uncle was tending a huge pot over a propane burner, steam curling up around his face.

Kids chased each other barefoot through the grass, and fireflies started to blink awake around them. Music drifted from a speaker propped on a cooler, a mix of old soul, and Emily could pick out Marvin Gaye and Sam Cooke. Now and then, someone would start humming or clapping along, and before long, half the table joined in.

She sat down beside David's aunt, who wore a bright scarf and told stories about "the old ways." Basket weaving, fishing the flats at dawn, the ghosts said to walk the marsh, and the root magic. Emily listened, rapt. It was like stepping into another world—one built on resilience and history, on knowing where you came from and carrying it forward.

When the sun finally disappeared, the party didn't slow down. Someone brought out shortcake and key lime pie. David pulled Emily up from her chair, spinning her barefoot in the grass while the music swelled. She laughed, dizzy from the food and the dancing and the sight of him so loose, so unguarded.

"Come on, baby," he said, grinning, "You can't come to a real low country boil and stay shy in the corner."

"I wasn't planning on it," she said, smiling.

The nighttime was rowdy. Every few minutes, someone shouted a joke or told a story—half in English, half in Gullah—and the group erupted in laughter. It was easy, unforced, like the music swelling around them.

David was in his element. Gone was the quiet, meticulous law student in a cardigan. Tonight, he was in jeans and a T-shirt, barefoot in the grass, dancing with Emily and his little nieces, laughing so hard he had to wipe his eyes. He cracked jokes with his cousins, told stories about growing up in the low country, and teased his mother about her "oversalted" crab legs.

Emily couldn't look away. He had this deep, easy laugh—the kind that took over his face and crinkled the corners of his eyes—and she realized how little she'd seen of his world until now.

On the drive home, the night air slid through the open windows, carrying the faint briny scent of the coast. David tapped his fingers on the steering wheel, humming along with the radio.

"That was fun," Emily said quietly.

He smiled. "Told you. Nothing better than good food and too many people talking over each other."

"Your family's incredible," she said. "They made me feel... welcome."

He glanced over. "They like you. Mama said you fit right in, even when Uncle Reggie tried to make you eat that hot sauce."

Emily laughed. "Oh my God, I almost died."

"That's how you earn respect," he said, grinning.

They drove in comfortable silence for a while, the lights of Charleston glowing in the distance.

David's tone softened.

"I've been thinking about D.C. again," he said. "After graduation, if the internship goes well... I think I want to stay."

Emily turned toward him. "You'd be great."

"You think?"

"I know it."

"You could come with me, you know. You'd kill it up there, too."

The words hung between them.

Emily looked out the window, the reflection of highway lights running across her face. She admired David—his drive, his calm, the way he always seemed to know who he was, where he came from, where he was going. Everything about him was solid and sure. And yet, beneath that admiration, something twisted in her gut.

With Ash, it had never been solid or sure. It had been chaos and fire and heartbreak. The kind of love that burned too hot to last. So why did she still ache for it? Why did the quiet goodness beside her feel good but… not good enough?

Why do I keep going back to someone who only leaves me bleeding?

David reached across the console, his hand warm over hers. "You okay?"

She forced a smile. "Yeah. Just tired."

He squeezed her hand, eyes on the road. "Then rest your eyes, baby. I'll wake you when we're home."

Emily closed her eyes, pretending to drift off, but her mind wouldn't quiet.

The next morning, sunlight filtered softly through the blinds—gentle, not severe, the way it had been at Ash's place. Emily blinked awake to the smell of coffee and the low hum of music from the kitchen.

David was at the stove in sweats, barefoot, flipping pancakes.

"Morning," he said when he saw her, smiling that easy, steady smile of his. "You looked like you needed sleep, so I let you."

She stretched, then pulled his hoodie tighter around her. "You didn't have to."

"I wanted to." He slid a plate toward her, topped with pancakes, bacon, and blackberries on the side. "Fuel for a big day of studying. Or procrastinating. Whichever."

She smiled, but it didn't quite reach her eyes. Everything about this felt… right. This was how mornings were supposed to feel.

David leaned against the counter, sipping his coffee.

"You were quiet on the drive home last night," he said casually. "Everything okay?"

Emily hesitated. "Yeah. Just tired, I guess."

He nodded. "I know school's been rough. L2 is no joke. You've been pushing yourself hard."

She looked at him, the faint stubble on his chin, the kind honey-colored eyes that never seemed to harden, the poise in the way he carried himself. He was the kind of man her parents always hoped she'd end up with. Yesterday, she'd come home to him from another man's bed. Her whole body ached with shame. She'd told herself it was grief, mixed with confusion, whiskey, and compassion. But she knew better.

David was talking about maybe going for a run later, about the forecast, about nothing, and everything, while she nodded, pretending to listen.

He's a good person. He doesn't deserve your shit. You have to bury that night with Ash down deep. Don't think about it. Commit to this version of life.

David looked over at her, smiling softly and breaking into her thoughts. "You're staring at me."

She blinked, startled. "What? No, I—"

"You do that when you're overthinking," he teased. "You forget to blink."

She forced a laugh. "Maybe I just like looking at you."

He grinned. "What a relief."

He crossed the kitchen, kissed her forehead, and she willed herself to feel something because this was what stability looked like. What love should look like. And she wasn't going to ruin it. Not if she could help it.

Chapter thirty-nine

The townhouse smelled like stale liquor and old takeout from the diner on one particular Sunday. Ash was on the couch, barely awake, watching football, an empty bottle half-buried beneath the crumpled blanket. His leg was healing up slowly; he could finally put most of his weight on it without limping.

The screen door slammed so hard it rattled the frame.

"Asher Dean Bell!"

He flinched, blinking as he sat up. "Mama?"

Cindy stood in the doorway, arms crossed, eyes blazing with that furious and terrifying look only a mother can pull off. She was wearing her church clothes, and that was a bad sign. Never mess with a Southern mama after she's been to church.

Ash had learned that lesson the hard way once, when he was sixteen. He'd skipped church service one Sunday and taken some of his daddy's beer down to the fishing pond. Then his mama showed up, hollering and swinging her Bible. She'd been ready to rain the Father, Son, and Holy Ghost down on his head.

She probably would have too, if she could have caught me.

He almost smiled at the memory.

"What's this?" she demanded, kicking an empty beer can across the floor. "Your baby boy is over at the Greens' house being cared for by a nanny, and you're sittin' here marinating in drink like you've got nothin' to live for!"

Ash groaned, dragging a hand over his face. "Mama, please—"

"No, you don't, 'Mama, please' me. You got a second chance when that wreck didn't kill you. I'm startin' to wonder if you even care that God gave it to you."

Her voice cracked, anger folding into fear.

"I buried your daddy, Ash. I watched him fade, but he fought. You hear me? He fought for every day he had left. And here you are throwin' your life away."

Ash pushed himself upright, grimacing as pain shot through his leg. "I'm tryin'. You don't understand—"

"I understand plenty." Her eyes glistened. "You're drownin' in grief and guilt because you think what happened to Mandy was somehow your fault. But drinkin' yourself into the grave ain't gonna bring her back. And it sure as hell ain't gonna raise your boy."

He went still.

"Jesse deserves more than this," she said, softly now. "He deserves a father who shows up. Not one who's too drunk to answer the phone."

Ash's throat worked, but no words came.

Cindy stepped closer. "I called a place upstate. Real rehab, not some weeklong vacation nonsense. They can take you tomorrow. You're goin'."

He shook his head, eyes glassy. "You can't just—"

"Oh, I can. And I will." She leaned in, voice shaking. "Because if you keep on like this, Asher, your mama is gonna be the next one in the grave."

The words hit harder than any slap.

Ash looked down at the floor, his breathing shallow. For the first time in months, something inside him cracked, this time not from anger, but from shame.

"Okay," he whispered finally. "I'll go."

Cindy exhaled like she'd been holding her breath for days.

"Good," she said, brushing a hand softly through his hair before turning for the door. "Pack a big bag. You're not comin' home until you remember whose son you are."

Ash sat there in the quiet after she left, the echo of his mama's voice settling like dust. The bottle of bourbon caught the afternoon light, amber and deceptive, the same way it always had.

He stared at it for a long time. He was tired. Tired of waking up with his mouth dry and his head pounding, of pretending the burn was comfort instead of punishment. Tired of the same old patterns, of letting people down and calling it fate.

He'd never quit anything in his life—not even the things that broke him. But maybe that was the problem. He'd fought against everything except himself. For once, he didn't want to fight. He just wanted to feel clean again. He wanted to see Jesse grow up. He wanted to show up for his mama. He wanted to be someone Mandy would have been proud of and someone Emily wouldn't have to save.

With a slow breath, he stood and reached for the bottle. The glass was warm in his hand. He twisted the cap, hesitated, then tipped it. The bourbon hit the sink in a steady stream, an ugly hiss rising as it swirled down the drain, like something evil that was slowly dying.

The next morning, the two-hour drive to the rehab center near Columbia was silent. The kind of silence that was full of things neither of them knew how to say.

Cindy kept both hands on the wheel, knuckles pale against the steering grip, her lips pressed tight. Every so often, she'd glance at the road signs or at the clouds hanging low, but never directly at Ash.

He didn't try to fill the space. He didn't have anything left to fill it with. He'd run out of excuses, run out of charm, run out of ways to make what he'd done sound smaller or softer than it was. The truth sat heavy in his throat, right where the bourbon used to burn.

He leaned his head against the window, watching the world pass in pieces: rusted barns, peeling billboards, lone gas stations swallowed by highway and pine. Everything looked washed out. Tired. Like him. It had been less than a year since Mandy died. But he felt decades older. He'd lost weight he couldn't afford to lose, his cheekbones were sharper, his clothes hanging wrong on a frame that used to feel solid. He felt weak—not just in his body, but somewhere deeper.

He wanted to get healthy again. Strong again. But a question he couldn't answer gnawed at him: Who the hell was he without Mandy?

He could hardly remember himself before her. Did he really want to find out who he became after her? What if he didn't like that man? What if Emily didn't either? Not that it mattered much, Emily didn't like the man he was now.

He let out a shaky exhale—half laugh, half ache.

Well... what do I have left to lose?

The truck hit a bump, jostling him slightly. Immediately, his mind flashed to Jesse. His little boy, the one person he couldn't afford to keep failing. That brought a different kind of ache. Closer to the bone. He wanted to be a good father—the kind Jesse could count on. The kind who showed up, who didn't let his own pain swallow him whole. But the responsibility felt overwhelming—like someone had handed him a future he wasn't sure he deserved.

Ash thought of his daddy. He had been the kind of father who showed up to every game if he wasn't on the road. The person who taught him how to throw a football and how to be a man. Someone who worked hard, loved harder, and made raising a family his priority from the age of eighteen until he passed away.

Those memories were scary. Right now, Ash didn't feel anything like the man who raised him. What if he couldn't be that kind of father for Jesse? What if all the mistakes he'd made, all the grief and guilt and spiraling, carved him into someone less? Someone smaller. Someone who couldn't measure up. He didn't want Jesse to grow up wishing his dad was different, stronger, better. He didn't want to fail his son before he ever got the chance to be a father at all.

The building came into view—plain brick, white trim, wholly unremarkable. But something in Ash started to hope as he looked at it. It wasn't inviting, but it looked like a doorway out of the life he had been living. A new beginning, if he wanted one.

He wrapped his hand around the door handle, holding it tighter than necessary.

"All right," he whispered to himself, voice barely there. "Time to quit for real."

He didn't know who he'd be on the other side of this. He didn't know if he'd like the man he'd find. But for once, the discomfort of staying the same outweighed the fear of making a change.

At check-in, after what felt like signing his life away, the woman behind the desk asked softly, "I'll need your phone and wallet."

He nodded. His hands felt heavy as he reached into his pocket.

"You'll get them back when you check out," she added, her voice kind but practiced. The sort of tone that suggested she had said this a thousand times before.

Ash looked down at his phone, thumb hovering over the screen. He typed out one last message.

Going to rehab. They're taking my phone.

He stared at the words—short, bare, honest—then hit send. No explanation. No apology. Just truth.

When the message disappeared, he turned the phone over in his palm once, then handed it across the counter.

Emily's phone buzzed as she sat hunched over a pile of constitutional law in the library. The text preview glowed up at her from the screen, short and straightforward.

Going to rehab.

Her heart clenched. She should have felt relief. She should have smiled, proud of him for finally trying.

Instead, her eyes stung, and she whispered, "About damn time," just to keep from crying.

Across the table, David looked up from his laptop. "Everything okay?"

She nodded quickly and lied mechanically. "Yeah. Just a text from my mom."

But her mind wouldn't settle. As much as Ash needed rehab, maybe she did too. A detox from the tall, dark-haired man she couldn't get enough of. A reset for the way she kept drifting back, for the high she got from his voice, for the crash that always followed.

That night, when David came up behind her while she brushed her teeth and said, "I love you, you know," she turned and said it back.

This time, she meant it with her whole heart. No more saving Ash. No more splitting her life in two. She buried herself in coursework, late nights at the library, mock trial prep. She and David fell into a healthy groove—studying, cooking together, mass on Saturday afternoons, running by the river. Routine became her recovery. Quiet practice became her healing.

Chapter forty

The first seventy-two hours broke him. Sweats. Tremors. Vomiting until his ribs ached. The staff called it detox. Ash called it punishment. Every drop of poison he'd poured into himself clawed its way out, leaving him faint and shaking. He didn't talk. Didn't look anyone in the eye. Just stared at the beige walls, trying not to think about how miserable he felt.

On day three, they assigned him a counselor, Dr. Lorraine Price. Fifty-something, African American woman with silver-streaked curls she wore in a tight bun. Her posture was stiff, as if she were still at parade rest.

Dr. Price was a retired drill sergeant who'd served twenty years in the Army before earning her PhD. Ash figured she'd be all rules and lectures—the kind who thought "warmth" was a weakness.

He was only half right.

"You can sit there in silence all you want, Mr. Bell," she said at their first session, crossing her arms. "I've stared down plenty of soldiers who thought they could out-stubborn me. You won't scare me, and you won't bullshit me either."

He blinked. "You're a therapist?"

"I'm whatever you need me to be," she said coolly. "Therapist, motivational speaker, pain in the ass. I don't do warm-and-fuzzy, Mr. Bell. I do results."

He almost laughed, but something in her eyes said, *don't try me.*

The days blurred. Group therapy. Chores. Twelve steps. Everything designed to strip you down until you couldn't hide from yourself.

Lorraine was relentless. When he blamed the drinking on Mandy's death, she leaned forward and said, "Grief didn't make you drink. It gave you permission."

When he said he was here for Jesse, she fired back, "That boy doesn't need a martyr. He needs a man."

Every word cut like he was crawling across broken glass. But for the first time, Ash started to hear it.

By the fourth week, he talked more. About his shoulder injury, his dad's cancer, Mandy's death, Emily, the pregnancy, the accident, the bottle, the guilt, and the pain. Somehow, all the emotions had tangled up into one unbearable ball deep in his gut. The only way to get away from it was to drink himself numb. But then that seemed to make everything worse. A vicious cycle of pain, numbing, then more pain behind it. Wave after wave.

Lorraine didn't coddle or comfort. She just said, "There's the truth. It's been pushed down too far, and it wants to come up. It hurts, but it's real. And that's where you start."

Six weeks in, the nightmares eased. His leg was almost one hundred percent, so he started running slow laps around the compound at dawn and lifting weights with some of the guys in the afternoon. He ate all the meals, even though most weren't great, kept to the routine, and did the work outlined in his treatment plan.

At night, he sat on the steps and watched the sun drop behind the trees—sober and still breathing.

Dr. Price found him there one evening.

"You ready to go home yet?"

"I don't know," he admitted.

"Good," she said, patting his shoulder. "People who say they're ready usually relapse before the week's over. You stay scared. It keeps you honest."

Graduation day at Oasis Recovery came with weak coffee in Styrofoam cups and metal folding chairs set up in a circle.

"My name's Asher," he said when it was his turn. "And I'm an alcoholic."

"Hi, Asher," the room echoed softly.

"I used to think my life ended the day my wife died," he said. "But now I know that wasn't the end, it was the reset. I don't know who I am yet, but I know who I don't want to be anymore."

From her seat, Dr. Price nodded once. "That's progress, Mr. Bell."

Outside, sunlight hit him like freedom. A familiar truck was parked out front, Arch leaning against it, sunglasses on, arms crossed.

"Damn," Arch said with a grin as Ash jogged out, duffel slung over his shoulder. "Didn't think you'd make it a day without whiskey and bad decisions."

Ash snorted. "Almost didn't."

They hugged quick and hard. The kind of hug men give when they've been through something ugly together, even if they never say it.

On the drive, Arch kept things easy at first—family, sports, small talk to fill the miles. Jessica was pregnant again, and while Ash was in rehab, they'd found out the gender.

"It's a girl," Arch said it like the words needed grounding. "Scares the shit outta me, man. I don't know how to be a girl dad."

Ash smiled as he took in the news, and then he thought about Jesse. The ache of missing him cut deep. He couldn't wait to see his son again—two months away felt like a lifetime.

Halfway back to Haven County, Arch's voice went deeper, the lightness falling away.

"Mama and I were scared shitless, Ash," he said. "You keep this up, and we'll bury you next. You can't let that happen."

Ash stared out the window. "I know."

Arch reached into his jacket and handed him a business card. "Call this guy. He's the best custody lawyer in the county. You get your act together; you'll get Jesse back. You screw it up again—"

"I won't," Ash cut in quietly. "I'm done drinking. For good this time."

Arch nodded, satisfied. "Good. Because we're out of lives to spare, brother."

That night, after dinner at his mama's, Ash sat on the faded plaid couch for a long time, watching some TV, scrolling through his messages until he stopped on her name. He punched out a short text: *Just wanted you to know I'm out. Doing better. Hope you're happy, Em.*

Then he set the phone down and didn't wait for a reply. He wasn't going to call or try to pull her back into his life. He meant what he typed. If that guy down in Charleston made her happy, he wouldn't try to stand in the way. Not this time.

He took a walk out to the pole barn. The old boat sat looking dilapidated as ever. Cracked paint, rotting wood, but still there, waiting for him.

He found a Sharpie on the workbench and knelt beside it, tracing the faded hull with steady hands. The letters came out uneven, but it didn't matter.

The Other Woman.

"The *only* woman in my life now," he said quietly, running his palm over the worn deck. "Thank God she don't talk back." He smiled a little, a tired kind of smile. "Guess it's time we both get another shot."

Ash sold the townhouse. Too many memories that could drag him backward. He moved back in with his mama—at least that way someone could keep him accountable.

The house smelled like coffee that first morning, as Cindy slid a plate of biscuits across the breakfast table and said, "You're up early. That's a good sign."

He smiled faintly. "Haven't been sleeping much."

She nodded, poured him coffee, and changed the subject to Jesse.

The first few weeks home were quiet. Too quiet sometimes. Sundays came slower. Sometimes he'd tag along with Cindy to church, even though he still wasn't sure where he stood with God.

He always sat in the back, the last pew by the door, hands shoved in his pockets. The preacher's voice boomed through the chapel—forgiveness, grace, redemption. Ash stared at the floorboards, convinced the sermons were aimed right at him. When the choir sang "Amazing Grace," he didn't join in. He just closed his eyes and listened.

He called the lawyer Arch recommended—a man named Paul Withers, gray suit, gray hair, soft-spoken but sharp as a tack. The Greens had been kind, even understanding, but Ash wasn't sure they would give up custody of Jesse without a fight. They'd requested mediation, and he didn't want to leave anything to chance. Consulting an attorney seemed like the smartest move.

The law office sat in a brick building in downtown Bellefontaine, wedged between the post office and a bail bonds place. It smelled like old coffee and copy toner. The walls were lined with thick leather-bound books, their spines faded from sun and use.

"I'll be honest with you, Asher," Mr. Withers said, flipping through the file. "It ain't exactly an easy sell, but it's not impossible either. You finished treatment, you've kept up with visitation, and you've got your family standin' behind you. That counts for a lot more than you think."

He leaned back in his chair, glasses sliding a little down his nose.

"Now, it helps some that Haven County's small. Folks know you, and they know your people. But they know the Greens too, and that's where you're gonna have to walk a line. Keep your head down, keep doin' right, and don't give this town any reason to start talkin'. You just let your actions speak for you, son."

Ash nodded. "I just want Jesse home."

"Then keep doin' what you have been," his lawyer replied reassuringly. "Stay sober, hold a job, keep your temper in check. Most importantly, don't break any more laws."

So that's what Ash did. He showed up to every visitation, even the ones that broke his heart. Jesse's chubby hands reaching for him when it was time to go back to Mandy's parents. He got his mechanic job back at the marina. Started lifting weights again at the high school with his old buddies, eating better, and keeping a schedule. He worked on fixing up The Other Woman in his spare time. He was living a boring, ordinary life. The kind he'd once thought he'd never have again.

Chapter forty-one

Their tiny apartment always smelled like something warm on the stove, thanks to David, who insisted on cooking actual meals, instead of surviving on frozen burritos, like everyone else in law school did.

Tonight, he was making gumbo. Real gumbo. The kind you had to stir for nearly an hour and season by instinct, not recipe. The kind that made the whole place feel homey and intentional. David didn't slack off at anything. He'd been an adult long before he should've had to be.

Emily sat on the couch with her laptop open, highlighting case law she could barely concentrate on. She'd been in her head all day since Ash had texted.

Just a short update about Jesse's custody hearing: *Everything seems to be worked out now but keep us in your prayers, okay?*

She still hadn't responded. She wanted desperately to call him, but she held back. Getting too close felt dangerous, yet distance felt wrong. Whatever they were now balanced on a thin edge, steady only as long as neither of them leaned too hard.

David walked in from the kitchen, wiping his hands on a towel, shoulders tight. He looked tired. Not the usual mid-terms tired. Something heavier. Something that looked like it came from years, not hours.

"You're quiet," he said, dropping beside her. "Even for you."

"Just cramming," she muttered, pushing up her reading glasses to rub her eyes.

He nodded tensely and stared at the wall.

"Did something happen?" she asked.

A scoff. "Terrence called."

Emily blinked. "Wait… your father?"

"Mm-hm." He tossed his phone onto the coffee table. "Ten years of nothing. And today he calls out of the blue."

Anger moved across David's face—not showy, but deep, old, layered. Emily had never seen it before. David didn't wear his emotions on his sleeve. He'd told her, almost jokingly, that he practically raised his brothers while his mom worked nights. That he'd been the one who packed lunches, broke up fights, helped with homework, and ran the washing machine wrong until he learned to do it right. He'd told the story like it was fine, like it wasn't childhood stolen. But this… this was the hurt he never said out loud.

"What did he say?" Emily asked softly.

"He said…" David exhaled hard. "'Hope you're good. Proud of you.' *Proud.*" He shook his head, a bitter, disbelieving laugh slipping out. “He doesn’t get to say that. He didn’t raise me. He didn’t raise *any* of us. He doesn’t know what I had to do just to keep our house from falling apart.”

Emily stayed quiet, letting him set the pace.

“My mama—” His voice caught, then steadied roughly. “She killed herself working two jobs to make sure we had food on the table. And he… he waltzes in now with ‘proud’ like he gets to attach himself to the finished product.”

He rubbed his fingertips over his brow, the same way he did before oral arguments. But this wasn’t nerves. This was someone trying not to crash into a past he’d spent his whole life outrunning.

“I spent my entire childhood terrified of messing up,” he said. “Like if I failed at something—school, taking care of my brothers, being the ‘good one’—everything would collapse. Like the whole damn family was hanging on me doing things right.”

Emily felt her heart pull. Not with pity but with recognition. The kind you only feel when someone finally shows you the wound they’d kept hidden under all that competence.

“You can be angry,” she whispered.

He finally met her eyes. And for the first time, she saw the brokenness there. It wasn’t weakness, just the exhaustion of someone who had carried too much, too early.

“I am,” he whispered back. “I’m furious. And I don’t know why it still feels like something I’m not allowed to feel.” His throat bobbed. “My mama depended on me. My brothers did. Hell, they still do. I worked my ass off to get here, to break the cycle so my kids don’t grow up the way I did. Now Terrence thinks he can… act like a dad when I’m too old to need one.”

Emily reached for him, and he didn't pull away. His hand found hers and held it tighter than necessary, like he was rooting himself in the assurance.

"You deserved better," she said. "So much better."

He let out a breath that sounded like something unclenching.

"I'm sorry. I don't usually let myself—" he gestured vaguely, "be like this."

"Maybe you should sometimes," she murmured. "You don't have to be perfect."

A quiet laugh slipped out. "Don't tell anyone."

The tension in his shoulders didn't fully ease until he kissed her. Soft at first, then deeper, like he was anchoring himself back into the present. His hands slid beneath her sweater, fingertips warm and searching, not rushed, not frantic. Needing closeness and needing *her*.

Emily went into his lap easily, her knees bracketing him, her fingers threading through his hair. She felt the shift in him—not lust, just relief. Relief at not having to be the unshakeable one for once.

He breathed her name against her skin, low and rough in a way she'd never heard from him. "Em... you're everything to me. You know that?"

She kissed him harder, wanting to meet him where he was. Wanting to quiet the part of her mind that still drifted toward someone whose drama felt like fate.

David's hands were gentle but firm, pulling her sweater over her head. His palms and lips traced her waist, her ribs, her shoulders like he was memorizing parts of her. He wasn't a storm. He wasn't a risk. He was the man who'd grown up too fast, who'd always taken care of everyone else, and who was terrified of failing, because failure meant people got hurt.

Right now?

He needed someone to take care of *him*.

Emily let him guide her down onto the couch cushions, their bodies finding that familiar, quiet rhythm built from comfort, not desperation. Clothes slipped away in soft motions. Their breath mingled. Everything settled. When he whispered her name again—not desperate, not possessive, just sure—she felt herself soften. She let herself be the thing he could lean on.

Afterward, he rested his head on her chest, his arm locked around her waist like he was afraid she might disappear. After a long stretch of quiet, David exhaled against her skin, his voice low and unguarded, the kind of honesty that only surfaces when someone feels safe.

"You know what scares me the most?" he murmured. "That I'll screw everything up one day. That I'll become him. That I'll disappear from my kids' lives the way he disappeared from mine."

Emily's chest tightened. "David, I know you. You'd never do something like that."

"I want to believe that," he said. "I do. But I don't know why I feel this pressure in my bones, like everything depends on me being perfect. Like if I slip up even once, the whole future I want… evaporates." He took a breath. "I want to build something real. A family that doesn't break up. Kids who never have to wonder why their father didn't stay."

Emily could admit she *wanted* that too. She wanted the warmth of that image, the normalcy, the promise. She wanted to picture herself with him in that life: a house, two kids with David's dark hair and serious eyes, him cooking on Sunday nights, her laughing at his corny jokes.

She *wanted* to see it. But when she tried to summon the picture, the edges blurred. The space beside David in that imagined kitchen felt… blank. Like a dream she could only recall in parts. A life she couldn't quite step into, no matter how hard she reached for it.

She swallowed.

"You'll be an amazing father," she whispered, and she meant it. "You're nothing like him."

David lifted his head just enough to meet her eyes.

"I want it more than anything, Em. A family, stability. A future that feels solid." His gaze softened. "With someone who believes in me."

Something inside her trembled—not out of fear of *him*, but fear of *herself.* Fear that no matter how good he was, some part of her was drifting toward a different storyline.

She pressed a kiss to his forehead, gentle, lingering.

"You deserve all of it," she said. "You're going to have it someday, I know it."

He smiled, tired but genuine, and tucked himself back against her like he'd finally let himself rest.

Emily held him, stroking his hair, feeling his warmth melt into her. Booger had joined them now, rubbing his soft head against Emily's arm, begging for attention or a meal.

Underneath the tenderness, an invisible truth pulsed quietly, painfully. She wanted the world for David, but she still couldn't see herself in the picture he was painting. Not fully. Not clearly. Not the way she knew she should.

Chapter forty-two

The courtroom for the final hearing was cold in the clinical way courthouses always are—tile that bit through Ash's shoes, the overwhelming smell of crisp paper and polished wood. They'd already been through mediation, and the outcome felt mostly settled, but he couldn't breathe easy. Not until it was official.

Mandy's parents sat together, hands clasped in a show of unity. Cindy was on the bench directly behind Ash, a warm, stubborn presence. She had reached over to pat his shoulder before taking her seat.

Before the judge entered, Mr. Withers leaned over and whispered, "Listen to me carefully. Judge Harlan's fair, but she's tough as nails. She's got no patience for self-pity or excuses. She's seen too many parents promise to do better and never follow through. So, if she asks you for a statement before the court enters the order, keep it straight, keep it short, and don't get emotional unless it's real. You understand, son?"

Ash nodded. "Yeah. I got it."

The bailiff called for order. The gavel cracked once. When the judge peered down over her glasses and asked if he had anything to say, Ash stood. His hands trembled at his sides; the room felt too quiet, every breath amplified.

"I know I messed up, your honor," he said, trying to keep his voice level. "I know I let people down—my son, my family. I drank. I broke the law. But I went to treatment. I've been sober for seven months now. I have a job, a stable place to stay, and a family who will help me raise Jesse the right way. I won't waste the chance to be his father."

For a moment, there was only the soft creak of a chair. The judge read through the file again, then looked up at him with an expression that balanced compassion and the kind of legal toughness that could cut through excuses.

"I have reviewed all the submissions," she said finally. "The record reflects compliance with visits, completed treatment, and proof of stability. You also have a particularly good letter of recommendation from Dr. Price at Oasis Recovery. I happen to know Dr. Price personally, and I know how hard it is to impress her, Mr. Bell."

She tapped her gavel lightly.

"The court is entering the final order granting full legal and physical custody of Jesse Carter Bell to his father, Mr. Asher Bell. Visitation for the maternal grandparents will continue as outlined in the agreement."

Her eyes locked on Ash for a minute longer.

"But hear me clearly—any substantial deviation from this order will bring you back before the court. This is not a reward. It is a responsibility."

Cindy wept softly into her handkerchief. Elizabeth's face, hard as stone for weeks, crumpled into something like reluctant acceptance. Ash sat down slowly, the decision settling over him like both a weight and a promise.

Outside the courthouse, when Jesse fell asleep with his head on Ash's shoulder, and Cindy wiped at her eyes, Ash felt a fierce and final sort of relief, not victory so much as the terrifying start of something he was ready to prove he could keep.

He whispered to his son, "We're gonna do it right, kiddo. I swear I'll keep my promise."

The drive home from the courthouse was quiet except for the whir of the truck tires on the pavement and the soft snore of a toddler in the back seat. The custody papers lay folded on the console. Proof that, somehow, he'd pulled himself out of the wreckage.

When they turned down the old dirt road toward his mama's double-wide, the sun was beginning to set. Ash parked in the drive, cut the engine, and sat for a second, staring at the house. He'd driven that stretch a thousand times, but this time it felt new, like he was coming home for the first time.

"Go on," Cindy said softly. "Take the baby inside."

He unbuckled Jesse from his car seat, the little body limp and warm against his shoulder. Jesse stirred as they walked up the steps, murmuring something that sounded like *Daddy*, and Ash froze just long enough to feel his throat close, and his eyes sting.

The house that evening smelled like fried chicken and cornbread. Cindy had gone all out for their "celebration dinner".

She set a pitcher of sweet tea down and said, "You did good, Asher."

He laughed softly, running his hands through his hair. "We did good."

After dinner, Cindy disappeared into the kitchen to clean up while he gave Jesse a bath. The smiling toddler splashed in the shallow water, giggling, soap bubbles clinging to his curls. It was such a simple sound, the kind that broke and mended your heart at the same time.

When Ash tucked Jesse into bed that night, the toddler clutched the stuffed dinosaur Cindy had bought him for his first birthday, eyelids fluttering. Ash stood there for a long time, one hand on the crib rail, watching his son sleep—peaceful, safe, and finally home. He didn't feel like the same man who'd stumbled into rehab back in the fall, tormented and trembling. He wasn't sure he believed in miracles, but this felt close.

Rehab had taught him things he wished he'd learned sooner—that control was a myth, at least the way he used to chase it. He couldn't change the past, couldn't rewrite Mandy's ending, couldn't make himself stop missing her, and he couldn't make Emily come back. All he could do was take ownership of his own story—one day, one breath, one choice at a time.

Dr. Price's voice still echoed in his head: *"You can't fix what's gone, Mr. Bell. But you can decide what comes next."*

That's what he tried to do. He kept his head down, showed up for Jesse, and prayed—not for forgiveness, not even for peace—but for the strength to hold steady when the next storm came.

Chapter forty-three

The air on Haven Island smelled like honeysuckle in the spring, a soft, sticky sweetness that clung to everything. Emily hadn't been back in months. She'd almost forgotten how different it felt from Charleston. Slower. Easier. The kind of place where time seemed to nap in the sun.

She'd come home over spring break to house-sit—and dog-sit—while her mother and Greg were in Europe. They had recently adopted a nine-week-old golden retriever named Cooper, who was all floppy ears and oversized paws.

Cooper followed Emily from room to room like a shadow and slept curled next to her in bed. She enjoyed the quiet of the beach house, interrupted now and then by the jingle of a tiny collar.

She spent her mornings studying, her afternoons running the overgrown trails near the old lighthouse, and her evenings cooking dinners for one while the sun melted into the water.

Now and then over the past few months, she and Ash had exchanged texts—nothing too heavy, just little check-ins that felt safe.

Ash: *I know it's early, but do you wanna put money on the Clemson v USC game this year?*

Emily: *Don't start. You jinxed us last time.*

Ash: *Marina job's going good, wish I had found this sooner.*

Emily: *Glad to hear it!*

Emily: *Almost finished with administrative law, thank God!*

Ash: *Keep killing it tiger!*

It was comfortable, that strange half-friendship they'd fallen into. Sporadically texting about Jesse, football, his work, and her classes. He'd told her he got a mechanic job at the marina and was working on his boat again, though he never said much more. Just enough to make her curious. She thought about texting him that afternoon—a *how's the boat coming?* But stopped herself. Some things were better left untouched. Especially with her being so close by this week, acutely aware she was on his turf now.

Emily was folding laundry when her phone rang. The sound jolted across the room, echoing off the vaulted ceilings. Cooper barked from the hallway—sharp and curious—as if he knew something important was happening. She glanced down at the screen.

Ash's name lit it up, and her stomach dropped.

"Hey," she said, breath catching. "Everything okay?"

His voice came out tight, rushed. "No, not really. Can you do me a favor? Mama's having chest pains. The neighbor is taking her to the

ER. Jesse's already asleep. I need to go be with Mama right now, and I can't take him with me. Jessica has Ryker and Katie Jo, the baby. Arch is on a call. I just… I don't have anybody else right now, Em. I'm sorry to bother you."

Emily's heart started hammering. "No problem. Of course I'll come. But—how'd you even know I was in town?"

He hesitated, then let out a half-laugh. "Ran into Jeanne at High Tide this afternoon. She said you'd stopped in for coffee and that you were here for a school break. Guess word still travels faster than the ferry around here."

Emily grabbed her keys, already rushing for the door.

"I'll be there in twenty."

"Thank you," he said softly. The kind of thank you that carried exhaustion and relief all at once.

Cooper trotted up to her, tail wagging, only to stop short when she opened his crate.

"I'm sorry, buddy," she said, crouching down to unclip his collar.

He gave her those big, heart-melting eyes and let out a soft whine.

"I know. I'll be right back, okay?" she promised.

He curled up inside, letting out a dramatic sigh, as if he understood.

She shut the crate door gently. He was so impossibly cute it made her feel guilty, but she knew her mother would never forgive her if he chewed a chair leg or had an accident on one of the Persian rugs.

Emily locked up the house, heart still pounding, wondering why, after everything, it still felt like the only direction she could ever run was toward Ash.

By the time Emily turned down the familiar dirt road to the Bells' property, the moon was high, silvering the tops of the pines. Ash's new truck was parked out front—black, polished, surprisingly nice—a clear sign that, at least on the outside, he had steadied.

The house looked the same as always, small and cozy, with warm light spilling from the kitchen window. Emily noticed the porch had been recently painted and didn't sag quite as much as it used to.

Ash met her at the door in jeans and a faded T-shirt, hair still damp from a hurried shower. His face was tight with worry, but his eyes softened when he saw her.

"Hey," he said, stepping aside. "Sorry for the late call."

"It's fine," she said, brushing past him. "How's Cindy?"

"Still at the ER. They're running tests. She's stubborn as hell, but I don't wanna be taking chances."

Emily nodded, glancing around. The house was tidy but lived in—a pile of toys on the coffee table, a blanket draped over the couch, laundry half-folded on the armchair. It was the kind of comfy disorder that came with a one-year-old.

Jesse's soft snores carried from the bedroom on the baby camera.

"He's down?" she whispered.

"Out cold," Ash said. "Kid could sleep through a hurricane."

She smiled faintly. "Sounds like someone else I know."

He chuckled softly. "I owe you one, Em. Really."

She shook her head. "You would do the same. Go take care of your mom."

He lingered a second, as if wanting to say more. Then he nodded and grabbed his keys. "I'll text you when I know something."

The screen door creaked shut behind him, and the rumble of his truck faded down the red dirt road until the night swallowed it whole.

Emily stood there for a long moment, letting the quiet settle around her. She toed off her shoes and wandered toward the back room. Jesse stirred in his crib and then started to fuss. She leaned over, brushing his wispy blond curls gently.

"Hey, hey, it's okay," she whispered. He blinked up at her with sleepy blue eyes, and something inside her melted.

She scooped him up, rocking him back and forth slowly until his head dropped back against her shoulder. The small weight of him, the warmth, the innocent trust, it undid her. She sank into the old rocker by the window, holding the baby, watching the moonlight shimmer across the yard. Her eyelids grew heavy, the sway of the chair lulling her until she drifted off with Jesse still sleeping soundly in her arms.

When the door finally squeaked open hours later, Ash stopped short at the sight. Emily was asleep in the chair, with Jesse nestled against her, both bathed in silver light. For a long moment, he didn't move. He just stood there, something gentle and longing moving across his face. Then he crossed the room and knelt beside them, his voice barely a whisper.

"Em," he said.

Her eyes fluttered open. "Hey, how's your mom?"

"They're keeping her overnight," he said quietly. "Chest pain's from high blood pressure, not a heart attack, thank God."

Relief washed over her. "That's good."

Ash's eyes softened as he brushed his hand over Jesse's head. "He likes you."

"Yeah," she said quietly. "I like him too."

Without thinking, he brushed a stray curl from her face. "You look tired."

"Thanks," she said dryly, but her lips curved into a slight grin.

Their eyes held for a moment too long, too familiar.

Ash hesitated, his hand still hovering near her cheek. "Em… you're beautiful like this, you know?"

Her breath caught. "Ash—"

He shook his head slightly, as if to stop himself, but then he moved closer, slow, uncertain. His lips brushed hers, barely there, testing the air between them.

Emily steadied herself for just an instant, then she leaned in. The world went still. Just the sound of their kiss and Jesse's soft, even breathing.

When they finally broke apart, her voice quivered slightly. "I should go."

He nodded, but his thumb lingered, hovering at the corner of her mouth.

"Yeah," he said quietly. "You probably should."

Emily eased the sleeping little boy down into his crib, kissed his soft curls, then turned to grab her bag.

She looked back at Ash once more. He was standing there barefoot, looking lost and found all at once, and she couldn't help it—she wanted to throw herself into his arms.

"Goodnight, Ash," she heard herself say softly instead.

"Goodnight, Em."

She slipped out into the pitch darkness, the screen door creaking shut behind her. The moon had disappeared, and the night air was thick with the scent of the marsh, swelling around her with guilt that felt oddly light and longing that was painfully clear.

Ash stood at the window long after Emily's taillights disappeared down the road, hand pressed against the windowsill, wishing he'd had the strength not to kiss her and knowing he'd never stood a chance.

Chapter forty-four

One Year Later

The spring was one of the hottest and most humid the Low Country had seen in years. In Charleston, the thermometer had already started to climb by midmorning, heat lines shimmering off the quad in waves. White tents dotted the lawn, a brass band tuning somewhere near the stage, the scent of magnolias thick in the air.

Emily adjusted her cap in the reflection of her phone screen, then laughed under her breath.

"Three years of law school," she muttered. "And I still can't keep a bobby pin straight."

David stood beside her, straight-backed in his black gown, his smile calm and confident.

"You look perfect," he said, taking her hand. "Ready to finally be free of the library?"

"God, yes," she said with a grin. "If I never see patents again, it'll be too soon."

He chuckled. "You'll miss it in a week."

"I'll miss *you* in a week," she admitted softly.

He squeezed her hand. "You don't have to."

Before she could answer, the procession started—a sea of caps and gowns moving in step to the band's march. Emily's heart swelled as they took their seats in front of the stage, the rows stretching endlessly down the green.

When David's name was called—*David DeWayne Jordan, juris doctor*—his family erupted. His mother waved a handkerchief, his brothers whooped from the back row, his aunts shouted, "That's my baby!" until the whole tent laughed. Emily couldn't help but beam.

Then, a few names later—*Emily Francine Kennedy, juris doctor.*

For a breath, it didn't feel real. She walked across the stage, shook the dean's hand, and when she turned, she saw them—her people. David's cheering section went wild again while he jumped to his feet and let out an excited whoop. Her mom and Greg were standing, clapping through tears. Joel and Mateo waved wildly from the side aisle. Cindy was smiling proudly beside Ash, who had Jesse perched on his knee. The little boy was pointing and babbling as if he somehow knew what was happening.

Even from a distance, Emily saw the pride in Ash's eyes and felt the familiar twist in her gut that came with it. She'd texted him a few weeks ago, fully aware it would complicate things. She made sure to run it by David first, half expecting him to shut it down. He hadn't exactly encouraged it, but he hadn't said no either.

When the ceremony ended, she wove through the crowd of robes and families, her classmates' arms full of flowers and hugs. Joel nearly tackled her when she reached him.

"Miss Esquire!" he said, dramatically fanning himself. "My best friend is officially a lawyer. Do I get immunity now?"

Emily laughed. "Absolutely not. You're my number one liability."

Mateo leaned in, holding up a bouquet of roses and an envelope.

"The note is from Kenzie," he said, his speech punctuated by his soft Spanish accent. "She made me swear to deliver it in person.'"

Emily rolled her eyes, tearing it open.

Inside was a postcard from Florence, a sketch of the Duomo on the front, and Kenzie's looping handwriting on the back: *'Proud of you, Em. Don't forget to enjoy this part before you go running off to your next thing. Love you always.'*

Joel peered over her shoulder. "She's annoyingly right, you know."

"Don't tell her that," Emily said, laughing through the happy tears that slipped anyway.

Her mom and Greg appeared then, both wrapping her in warm hugs and congratulations.

Next came Cindy, Ash, and Jesse.

Cindy wrapped her up first in a soft, motherly bear hug. "We're all so proud of you, sweetheart."

Ash came next, a soft side hug. His tie hung slightly askew, sleeves rolled to show the same tattoos. He was clean-shaven and looking stronger than she'd seen him in years.

“Didn’t know your middle name was Francine,” he teased. “Explains a lot.”

“Shut up,” she said, laughing.

He grinned. “On a serious note, congratulations, Em. You did it, I’m proud of you.”

She looked up at him, that warmth in his eyes was still capable of undoing her in one second flat. “Thanks, Ash. That means a lot.”

“Let me take you to lunch,” he said suddenly. “You, me, Mama, Jesse. You can invite your parents and Joel and his partner, if you want. My treat. A proper celebration.”

She hesitated. “That’s really sweet of you, but I already have plans. David’s mom organized a family brunch at Magnolia’s.”

He nodded, doing his best to mask the flicker of disappointment that crossed his face. “Fancy. Makes sense. It’s a big day.”

She smiled softly. “Maybe another time.”

“Yeah,” he said. “Another time.”

They stood there a moment longer as the crowd moved around them—her clutching flowers, him with Jesse tugging at his hand—two people on opposite sides of a chapter they’d both survived, but hadn't yet closed.

The following evening, Hall’s Chophouse hummed with low conversation, the clink of wine glasses, and the soft jazz of a live band weaving through the air like silk. Every table was lit by candlelight, the glow spilling over the dark mahogany walls and crisp linen like liquid gold.

Emily sat across from David in the intimate corner booth he had reserved weeks ago as a special celebration for just the two of them. A bottle of Dom Pérignon chilled between them, the condensation tracing slow paths down the glass.

David had dressed for the occasion in a dark suit, crisp and classic, with a thin striped tie. It was the kind of look that made him stand out in every room he entered. Emily matched his effort without really meaning to, in a black strappy dress that bared her shoulders and shimmered faintly when she moved.

Tonight, David reminded her of someone who'd never once doubted the trajectory of his life, the kind of man who made decisions once and didn't look back.

The waiter brought oysters on crushed ice, shrimp cocktail, and two perfect filets with truffle butter. The smell alone could've made her cry.

"We deserve to celebrate tonight," David said, smiling over his champagne glass. "All those late nights and outlines. I'm proud of you, Em. Proud of us!"

She smiled back. "Thank you. For… everything. For putting up with me."

He reached across the table, fingers brushing hers. "That's not something I *have* to do. That's something I *want* to do."

The band shifted to slow, soft saxophone, and as the velvet notes drifted toward them, the atmosphere seemed to change. David reached into his jacket pocket, and Emily's eyes widened. He opened the small velvet box quietly, no grand gesture, just him, sure as he ever was, holding up a gold ring with a marquise solitaire diamond that shimmered in the candlelight.

"Emily Kennedy," he said, his voice calm, deep, deliberate. "You've made my life better since the day I met you. You challenge me, you make me laugh, you make me want to be more than I am. I want a life with you—wherever it takes us. Will you marry me?"

The words hit her in phases, first like a soft wave and then like a tsunami.

Her throat went dry. "David…"

His eyes searched hers, patient, kind, but already sensing it.

She swallowed hard. "Before you say anything else, I need to tell you something."

He didn't flinch. "Okay."

He knew. He'd probably always known. Maybe everyone had. But there was a difference between suspicion and hearing me say the words. If I accepted his proposal without saying them out loud, it would feel like one last lie between us.

Emily took a deep breath. "It was two years ago," she whispered. "After everything that happened with Mandy passing and with Ash wrecking his car. He called me, and I… I went to his house. I shouldn't have. It was a mistake. He was feeling lost, and oh my God, I was so confused back then. We—" she stuttered out the words, "We slept together."

David's hands were still. He didn't interrupt, didn't even blink.

"I never meant to hurt you," she said, tears brimming, threatening to fall. "But I know I did. I'm so sorry, David."

He leaned back slowly, exhaling through his nose.

When he finally spoke, his voice was quiet, almost too passive. "I was afraid you were going to say that. I'm not completely oblivious, Emily. You came back that morning looking like hell, saying you spent the night on Haven Island. Do you know what that makes me want to do? Drive up there and jack the guy's jaw."

Emily flinched.

He half smiled—small and sad. "But that's not me, Em. That's never been me."

"I know that," she whispered.

He studied her face, his expression heartbreakingly composed. "I'm not angry. Not like you think. I'm just sad… and disappointed. I thought we were building something."

"We were," she said. "We are. I love you."

He nodded slowly, taking that in, weighing it like evidence. "Then why does it feel like part of you is still somewhere else?"

She didn't answer—she couldn't.

After a long silence, he put the ring inside the box, snapped the lid closed, and put it back in his pocket.

"I'm leaving for D.C. next week. I want you to come with me, as my fiancée. But if you don't want that—if you're not all in—I won't force it. I don't want half of someone. You deserve more than that in this life. And so do I."

Her vision blurred, tears spilling over.

David reached across, brushing one away. "You're not a bad person, Em. You're just still figuring out who you want to be. Maybe I'm not part of your story anymore."

The words were gentle. Too gentle. Somehow, that made them hurt worse.

When David stood, he didn't rush. He moved with that calm, measured composure he always wore—the kind that made him look collected even when he was bleeding inside. He pulled a few bills from his wallet and set them on the table, more than enough to cover the check. His hand lingered there for a second, like he was gathering whatever pieces of himself he still had the ability to keep. Then he looked at her.

Emily had seen him sad before. Frustrated. Scared of failure. But this… this was different. This was David closing a door inside himself—quietly and deliberately—the kind of door she used to be allowed to walk through without knocking. The pain was still in his eyes, unmistakable, but he held it at a distance now, tucked behind a wall she no longer had the privilege to see past.

In the dim restaurant lighting, he looked like the version of himself she would never forget—quiet steadiness and old-soul charm—the kind of man who quoted *Casablanca* without irony.

With the shadows softening the edges of his face, he looked a little like he was imitating Humphrey Bogart: wounded, dignified, pretending he wasn't breaking because the love he felt wasn't enough to keep someone. She half expected him to whisper, "Here's looking at you, kid." But he didn't give her that. He didn't give her anything sentimental, cinematic, or open. Just a slight, careful nod. A version of himself that was still polite, still kind… but no longer hers.

"Goodnight, Em," he said.

Then he was gone, leaving nothing but the muted hum of jazz and the flicker of candlelight.

Emily sat numbly staring at the empty chair across from her, the one David had occupied moments ago as she shattered everything between them. She poured herself the last of the champagne; it had been meant for a celebration and had instead witnessed a betrayal. She drank it all down in one gulp.

The waiter passed by once, paused, then quietly turned away. Tears fell soundlessly onto the white tablecloth, each one dissolving into a wet blob that marred the fabric. David had been with her for the last three years of her life. He was what she should be moving toward. And yet, as the candles burned low, she felt that slow, familiar hole opening inside her.

Letting him go didn't feel like a mistake. It felt unavoidable. Almost as if no matter how many times she tried to rewrite her story, it would always find its way back to the same fault line, the one with Ash's name carved into it.

Chapter forty-five

The apartment was empty now. The walls, once lined with books and coffee mugs, echoed when Emily walked by them. The space smelled faintly of Chlorox cleaner and cardboard. David's desk was gone. So were his suits. Even Booger, fat and judgmental to the end, had gone with him to D.C.

For weeks after he left, she told herself the silence was what she needed—space to breathe, to think, to start over. But the silence didn't feel like freedom. It still felt like loss.

Her lease ended the same week in August that her bar exam results came in. The odds were against her passing on the first try, but somehow, she had defied them. The word *Congratulations* flashed on her laptop screen, and she sat staring at it for a long time—not crying, not cheering—just breathing.

Before she left Charleston, she laced up her running shoes and went down to the river one last time. The path was quiet, the water glassy and slow beside her. She ran without music, without pushing the pace, without trying to outrun anything. With every mile, something inside her settled: she was Emily. Just Emily. That finally felt good enough.

She let herself admit the hard truth there, in the quiet: there were a lot of things she hadn't handled well. Loving two people hadn't excused it, and it certainly hadn't spared David's heart. Still, she knew her abilities and the values she aspired to. She chose to let go of judgment and step into her next chapter with a heart full of gratitude.

That weekend, she moved back to Haven Island. The pristine white beach house in Haven Lakes was comfortable but suffocating, full of advice she never asked for. By twenty-five, Emily was ready to stop being a guest in her own life. She missed Ash more than she cared to admit, but that wasn't why she came back home. There was too much history between them, too much guilt and too many unanswered questions for her to believe they could simply pick up where they'd left off.

The cottage she bought out past the Point wasn't perfect—but it was *hers*. The sea air slipped in through loose windowpanes, the walls needed paint, and the floors creaked. She chose to see the charm, good bones, and potential. She spent her weekends trying to fix it up, though she'd readily admit she was no handyman. She was just a woman claiming a space that belonged to her alone.

With each passing day, she realized she wasn't chasing a man or clinging to one who made her feel safe. She was standing on her own for the first time in her life. It was terrifying, sure. But damn… it was the most liberating thing she'd ever felt.

She'd taken a job at a family law firm in downtown Bellefontaine and spent most weekends volunteering as legal counsel for Safe Haven, the women's shelter. Her days were long and heavy with stories that rarely had happy endings. But every once in a while, she felt like she truly made a difference—a small win here, a protected client there—and those moments were enough to keep her going.

Her days off were quiet, but she liked it that way. It was nice to have a routine, even though sometimes it felt a little predictable. She ran most mornings, tracing old paths around the Point where the sand gave way to broken shells and salt-slick rocks. Sometimes she made it all the way down the main road to the lighthouse, feeling the burn in her lungs and the salty ocean air on her face. She never went near the marina. Or the pier. Her legs always seemed to find another route.

She went on a few dates—dinners, coffees, the occasional drink after work—but nothing ever caught. The men were kind, polite, and normal. She'd smile, make small talk, and decline the second date with a gentle excuse. There was no spark. No pull.

Ash drifted through her mind now and then—the ghost of a voice, a half-seen photo. She kept up with him in pieces on social media: a post about his boat project, a picture of Jesse holding a fishing pole, the occasional like he gave on something she shared. They rarely texted, and he never called anymore. And yet, some nights, she'd catch herself scrolling back through their old messages and wonder how something, once so familiar, could now feel so far away.

Maybe, she thought, loving her had asked more than he could give. She understood it, even if she wished it weren't true.

On an ordinary Friday afternoon at the library, Emily saw Ash standing near the community board—pinning up flyers for the weekly AA meeting. He looked even better than he had the last time she'd seen him—six months ago, at her graduation. Leaner, clearer, and somehow more mature. There was a new calm in him, a different kind of confidence she hadn't noticed before. It was as if a quiet reserve had replaced his youthful swagger.

"Hey, stranger," she said, trying to sound casual.

Ash turned, and that familiar slow smile spread across his face. "Hey, Em. I heard you moved back in with your folks. How have you been?"

"There really are no secrets in this county!" she said, laughing. "I bought a house, actually. It's over near the Point. Two bedrooms, leaky roof, and a porch that sounds like it's crying when the wind hits it."

He laughed. "The Point, yeah, it's nice out there."

Emily could feel the instantaneous red flush on her cheeks.

He's not seriously trying to bring up that night at his cousin's beach house, is he?

Even more than three years later, she could still remember the storm and the passion of that night. She wasn't twenty-two anymore, she wasn't about to fall apart, but his eyes and that smile could still move something in her.

"You still working at the marina?" she asked, trying to change the subject quickly.

"Yeah. Over two years sober, too." He held up a flyer for her to see. "I'm helping lead meetings now, and I'm coaching football at Haven High. Big game tonight. Go Pirates!"

She smiled. "I'm happy for you, Ash."

He shrugged. "Just keeping myself busy."

She hesitated in the silence that followed, then surprised herself by blurting out, "You should come by my place for dinner tomorrow night. I could use a break from frozen meals."

"Dinner, huh? Yeah, I'd like that."

When he smiled again, she found herself mirroring it. This felt different. Warm, but not a forest fire roaring out of control. Something contained. Something she could trust.

By Saturday, Emily was a bundle of nerves. She spent the late afternoon scrubbing the house, prepping the food, and—against her better judgment—drinking.

One glass of wine to calm down turned into two, then three, while the chicken piccata sizzled on the stove. When the knock on the screen door came, she nearly dropped her spatula.

Ash stood on the porch, wearing jeans, a white T-shirt, and cowboy boots, holding a brown paper bag and a bouquet.

"Hey," he said, smiling. "I brought you something."

She blinked. "You brought me flowers?"

"Of course," he smiled, "I'm trying to be a good dinner guest. You're cooking for me, after all."

She laughed and thanked him nervously.

The kitchen smelled of lemon and butter. A candle flickered next to the table settings. It was unintentionally romantic and instantly made her flustered.

Emily reached for the wine bottle, her mouth moving before her brain caught up. "Can I pour you a glass?"

He paused, gentle but firm. "Em, I don't drink."

Her stomach dropped. "Oh—shit. Oh my God. I'm so sorry. I wasn't thinking. That was—"

"It's fine," he said, smiling easily. "That's why I brought my own." He lifted the grocery bag, pulling out cold cans of Diet Coke. "I came prepared."

She exhaled, half laughing, half mortified. "Good thing you did."

"It happens a lot," he said. "Trust me, you didn't hurt my feelings."

Dinner went better than Emily could have imagined. They talked about the high school football schedule, her work, Jesse, and the marina. She even told him about David, about D.C., about how she'd wanted so badly for it to work, but in the end, she couldn't commit.

Conversation was easy. Like they had never spent more than a day apart. Somewhere between the shared stories and the quiet smiles, she began to sense that they weren't free-falling this time. They were choosing their steps, slow and measured, walking back deliberately toward something that had once felt right, instead of tumbling into it.

When Ash noticed the uneven paint line on her kitchen wall, he chuckled. "You do that yourself?"

"I did, and what's wrong with it?" she asked defensively, crossing her arms.

"It looks terrible," he teased. "But it's fixable."

"Oh, really? And what would that cost me?"

He leaned back, considering. "Dinner. Every Saturday. Payment in food and Diet Coke."

She smiled despite herself. "I think I can afford that. I accept the terms."

She extended her hand to shake his, closing the deal, and for one instant, she felt like she was back at High Tide, back in that summer when she was shaking his hand for the very first time.

That was how it started. Every Saturday, Ash showed up with his toolbox, and Emily was waiting with dinner and cold cans of Diet Coke. Sometimes he brought Jesse, who ran around the yard with his bucket of toy frogs. Sometimes it was just the two of them.

Emily's cottage began to change—new paint, new bookshelves, a working porch light—and so did she.

One night, after Jesse had fallen asleep in the spare room, they sat on the couch finishing a movie neither of them had been watching.

Ash turned toward her. "You want me to go? I can throw Jesse in the truck; he won't even wake up."

She hesitated, then shook her head.

"No, don't go," she whispered, pulling him close.

He didn't need more than that. The kiss that followed was slow and lingering. As she led him to her bedroom, there was no frantic rush. Their clothes fell away gently, and the kisses came softly.

Ash lay back, propping himself on her pillows, and he looked at her with a tenderness she had never seen in him before. Emily pressed her body against him, feeling her nipples brush softly against his hard chest. She held his chin in her hands, looking down at him, and lowered her mouth to meet his.

Ash pushed inside her as she moaned softly, feeling his warm breath in her ear when he whispered her name. They moved together slowly at first, and then into a gradual crescendo. She collapsed on top of him and lay there for a long time, letting him gently stroke her hair.

The next morning in her bed, with Ash's arm draped over the curve of her hip, Emily noticed how the sunlight streaming in seemed soft and warm. It wasn't a glaring, accusatory spotlight; it felt more like a halo glow.

As she lay there, wide awake while Ash's breathing stayed steady and deep, a comfortable silence pressed in all around her. Her gaze traced the ceiling, questions crowding her mind. For a long moment, she felt every possible consequence—desire threading with vulnerability, satisfaction muddled with a thrill still tingling beneath her skin. She let the ache and the hope settle side by side in her chest, not rushing to resolve either.

She didn't have to throw her clothes on in a rush or run off anywhere. When Ash shifted and murmured her name, she pulled him closer. They didn't define it. They didn't need to. Whatever this was, it was theirs.

Chapter forty-six

One Saturday, Ash showed up at Emily's door in a cowboy hat, boots, and jeans that fit a little too well. A familiar grin tugged at his mouth, and mischief sparkled in his eyes.

"Get dressed up, honey," he said. "I'm takin' you out tonight."

Out turned out to mean The Dusty Spur, a country bar on the mainland with neon lights in the windows and the faint twang of guitar pouring out through the open door.

Inside, warm light spilled from chandeliers made of wagon wheels and neon beer signs glowing against the paneled walls. The dance floor was worn smooth from years of boots dragging across it, and the air smelled faintly of whiskey and sawdust. A band played energetically from the small stage in the corner, the fiddle and steel guitar weaving through the thump of the bass.

In the center of the room, rows of line dancers moved in perfect synchronicity, boots stomping, the sound echoing through the floorboards. Around them, couples two-stepped in a slow, steady circle that looped the edges of the dance floor, all easy smiles and practiced turns.

Emily glanced down at her sleeveless top, peplum skirt, and wedge heels and couldn't help but laugh.

"I'm so not dressed for the occasion," she said, taking in the crowd of women in cutoff shorts, flannel tops, and boots, and men in ball caps or Stetsons wearing pearl snaps.

Ash grinned.

"You look perfect," he said, his voice low and easy.

Emily paused near the edge of the bar, taking it all in—the outfits, the laughter, and the sheer confidence of people who knew every note of the song by heart.

She'd never been a fan of country music. In high school, she'd rolled her eyes at it, but over the past few years, it had grown on her. She'd even admit she liked some of the slightly older stuff—'80s and '90s country. Still, she felt out of her element, categorically the only person present in heels.

When the next song started, keyboard notes mixed with the guitar and smooth vocals floated through the bar.

Emily's face lit up in recognition.

"'It Ain't Cool to Be Crazy About You,'" she said, smiling. "I actually know this one."

Ash glanced down at her, surprised. "You do?"

She nodded. "I said I wasn't *that* into country music. It's growing on me, though. It's kind of like farm emo."

He laughed, the sound low and warm.

"George Straight, wow," he said, pulling her close. "You've got better taste in music than I thought."

Before she could answer, he guided her onto the dance floor, his hand finding the small of her back.

The crowd around them faded into motion and light, their steps falling in sync. He held her firmly, and their movements kept time so naturally it was hard to tell who was leading anymore. She tilted her head back to meet his eyes, and under the neon glow, everything else—the noise, the dance floor, the struggles, the years—fell away.

The drive back to the island was quiet at first. The sound of the truck's engine and the radio softly filled the space between them. The sky was ink-dark now, the stars scattered across it like rhinestones spilled on velvet.

Emily leaned her head against the window and smiled to herself.

"You're full of surprises, Ash," she said finally. "I had no idea you could dance like that."

He chuckled, his hand drumming lightly on the steering wheel. "Guess I've still got a few hidden talents."

She shot him a look, playful but curious. "Seriously, though—where'd you learn to two-step? You made it look easy."

He hesitated, eyes still on the road. "Took a few lessons, actually. I dated someone for a little while last year. She loved to dance. The Spur was her favorite place."

"Oh," Emily said quietly, her fingers tightening around the hem of her skirt.

She had no right to feel it—that pang of jealousy, the small sting of imagining him there, moving intimately across the dance floor with someone else. But it came anyway, curling through her body warm and hostile.

Ash glanced over, flashing her a faint knowing smile.

"Didn't last," he said. "There was just… no spark. Something missing, I guess."

Emily nodded, forcing herself to look out the window, watching the reflection of the moon ripple across the water as they crossed the bridge.

"I get that," she said, voice low. "You can't force what isn't there."

He didn't reply right away, but she could feel him looking at her, his gaze lingering just long enough.

"Yeah," he said finally. "I've learned you just can't."

The rest of the drive passed in comfortable silence. When he pulled into her driveway, the porch light flickered on, illuminating their faces in the darkness.

"Thanks for tonight," Emily said, her voice barely above a whisper.

"Anytime," he replied. "Next weekend, you can pick the date night spot."

She smiled as she reached for the door handle. "Deal."

When she stepped out and shut the door, the sound of the truck idling behind her made her hesitate. It was a *date*. The first of many, she hoped. Something in her wouldn't let it end there. She turned back, tugged open the door, and climbed up in the cab.

Ash looked up, surprised, his hand still resting on the gearshift. Neither of them moved at first, then she reached for him, her lips finding his, long enough to leave him breathless.

"Goodnight," she murmured as she stepped back and shut the door.

The truck's headlights swept over her as she walked toward her front porch, heart racing, a broad smile she couldn't fight spreading across her face.

Time started to slip by unnoticed. Some weekends, they stayed in at Emily's place. Other times, they went out to a movie, bowling, or wherever the night took them. Once, they even dropped by High Tide and had dinner sitting at the bar, joking with Jeanne about the "good old days."

By New Year's, the air on the island had turned crisp and clean, the kind that made the windows fog when Emily boiled water for tea. She read *Wuthering Heights* again, like she did every year—only this time she read it out loud to Ash on the nights they stayed in.

He listened in that intent way of his—head tilted, eyes steady, saying almost nothing. Sometimes he'd interrupt with a laugh when she tried to imitate a Yorkshire accent.

When she finally closed the book, the room was quiet except for the hum of the space heater.

Ash leaned back on the couch with his arms folded behind his head. "Wow," he said after a long pause. "That was intense. Kind of dark."

Emily smiled faintly. "Yeah, it is."

He studied her face for a moment, then said, "Now I think I'm starting to understand the tattoo."

He touched her shoulder, tracing the spot where the familiar ink lay beneath her sweater.

She didn't answer; she only nodded. Because for the first time, she was starting to see it differently—not as a scar from something unfinished, but as a promise still waiting for its other half.

Chapter forty-seven

Ash didn't visit her often anymore. Not because he didn't care, he did, but because it wasn't about punishment anymore. It used to gut him. Lately, it felt different.

Some Sundays, while Jesse stayed with Mandy's parents, he'd drive the two and a half hours to Savannah and park beneath the sprawling oaks at Bonaventure. There, the Spanish moss hung like silver curtains, and the breeze off the water carried the scent of earth and camellias.

Her headstone stood near the edge of a hedge-lined garden—a marble sculpture of an angel with her face turned upward, graceful and luminous even under the filtered sun.

Amanda Elizabeth Green Bell

February 10, 1980-March 12, 2006

Beloved daughter, wife, and mother. Light of our lives. Forever in our hearts.

The words caught the filtered sunlight, soft and clean. She'd been like that—bright, deliberate, never halfway anything.

He knelt to brush cut grass off the base, his hand tracing the smooth stone. He used to come here angry—angry at fate, at himself, at God for taking her and leaving him hurting. But lately, sitting under the low-hanging moss, he just felt still. It wasn't right or fair that she was gone, but he had somehow been able to untangle the tight ball of emotions that used to drag him down to a self-loathing hell.

He rolled up his sleeve absentmindedly, dark ink catching the sun. There was a delicate script wrapping the inside of his wrist—*Fiat lux*. Let there be light. He'd gotten it a few months after she died. Not to remember her—she was impossible to forget—but to remember what she had been to him.

Light.

There'd been a time he'd felt torn straight down the middle. Mandy was day, and Emily was night. He used to think he had to choose between them, between who he'd been and who he was becoming. Now he understood. They were both part of him. Mandy's brightness, her order, her certainty. Emily's dangerous spark, her depth, her untamable will. Day and night didn't compete; they completed the same sky.

He brushed his thumb across her name one more time.

"Thank you for teaching me so much, Mandy," he said softly. "You'd like Emily. I wish you had got to know her better. She's not like you, but she's good to Jesse. I know you would want that."

He couldn't help but thank her. So much of who he was had been shaped by Mandy—not just the love they shared, but the grief he carried after. Even the heartbreak of losing her had carved out space for him to become someone steadier, someone rebuilt.

His life had scars, just like his shoulder, and maybe it would never look the way he had once imagined. But he was still here. Still above ground and breathing. Grateful for the chance to find out what came next.

He stood, set a single white rose at the foot of the marble, and walked back toward his truck. He didn't feel cursed anymore. He felt whole.

Chapter forty-eight

Cindy's small kitchen smelled like cocoa powder and butter, just the way it always had when Ash was a kid. The counters were crowded with casserole dishes, and the room swelled with laughter—the kind that made everything else fade away.

Emily sat at the table beside Jesse, now three and full of personality, grinning with icing on his nose. Cindy cut the first slice of her famous birthday cake. Chocolate cake with fudge frosting, the same recipe she'd made for Ash every year of his life.

"It's a family tradition," she said proudly, sliding a plate to Emily. "Now it's your turn, sugar."

"Lucky me," Emily said, smiling. "It smells amazing."

Ash leaned back in his chair, watching them both. "You have no idea. One time me and Arch ate the entire thing before my dad got home. We got whoopin's from Daddy and Mama that night."

Cindy, Emily, and Jesse howled. The night rolled on easily after that. A southern summer evening filled with old stories, laughter, and sweet tea. It felt like peaceful belonging.

After dinner, Cindy stood and started clearing plates.

"You two go," she said, waving them off. "I'll get Jesse to bed tonight. I can spoil him and let him stay up too late. Go do something fun."

Ash raised an eyebrow. "You sure?"

Cindy smiled knowingly. "Go on, honey. She deserves a birthday surprise."

The marina was quiet when they arrived, and the moon hung like a luminous pearl over the water. Ash led Emily down the dock to the end slip, where a sleek, white, center console fishing boat waited, freshly painted and gleaming.

"*The Other Woman*. Really?" Emily read the name with a laugh. "She's beautiful."

"Finally finished her," Ash said, pride and relief in his voice. "Figured it was about time she had her maiden voyage."

He handed her a small bottle of champagne.

"Do the honors? It is your birthday."

Emily grinned, shaking it slightly before smashing it against the bow. Bubbles sprayed into the air, glittering under the moonlight.

"To new beginnings," she said.

"To this one," he replied, his voice quiet but confident.

They climbed aboard, the engine rumbling softly as Ash steered them away from the dock. The water shimmered silver and black, the salt air wrapping around them like a memory. When he cut the engine, the world went still except for the sound of the waves tapping against the hull. In the distance, they could see the Fourth of July fireworks exploding off the pier.

Ash turned toward her. "You know, I was thinking…" he began. "I can't imagine my life growing up without Arch. Having a brother was everything to me. I want that for Jesse—a little brother, or a sister."

Emily smiled, shaking her head. "Slow your roll, Coach. Not happening without a ring."

He chuckled, then reached into his pocket and pulled out a small box.

Emily's heart stopped.

The ring wasn't flashy. It was simple and elegant—a thin gold band, a pear-cut solitaire—perfectly timeless.

"Guess I came prepared," he said softly. "Marry me, Emily."

Tears choked her. "Ash—"

"I lost a lot of things trying to be the man everyone wanted me to be. But this—you, Jesse, all of it—this is who I'm supposed to be."

She nodded. "Yes."

He slipped the ring onto her finger, and she kissed him, slow and sure. Every wrong turn, heartbreak, and painful memory had finally led them right here.

Later, they lay entangled on the boat deck beneath the stars, the moon spilling silver light over their skin. The waves rocked them gently, in a calm coastal lullaby.

Emily traced Ash's scar with the tip of her finger.

"I'm twenty-six today," she murmured. "Same age you were when we met."

Ash smiled, eyes half-closed. "Full circle."

She looked up at the moon—the same one that had watched over them on the beach years ago when everything first began.

"It's the same moon," she whispered. "Only now, it doesn't feel like something's about to end."

"No," he said softly, pulling her closer. "This time, it feels like forever is beginning."

Epilogue

The little country church shimmered in the sunlight, its white clapboard walls bright against the blue South Carolina sky. The doors were open to catch the faint breeze drifting in from the marsh, carrying the scent of sea grass.

It wasn't a grand wedding—just family and the people who had walked through every storm beside them.

Jesse, now four with sun-bleached, sandy-colored hair and bright blue eyes, walked down the aisle proudly in his miniature seersucker suit, clutching Cooper's leash as he trotted along with the rings tied neatly to his collar.

The crowd laughed as Jesse turned and announced, "Ring bearers, reporting for duty!"

Jesse's cousin Katie Jo cried the whole way down the aisle, her flower girl petals trailing behind until she reached the front, and Jessica scooped her up in a hug.

Arch was the best man, Ryker a junior groomsman. Joel stood opposite as man of honor, his silk pocket square gleaming in the sunlight. Beside him, Kenzie smiled, radiant in her soft blush bridesmaid dress.

In the second pew, Marinda and Greg sat with Cindy, both women misty-eyed and beaming. In Marinda's arms slept two-month-old Owen Asher Bell, swaddled in pale blue, his tiny chest rising and falling evenly.

The doors opened, and Emily appeared in a simple lace gown, bare shoulders kissed by sunlight, her hair swept loosely back. She was barely wearing a touch of make-up, and yet her green eyes sparkled. Ash turned toward her, their eyes met, and time stood still. She smiled at him, and felt it all over again—that quiet certainty that some loves don't fade; they only grow deeper, stronger, and more sure.

When she reached the altar, Jesse grinned up at his dad and whispered loudly, "Miss Emmy looks like a princess!"

Everyone laughed softly.

Ash took her hand, his thumb tracing her knuckles.

"You ready?" he murmured.

She nodded. "I've been ready."

They said their vows—simple, honest, unpretentious—but every word carried the weight of what they'd survived. Ash promised to keep choosing her even on the hard days, the ones where love felt less like fireworks and more like forgiveness. Emily's voice trembled when she said she'd never stop believing in the man he was—the one who fought his way back, who did all the little things, who stayed. They didn't need flowery language. Their history spoke for them.

When the pastor pronounced them husband and wife, the church bells rang through the summer air, echoing across the island, clear and bright.

The reception was held later that evening down on the beach in front of High Tide. Jeanne had strung lights from palm to palm, and a local band played barefoot in the sand. Joel and Mateo danced like they'd been rehearsing all week. Kenzie laughed and danced wildly. She caught up with Emily and introduced everyone to her plus-one, João, whom she had met while backpacking in Portugal.

Jesse and Ryker chased little Katie Jo through the dunes while Cindy clapped along to the music. The smell of grilled shrimp and bonfire smoke mixed with the salt air, and the new Mr. and Mrs. Bell toasted the speeches with cans of Diet Coke.

When the photographer called for sunset pictures, Emily turned, and the wind took her veil, the fabric slipping away from her shoulder. That's when Ash saw it—the familiar script in ink, now completed.

"*Whatever our souls are made of... his and mine are the same*"

His breath caught, and he smiled softly, brushing his fingers along the text.

"Finished it, huh?" he whispered, kissing her bare shoulder.

She looked back at him, eyes bright. "I had to."

He nodded. "Looks perfect."

"It feels that way," she said, smiling.

Late that night, long after the last sparkler went out and Jesse had fallen asleep in a pile of blankets, Emily sat in the rocking chair by the window of their cottage holding baby Owen as he slept. Moonlight spilled through the curtains, and Emily's mind drifted back over the months since she'd said *yes* on the bow of the boat.

Life had unfolded in a collection of beautiful moments after that. Ash and Jesse had moved into her cottage on the Point. It had felt strange at first—toothbrushes sharing a too-small sink, Jesse's toys scattered through the tiny living room, Ash humming to himself in the kitchen while he burned dinner. But soon it all became the rhythm of family: Sunday dinners at her mom's house, fishing off the pier until dark, movie nights with Jesse falling asleep between them, his small hand clutching Emily's arm.

Then came the cool October morning that changed everything. Two pink lines on a dollar-store test trembled in Emily's hand. She'd stared at them for a long time, heart pounding, the world narrowing to that tiny window—feeling a rush of fear, disbelief, and then excitement.

When she told Ash, a grin split across his face. He pulled her into his arms, laughing and crying all at once.

"We're really doing this," he'd said.

She'd been scared, of course, she had. But ready, too. It wasn't *planned,* exactly, but it wasn't *unwelcome.*

The months that followed were a blur of small, unforgettable moments: morning sickness and sheer exhaustion, Jesse kissing her growing belly goodnight, Ash's calloused hand resting protectively across her stomach. She loved feeling the baby move—the gentle rolls, the sharp kicks, and the way he seemed to respond when Ash talked to him.

Then came that night in early June. Her back had been aching all day, dull and low. She thought it was nothing, just the usual late-pregnancy stiffness. She tried to sleep, but the pains came steadily, then stronger, then pulling her under in waves.

"Ash," she whispered, shaking his shoulder in the dark. "You'd better call your mom."

By the time Cindy arrived to stay with Jesse, Emily could barely walk. Ash scooped her up and carried her to the truck, rain tapping the windshield as he drove faster than he should have.

Labor was hard and fast. The kind of agony that swallowed her whole. Ash held her hand, rubbed her back, whispered that she was stronger than she knew. When she screamed, he let her, holding on tighter.

Toward the end, it felt like her body was splitting in two. For one terrifying moment, her mind flashed to Mandy—a shadow she'd never quite outran.

What if it happens to me, too?

But then the nurse said, "One more push, honey."

Emily gathered the last ounce of her strength and gave it everything she had—dizzying silence was followed by the piercing, fierce cry of new life.

When they placed Owen on her chest—red-faced, furious, perfect—Emily felt something inside her shift. Maybe she *had* died that night. Or maybe she was reborn. Because in that moment—with Ash kissing her forehead, Jesse waiting at home, and her newborn son curled against her heart, she knew this was the beginning of everything. Becoming his mama wasn't the next chapter. It was the start of an entirely new story.

One Year Later

The late afternoon sun spilled across Haven Inlet, turning the water to gold. *The Other Woman* rocked gently at her slip, paint bright and hull polished, her name freshly stenciled across the bow in clean black letters.

Emily stood barefoot on the dock, a cup of tea warm in her hands, her hair pulled into a loose braid. A pelican skimmed the surface of the inlet, wings brushing the reflection.

Jesse stood beside her, gap-toothed and tan, a bundle of endless five-year-old energy. He wore his favorite shark-print pajamas and narrated every move Ash made as he secured the moorings.

"Dad says she's gonna be the fastest boat on the whole island," he declared proudly, his voice carrying across the water.

Emily smiled, glancing up toward their new house. They'd sold the little cottage at the Point over the winter, trading it for something bigger—a weathered beach house on the inlet side of the island, white siding with pale blue shutters and a wide porch that caught the sea breeze just right. It had its own dock, a place for the boat and for Jesse to fish off with his miniature rod and endless optimism. It was also big enough to house the family they hoped would keep growing.

Ash looked up from the deck and caught her watching him.

He grinned, that easy, boyish grin that still made her heart skip. "You gonna stand there all day or come and help me?"

Emily rolled her eyes, taking another sip of tea. "I'm supervising."

He laughed, looping the final line around the cleat, and climbed up to join her. He brushed a stray strand of hair from her cheek by habit before leaning in to kiss her. The inlet shimmered around them, the sunlight glinting off the rings on their fingers.

"Dad, can I throw one now?" Jesse asked, clutching a small smooth stone.

Ash laughed, steadying him by the shoulders. "Go ahead, bud. Just don't hit the boat this time."

The rock plunked into the water, sending ripples fanning out toward the horizon, and Jesse whooped in triumph.

From the shade of the porch, Emily heard a soft coo. She turned to look at Owen sitting in his playpen, gumming a toy. His hair fell over his bright hazel eyes in the same dark, unruly waves as hers. She walked to him and picked him up, pressing her lips to his warm cheek.

"See that?" she whispered. "Your big brother's trying to make waves."

The sun was barely starting to sink in the sky. Soon, Marinda and Greg would have Sunday supper waiting. Cindy was bringing her chocolate cake.

Ash came over, wrapping an arm around Emily's waist, his eyes studying Jesse as the boy leaned over the rail.

"We should head that way soon," he said.

Emily smiled, leaning against him, struck by how this moment felt both ordinary and hard-won.

Life wasn't perfect. Sometimes it dragged you under, spun you in circles like a riptide until you couldn't tell which way was up. But then it gentled again, like soft waves kissing the shore, buoying you upward, letting you breathe.

Nothing had come easily for them. But maybe that was the truth about love: two people meant to be together would face the roughest storms. Not because it wasn't meant to be, but because everything real is tested.

Emily wasn't even sure anymore where choice ended, and fate began—how much of what had happened between them was written in the stars, and how much was just them stubbornly choosing each other, again and again. Maybe it didn't matter, because they had somehow held on through all of it and came out stronger. Unbreakable, not regardless of the struggle, but *because* of it.

Over the water, the first curve of the moon rose pale and full. Ash bent his head, his lips brushing his wife's temple.

"Same tide, same moon," he murmured.

Emily smiled, voice barely audible above the rush of the sea. "Forever."

Jesse tossed another stone from the dock, and Owen's laugh rang out—high, pure, and impossibly bright.

Just like that, under the endless Carolina sky, they kept going. Not a story beginning or ending. One continuing, steady as the tide, sure as the pull of the moon.

A Look at Book Two

When the Flood Tide Rises

The Haven Island series shifts its focus over the remaining books to the adult children of Emily and Ash, as they navigate early adulthood, first loves, and the complicated inheritance of family traits. Their children, Jesse, Owen, and Rose, have grown up on the island. The coming books in the series will follow their own love stories.

Book two mainly follows Jesse, as a new romance unfolds and old family dynamics resurface. It also follows other members of the Bell family who find themselves reckoning with desire, regret, and choices that blur the lines between what they want and what they know.

Themes in *When the Flood Tide Rises* include first love, coming-of-age romance, age-gap relationships, and the messy ways people repeat—or resist—the patterns they were raised in.

This book includes explicit sexual content, physical violence, cheating, and other emotionally messy romantic dynamics among adult characters. Themes may be challenging for some readers. Book two is written exclusively for adult audiences; reader discretion is advised.

Excerpt From When the Flood Tide Rises

"You slept with her?" Owen asked quietly.

Jesse didn't answer right away. The headlights swept across the marsh grass as the truck curved around the inlet.

"Yeah," he admitted.

Owen stared out the window. "Jesus, Jesse."

"What?"

"You know what," Owen said. "She's not like the other girls you've messed around with."

Jesse laughed, but it came out sharper than he meant it to. "You jealous?"

Owen turned his head slowly. "You don't even see it, do you?"

"See what?"

"What you do. You crash into people. You make them feel like they're the only one in the room, and then you move on like it never mattered. You can't do that to someone like Claire. She's special."

Jesse's grin faltered. "You done with the lecture, daddy? I feel like you have a huge secret crush on her. It's not my fault you didn't do anything about it."

Owen didn't respond.

The silence that followed wasn't comfortable. It wasn't brotherly. It was brewing—like something about to erupt. Outside, the lights of the Country Club flickered across the windshield, soft and golden and careless—utterly unaware.

About the Author

ERIN CANTRELL

Erin is an author of emotional, immersive contemporary romance with the occasional satirical short story or smutty novella thrown in.

She loves writing stories that blend atmosphere, depth, heartache, and hope. A lifelong coastal dreamer, she builds worlds filled with flawed characters, slow-burn longing, and the kind of love that leaves an imprint.

When she's not writing, Erin competes in trail races and sometimes manages to outrun her own anxieties. She lives to plan travel, and drinks more decaf green tea than any doctor would recommend.

She lives in South Carolina with her family and two spoiled felines named Simba and Gary.

Get In Touch

Stay Connected To Haven Island

Thank you for spending time on Haven Island.

If this story meant something to you—if you underlined a sentence, cried over a character, or wanted to throw this book across the room at least once—I'd love to hear from you.

Connect with me on Instagram and Goodreads!

Want bonus scenes, early excerpts, and first access to new releases? Join my newsletter at: www.erincantrellauthor.com

Reader messages are my favorite part of this whole process. Truly.

With gratitude,

Erin

Acknowledgements

This book exists because of a long list of people who supported me, challenged me, and reminded me why I wanted to tell this story in the first place.

To my family—thank you for loving me through long days, late nights, and the quiet stretches where my head was somewhere else entirely. Your patience and belief mean more than you know.

To my editor, Julie—thank you for your sharp eye, thoughtful questions, and for helping me make this story stronger without ever asking me to sand down its edges. I'm grateful for your guidance and your care for these characters.

To my friends—especially R.B., who listened to me talk through plot points, emotional beats, and self-doubt far more than was reasonable—thank you for holding space for both the work and the worry.

To my ARC team—thank you for supporting me through this debut. I mean it when I say this has been the most humbling process, and every one of you made this seamless for me!

To the readers who love stories about summer, the coast, and the moments that change us quietly and forever—this one is for you. Thank you for trusting me with your time and your hearts.

And finally, to the beautiful places along the Carolina coast that inspired this book—the water, the salt air, the beach towns that hum with memory and longing—thank you for the prompting. I followed your lead as honestly as I could.

Book Club Questions

Book Club Discussion Questions

Book Club Big Question: *What does it mean to choose messy love?* Let that guide the discussion.

1. **Emily is self-aware, but she still makes choices that hurt people she cares about.**
   Do you think self-awareness mitigates harm, or can it sometimes make selfish choices harder to excuse?
2. **David represents stability, safety, and emotional generosity.**
   Why do you think that wasn't enough for Emily—and do you think that makes her unfair, honest, or simply human?
3. **Ash is often described less by what he says and more by how he *is*.**
   What do you think ultimately draws Emily back to him: love, familiarity, unfinished business, or something else?
4. **The novel frequently explores the idea of wanting versus deserving.**
   Do you believe Emily ends up with what she deserves—or simply what she chooses to live with?
5. **Several characters act with restraint rather than confrontation.**
   How does silence function in the story—as protection, avoidance, or quiet power?

6. **The book resists framing anyone as a villain.** Did that make the emotional stakes stronger or more frustrating for you as a reader?
7. **Emily acknowledges that loving two people didn't excuse the harm it caused.** How important was it for you, as a reader, that she named this explicitly?
8. **David's ending is unresolved, while Emily's feels settled.**

   Did that imbalance bother you—or did it feel true to life?
9. **The epilogue focuses on ordinary, domestic moments rather than grand declarations.** What did "ordinary and hard-won" mean to you by the end of the book?
10. **If this story were told from David's or Mandy's point of view, how do you think it would change?** Would your sympathies shift or stay the same?
11. **Do you see Emily's final sense of peace as growth, compromise, or self-forgiveness?**
12. **What line or moment stayed with you the longest after finishing the book—and why?**

Relationships fail not because love is flawed, but because the people inside them are still unfinished.

www.ingramcontent.com/pod-product-compliance
Lightning Source LLC
LaVergne TN
LVHW100508110826
845146LV00002B/560

* 9 7 9 8 9 9 4 1 8 7 5 2 4 *